A CURSE BEFORE DYING

Coughing, the old man leaned on his ornately carved wooden stick. A mosaic of colorful tattoos covered his bald head and scrawny torso. Conan, who knew something of Iranistani tribes, guessed rightly that he faced a Kaklani shaman.

The shaman swayed and fell to one knee. Looking up at Conan, the old man gripped the ends of the stick in both hands, bowing it in the middle until it snapped. He gibbered in an unfamiliar tongue, and ribbons of luminous red vapors issued from the stick's halves. They coalesced in a mist that swirled around Conan's head. The shaman shrieked, his voice loud and harsh; then he ceased his chant and died.

Conan waved his arms about trying to ward off the red cloud burning his eyes . . . painful flashes filled his head, like needles piercing his skull . . . lodging in his brain. . . .

Conan Adventures by Tor Books

CONAN

AND THE SHAMAN'S CURSE

—— BY ——

SEAN A. MOORE

A TOM DOHERTY ASSOCIATES BOOK
NEW YORK

This is a work of fiction. All the characters and events portrayed in this book are fictitious, and any resemblance to real people or events is purely coincidental.

CONAN AND THE SHAMAN'S CURSE

Cover art by Ken Kelly
Maps by Chazaud

A Tor Book
Published by Tom Doherty Associates, Inc.
175 Fifth Avenue
New York, NY 10010

Tor Books on the World-Wide Web:
http://www.tor.com

Tor® is a registered trademark of Tom Doherty Associates, Inc.

ISBN: 0-812-55265-2

First edition: January 1996

Printed in the United States of America

0   9   8   7   6   5   4   3   2   1

For Raven
Still beguiling all my fancy into smiling

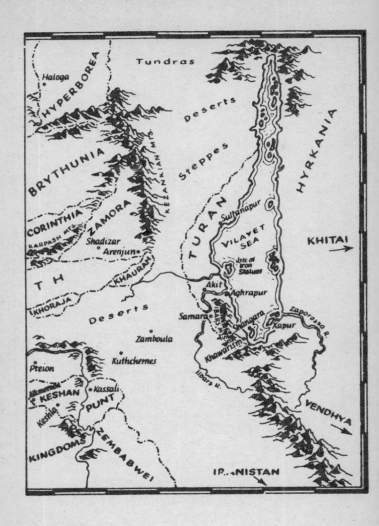

Contents

Historian's Note

After the events chronicled in "The Flame Knife," Conan rides east with his free company of mercenaries. Nanaia, the beautiful but feisty girl whom he rescued from the ghoul-haunted city of Yanaidar, returns to the Islands of Pearl.

Conan journeys toward Anshan, Iranistan's capital city. He commands a band of some two hundred men. They plan to join King Arshak's army for gold and glory—more for the former than the latter. But the winds of fortune swirl chaotically about the mighty Cimmerian, hindering his plans with fateful gusts.

Here begins the tale of Conan and the Shaman's Curse.

One
Red Mist

Carrion birds circled above a small stretch of rocky beach, squawking in anticipation. The stench of blood mingled with the pungent reek of carnage that rose from below, luring more vultures and fouling the humid air.

Thousands of human corpses choked the beach, spreading over it like a grisly carpet of death. Many of them still clutched weapons in their stiff fingers; others lay twisted beneath the bodies of foemen, snarls frozen upon their lifeless faces. The slashed, bloodied robes and crimson-soaked kaffiyehs were those of Iranistani tribesmen. The scattering of broken weapons, hacked bodies, and severed limbs told a silent tale of a savage war.

But not all were slain, though the cawing carrion birds swooped closer. A band of fourteen warriors had survived the battle. They wore yellow robes striped with red in the fashion of southern Iranistan's Kaklani tribe. Behind them limped an old man with a long white beard, leaning heavily upon a short wooden stick. Snarling and panting, the band moved through the sprawled cadavers to surround a lone man.

The man stood his ground. Shoulder-length black hair streamed from a battered iron cap perched crookedly upon his head. His chest swelled powerfully beneath his leather-lined shirt of mail. Corded muscles bulged along his arms, and in his scarred right fist he gripped a massive broadsword that glinted in the waning afternoon sun. Blood from countless Kaklanis smeared him from head to toe and dripped from the edge of his blade. Blue eyes blazing, he bared his teeth in a savage grimace.

His name was Conan, a barbarian from Cimmeria—a land of frozen plains lying so far north that here, on Hyboria's southern coast, its very name was little-known. The people of Cimmeria, tempered by hard living, were as grim and ferocious as their homeland. Cimmerians never sold their lives cheaply in battle, and Conan was no exception. At his feet lay the heaped bodies of Kaklanis. But deeper were the piled corpses of Zariris, the men who had fought side-by-side with Conan.

The Zariris, bitter ancestral foes of the Kaklanis, had hired Conan and his free company of warriors to join them in the ill-fated assault upon the Kaklanis. The bloody fight raged at the foot of the Mountains of Gold. The tide of battle had swept both forces toward the beach, where the last Zariri perished with the last man of Conan's free company.

Conan unsheathed his sword at sunrise, leading his men into battle. Throughout the day, the fighting had been thickest around him. The sun was now sinking toward the western horizon, but Conan showed no signs of fatigue. He held high his unwavering sword, ready to meet the advancing Kaklanis.

These weary warriors, sensing that victory was close at hand, moved as one, eager to strike. Fourteen faces contorted into menacing masks of fury. Fourteen curved knives drew closer and closer, like steel teeth ready to snap shut around the red-eyed Cimmerian. "Foreign jackal," the foremost of them snarled, rushing forward. He spat at Conan's feet. "The fighting is done. I sheath my blade in your foul heat!" He lunged with the speed of a striking viper, thrusting his blade at the Cimmerian's breast.

But Conan parried, his ferocious riposte knocking the blade from the Kaklani's hand, lopping off his sword-arm and smashing through his ribs. The clang of steel and the stricken warrior's shriek mingled with Conan's savage war-cry. The Kaklani collapsed onto the carrion heap at Conan's feet.

Conan tore his dripping sword free, charging toward the nearest Kaklani. The Cimmerian's mighty downward stroke shattered his foeman's blade and split his skull to the jawbone in a spray of blood, brains, and teeth. Before the other warriors could strike, Conan was through their circle. He could have fled, but he was sworn to avenge his men: loyal companions who had died at the Kaklanis' hands. He turned to face the twelve enraged tribesmen.

They rushed toward him, like a wave of slashing steel—a wave that broke upon the indomitable Cimmerian. With his every sword-stroke, a screaming Kaklani went down with a cloven skull, a hewn torso, or a severed neck. Their murderous blows rained upon the frenzied Cimmerian, but the links of his mail shirt turned aside their blades. A few of their thrusts nicked the barbarian, but all suffered who strayed within reach of Conan's whirling web of steel.

Battle lust seized the Cimmerian, pumping through his veins and filling his head with fire. He fought with relentless fury until the last Kaklani dropped to the ground, clutching the dangling coils of his shredded entrails. Conan lifted his sword, seeking another foe. Panting from exertion, his heart pounding like a Pictish wardrum, he carefully watched the bodies of his enemies for signs of feigned death.

Only one of the Kaklanis even twitched—the old, white-haired man. Coughing, he leaned on his ornately carved wooden stick and rose from the crimson ground. Blood dribbled from his wounded side, and he dragged a nearly severed leg behind him. A mosaic of colorful tattoos covered his bald head and scrawny torso. Crusted blood caked one side of his wrinkled face. Conan, who knew something of Iranistani tribes, guessed rightly that he faced a Kaklani shaman.

Although the Cimmerian feared that this shaman might invoke some deadly spell, he was too exhausted to strike down the unarmed man—his fiery berserker blood had cooled. Besides, the old man's injuries would soon send him to whatever hell awaited these Kaklanis. "Peace, old man," Conan rumbled in rough Iranistani. "I shall not harm you."

The shaman swayed on his good leg, raising his stick as if to smite the Cimmerian. Conan stepped back, and the shaman overbalanced and fell to one knee. Looking up at Conan, the old man gripped the ends of the stick in both hands, bowing it in the middle until it snapped. He gibbered in a tongue unfamiliar to the Cimmerian, and ribbons of luminous red vapors issued from the stick's halves. They floated aimlessly through the air, coalescing in a mist that swirled around Conan's head. The shaman shrieked, his voice loud and harsh. Billowing, the crimson mist sparkled in the sunset. Then the shaman ceased his chant and died before his body slumped to the blood-slimed ground.

Conan waved his arms about, trying to ward off the red cloud burning his eyes. Painful flashes filled his head, like needles piercing his skull and lodging in his brain. He gasped for air but inhaled only the chokingly sweet fog. Wheezing, he put a hand to his throat and toppled onto the shaman's stiffening corpse.

Two
Beach of Blood

Conan raced through the dense, sweltering jungle, panting from the long chase. He had forgotten what he was pursuing, but his quarry was swift and nimble. The Cimmerian was naked and carried no sword, but this did not bother him. Glancing upward as he dashed into a clearing, he noticed the full moon filling the night sky, staring down like a glowing, malevolent eye. It somehow maddened him, spurring him to run faster.

The smell of his prey filled his nostrils. Salivating, he raced toward the four-legged beast, sensing its fear. Red mist swam before his eyes and blood boiled in his veins. Crashing through leafy vegetation, he reached out, startled by the sight of coarse, white hair sprouting from his arms. Sharp, black talons grew from his thick, misshapen fingertips.

Leaping forward, he seized the squealing beast with those talons, rending and shredding its flesh . . .

* * *

Conan awoke, yelling. He jumped to his feet, shaking droplets of sweat from his face and hair. He blinked at the painful glare of the Iranistani sunrise and reached for his sword instinctively before realizing that he had been dreaming.

Lifting his foot from the shaman's stiff corpse, he stepped back in disgust, nearly tripping over a severed leg. All around him lolled the bodies of the slain. He walked to a patch of bare ground, letting his eyes adjust to the light and feeling his heartbeat slow to its normal rhythm. The tide was coming in, lapping at the carcasses scattered along the beach's edge.

On the morning after battle, most men would have moved sluggishly, feeling every nick and ache. Not so Conan; his endurance was that of a wolf, his strength that of a lion. He had fought in campaigns where battles were waged from dawn to dusk, for days on end, by soldiers fed on meager victuals and rationed water. This war had lasted but one bloody day.

Conan rubbed his aching skull and shook off the memory of the strange dream. No nightmare could match the hellish scene of the battlefield around him. The gruesome sights on the beach would have turned the stomachs of many seasoned soldiers, but Conan was no stranger to the aftermath of battle. He had been born on a battlefield in Cimmeria nearly thirty years ago. By his eighteenth birthday, he had fought in more wars than many men saw in their lifetimes.

His eyes and nose registered the familiar details of the savage tribal feud. Conan deemed it unmanly to hew at the body of a slain foe. But the Iranistani tribes seemed to delight in this practice, by the look of atrocities committed upon the bodies that littered the sand. The beach was a vast tapestry of death, woven from grisly human threads.

The rising sun lifted the morning chill, but did little to warm Conan's spirits. He bitterly cursed the circumstances of his involvement in this catastrophic battle. A week ago, he and his free company had been on their way to the Turanian steppes to join the army of Arshak, Iranistan's new king.

Conan's men had been seasoned Hyrkanians, hungry for gold and glory. When passing through Zariri lands on their way to the steppes, they had been invited into the tent of Jaral, sheikh of the Zariris.

Jaral had heard of Conan's legendary battle prowess. He told the Cimmerian about outrageous acts of Kaklani barbarity. So graphic were Jaral's accounts of these acts that the obdurate Cimmerian had grunted while listening. Jaral pleaded for Conan's aid, appealing to the Cimmerian's barbaric yet curiously chivalrous code of honor.

At first Conan had declined, eager to reach the steppes and fill his purse with gold from Arshak's treasury. But as the evening wore on, Jaral filled Conan's wine goblet again and again, while filling Conan's ears with promises of rich rewards. Scantily clad, sultry-eyed wenches served delicious spiced meats, quelling the rumbling in Conan's belly. Jaral offered the Cimmerian his choice of the voluptuous Zariri dancing girls. When Conan put each of his burly arms around a soft-skinned, ebony-haired girl, the sheikh had made the Cimmerian a generous final offer: half of the Kaklani tribe's treasure, to be divided among the free company. He told Conan of the Zariri tribal jewels, stolen by the Kaklanis. He even promised Conan a personal share when the Kaklanis were defeated.

Conan accepted—an ill decision that he now regretted. The Kaklanis outnumbered their attackers by at least two to one, turning the invasion into a massacre. The Cimmerian was forced to fight or die. He had considered fleeing, but his own men had been penned in, and he was responsible for them. They had died bravely in the last stand, dragging many Kaklanis to Hell with them. To the last man, they had stayed at his side.

To the last man, they had perished.

Cursing, Conan shoved the memory aside. He watched bold carrion fowl rip chunks of meat from putrefying corpses. The gentle slosh of the surf was accompanied by the flap of wings, the shrill cries of feasting birds, and the rude tearing of ravening beaks.

Conan pondered his options, looking away from the battlefield to the sparkling water. Thin ribbons of cloud hovered in the sky, unmoving. In the distance, he saw a cross-shaped speck that might have been a ship, its mast and furled sail drifting slowly. He heard the gentle whisper of the ocean beckon him, but he refused to heed its call. His prospects were better here, with his feet planted on firm ground.

Besides, he had work to do yet. He yawned, returning his eyes to the grim sights around him. He felt unrested, although he had slept all night. He rubbed at the base of his aching skull, unable to recall having been struck. Of course, when the fever of battle seized him, he often failed to notice such injuries until his bruised body reminded him later. Perhaps his nightmare had been the residue of a nasty knock. Drawing in a breath of pungent sea air, he set himself to the unpleasant task at hand.

Conan began to gather the bodies of his men. He piled them and their weapons atop a mound of sticks and lit a pyre, as befitted their custom. For their loyalty and bravery, they deserved better than the belly of a bird.

For hours, Conan bent his back to the disheartening task of retrieving his dead. He shed no tears for the fallen and shouldered no further guilt for their fate. They had accompanied him of their own free will and died bravely. He had avenged them. The Cimmerian dragged the last few from the water's edge, noting that the lips of one of his men—Ari, his second-in-command and a worthy rogue—were slowly moving.

Ari's eyes were closed. Conan bent down to revive him and offer him a waterskin, before jerking it back with a grunt of surprise. The movement he had seen came from a small crab inside Ari's mouth, feasting upon the tender meat inside. The Cimmerian brushed off this scavenger as it emerged from the dead man's mouth. Skewering the thing with his sword, he pulled a raw, pink chunk from the crab's claw. It was all that remained of Ari's tongue.

Conan placed the corpse on the mound of bodies, now numbering almost two hundred. The barbarian's shoulders had begun to throb, and the day's heat and humidity beat at him like invisible fists. Yawning, he trudged back to the Zariri camp that lay a half-league away, where the Mountains of Gold touched the shore by the vast Southern Ocean. There he would slake his thirst with a skin of wine, take the Zariri sheikh's horse, and gather wood from the nearby forested hills.

He had seen Jaral slip away the night before the battle, lugging a wooden chest into those hills. Curiosity had prompted him to follow the crafty sheikh, who buried the chest near a short, distinctively gnarled tree. The Cimmerian guessed that the chest contained the balance of the gold due to Conan's free company, so he had marked the spot well to ensure payment if a dispute arose later.

Conan passed through the camp, riding to the tree. He retrieved the heavy pay chest and strapped it to his mount, then gathered the kindling he needed for the pyre. The wood he had collected was green, but he cared not. He would be far away before smoke began pouring from the bonfire. He had already decided where to ride.

With his chest of Iranistani gold, he could spend a few months in the nearby port city of Denizkenar. A month of strong wine and soft women would clear the bitter taint of this battle from his mind, leaving him refreshed. He had been away from the pleasures of civilization for too long, living the oft-cheerless life of a mercenary.

Returning to the burial mound, he ignited the kindling and watched briefly as the wood caught fire, pungent smoke curling into the sapphire sky. But when he straddled his horse, he saw riders approaching—hundreds of men on horseback, their mounts galloping at breakneck speed.

"Crom!" Conan cursed, digging his heels into his horse's flanks and spurring the beast away at full gallop. Those riders wore the distinctively striped kaffiyehs of the Baj-karis—eastern allies of the Kaklanis, doubtless summoned by a messenger.

These allies had come too late, but Conan knew that they would seek vengeance. Sand sprayed from their horses' pounding hooves, which bore them toward the smoke-wreathed pyre. The foremost ranks slapped the sweaty rumps of their mounts, spurring the horses forward. They swept menacing tulwars from their belts and waved them in the air.

Conan rode west toward the Mountains of Gold, hoping to hide in their rock-shadowed recesses and discourage pursuit. The wind tore at the Cimmerian's yellow-banded kaffiyeh, which marked him as a friend of the Zariri. He had not bothered to doff the incriminating headgear, doubting that it would make a difference.

His laboring horse slowed, overburdened by the com-bined weight of its rider and the gold-filled chest. The Cimmerian looked over his shoulder at the enraged Bajkaris, who were gaining ground. As Conan rode be-tween two stone-covered hillocks, he saw a group of Bajkari bowmen lying in wait—arrows nocked, ready to fire. Others raised crossbows, drawing a bead on him. "Crom and Badb!" he swore, jerking the reins and turning his horse southward an instant before the archers loosed their storm of shafts.

Arrows and quarrels hissed through the air like wooden serpents, clattering from rocks around him. A few shafts fleshed his horse; others rebounded from the back of his mail shirt. Panicking, his steed bolted while Conan clung to its mane as it galloped southward, down the gentle east-ern slope of the Mountains of Gold. He guided his horse toward the narrow strip of stone-covered beach at Irani-stan's farthest southwestern shore.

The Bajkari horsemen spread out, cutting off any hope of escape. Conan considered his few options: make a stand while they ran him down, ride into their midst and try to break through, or swim to safety. From his freebooting years with Bêlit, Conan knew that Vendhyan merchants made frequent voyages along this Southern Ocean route. They traded wares with coastal tribes of Zembabwei and the Gwadiri people on the Islands of Pearl.

Scanning the southern horizon, his sharp eyes picked out the shape of a vessel. It was distant, a long swim, but the calm sea provided a better chance for escape than he would have here.

He leapt from the back of his snorting horse, still holding its reins. Tearing off his ragged shirt of mail, he flung it aside and doffed his kaffiyeh. Turning the headdress into a cloth sack with deft moves, he filled it with what little gold he dared to carry. After a moment's consideration, the Cimmerian sheathed his sword in its scabbard and tied the sack to his thick leather belt. Drawing a deep breath, he dove into the warm blue water.

The shouts of the Bajkari filled his ears as he struggled against the tide, swimming in powerful strokes and fighting the temptation to drop the small sack of gold that might secure him passage aboard the ship . . . if he reached that faraway haven. Behind him, the howling avengers were shedding their heavy gear and plunging into the water, curved daggers clamped between their teeth.

The bowmen—left behind when Conan's horse had bolted—now reached the shoreline and began shooting. The Cimmerian thanked the fates that the Iranistani were among the poorer of arbalesters, or they would have speared him like a fish ere he swam beyond their range.

"Zariri swine!" they cried, hurling oaths at the escaping barbarian. "May the sea-beasts gnaw your accursed bones!"

Conan would have laughed, but he saved his breath for the swim. He had escaped the archers, but dozens of Bajkari warriors still relentlessly pursued him. Weighted by his sack of gold and heavy sword, he felt his pace slacken. The Bajkaris swam within a stone's throw, closing in with every stroke.

Three

"Welcome aboard
the *Mistress* . . ."

Conan quickened his pace, drawing deeply from his well of reserve vitality. The burden of a heavy broadsword and a gold-filled sack would have dragged a lesser man to the ocean's floor, but the Cimmerian's muscular frame and powerful thews carried him through the placid ocean waters with a swiftness that would have shamed many a sea creature.

Exhaling and inhaling rhythmically, Conan pumped his arms and legs for every measure of speed that he could muster. When his destination loomed ahead, he lifted his head, tossing his hair back in a spray of saltwater as he looked over his shoulder.

Many Bajkari, more accustomed to their saddles than the sea, had begun to flag. A few had stopped and were simply treading water, too exhausted to swim back. The bowmen on the beach looked like mere insects. "Dogs!" Conan yelled.

This epithet left him short of breath, and he paused before renewing his efforts to reach the ship. He was close enough to study her in detail. She was a high-sterned, broad-waisted craft, a design similar to many Vendhyan costal vessels. She accommodated ten rowers on each side, but her captain may have crewed her sparingly, for Conan saw only ten oarsmen at work. Perhaps the shipmaster had counted more on trade winds than on bowed backs. Her single sail was bundled against the yard by its brails, and she bore no standard that indicated her origin.

To Conan's practiced eye, she had the look of a cargo-laden Vendhyan merchant. Sniffing the air, he also judged that she was not a slaver. Such vessels carried an unmistakable stench that fouled the air around them. A ship rowed by free men might welcome the Cimmerian, who knew his way around an oar. Better to pay for his passage with labor than part with any of his loot.

He knew that a strong rower and skilled swordsman would be welcome aboard—captains of small merchant ships lived in constant fear of pirate attacks. Years ago, Conan and Bêlit—the beautiful but deadly piratess—had preyed upon many such vessels. Bêlit's *Tigress*, with her eighty oarsmen and steel-beaked ram, would have made short work of this seagoing morsel.

As he swam on, exhaustion led Conan into sadly but fondly remembering the Shemite lover with whom he had spent many happy years. The two of them had terrorized countless Stygian vessels—their raiding, plundering, and slaying had made them infamous among those who dwelled along the southern coasts of the Western Ocean.

He had never before—or since—known a woman like Bêlit. She had reveled in her life of roaming, fighting, and plundering, as Conan did. And of the many women Conan had bedded, none had matched her raw, insatiable passion for lovemaking. Bloody battles fueled the fires of her lust as much as they fueled Conan's. In his arms, she was as wild and untamed as a jungle cat. After every conquest, the two would quench their thirst for each other—often from sunset to sunrise.

Bêlit's hunger for pleasure of the flesh had been exceeded only by her appetite for loot. It was the latter, and a vile legacy of tainted treasure, that had long ago taken her from him.

Conan missed his pirate queen, and he realized that he had—perhaps deliberately—avoided the sea since the Queen of the Black Coast's untimely death. Without her, the seafaring life had lost its luster.

His face hardened like a mask chiseled from stone. Now was not the time for reminiscing. Conan pushed aside the haunting memories, focusing on his goal. A few Bajkari doggedly swam after him, and the Cimmerian did not yet wish to join Bêlit in Hell.

Glancing back toward the beach, he saw that only three men had stayed in the race. As they closed the distance, he saw water streaming from their reddened faces. Sunlight flashed wickedly from daggers clenched between their teeth.

The Cimmerian considered facing them. His sword, however, would be unwieldy in a free-floating fight, and he had no mail to turn their blades. To worsen matters, his heavy sack of loot hindered him. He knew that he should cut it loose, but after hauling it this far, he was loathe to drop it.

A furtive movement caught Conan's eye, and he spun his head toward it. Rippling under the water's surface just a few feet from his side, he saw a long, silvery shape darting toward him. Backpedaling with his legs, he drew his broadsword. It just cleared its sheath before the gigantic barracuda was upon him. Sharpened teeth brushed the flesh of his calf as he desperately thrust his blade toward the vicious beast.

The point struck home, spearing the barracuda, sinking deep into its vitals and lodging in bone. Thrashing in agony, the wounded fish tried to dislodge the blade, but the sword was stuck fast. Conan clung to the hilt, vainly tugging at the blade. The maddened barracuda lunged toward him, forcing back his arms and clamping his belt between its jaws.

Conan's sword had not weakened the fish. With a violent tug the beast pulled him under. He sucked in a lungful of air before sinking, placing his feet against the slippery scales of the impaled predator and wrenching at the trapped blade.

Man and beast waged a tense tug-of-war. Conan hung on to his sword-hilt while the dying barracuda pulled its stubborn passenger through the water. Conan ached to expel stale air, and pounding blood sent waves of dizziness through his head. He held the air in, knowing that a watery grave awaited him if he exhaled. His only chance was to free his sword and skewer the thing again.

He could not will his arms to move.

Shadowy fog engulfed his vision. He was only dimly aware of the barracuda's final spasm. Chest heaving, he broke the paralysis that had seized him and ripped his broadsword from the fish's guts. The dead creature relinquished its grip, drifting away in a red ruin. Resisting his body's involuntary urge to open his mouth wide and take in what would be a drowning breath, the Cimmerian kicked his legs frantically, swimming toward the light. He knew that the blood and thrashing might attract even worse creatures—great striped sharks who were said to infest these waters.

After several moments of nearly unbearable agony, Conan's head cleared the surface. Gasping, he gulped the sweet, lifegiving air, expelling several lungfuls before his eyesight returned. He gazed with astonishment at the faraway beach, and almost smiled. The barracuda had towed him *away* from the Bajkari, closer to the safety of the Vendhyan ship.

His hunters had apparently abandoned the chase. They receded to tiny specks as Conan forced his aching limbs to swim the remainder of his harrowing escape route. No telltale fins broke the surface; perhaps the sea predators lurked elsewhere today.

A bored-looking Argossean leaned against the ship's taffrail, straightening with a jerk when he sighted the approaching Cimmerian. His shouts roused a few other sailors, and they tossed a knotted rope overboard, which Conan seized. He pulled himself up the rope and over the rail, thumping wetly to the starboard thwart between two cursing, sweating rowers. They and the other rowers stopped, raising their twenty-foot oars and gaping at the drenched barbarian.

The tall, bearded Argossean strolled amid the thwarts toward Conan, keeping a beefy hand upon the brass hilt of an enormous tulwar thrust through his wide belt. The other sailors—olive-skinned Vendhyans, stout Argosseans, and a few shifty-eyed Zingarans—fingered the hilts of their keen-edged scimitars. The tall Argossean barked a greeting in his native tongue. "Bel's beard! A blue-eyed giant—a northerner, by yer looks. Welcome aboard *Zarkhan's Mistress*. I'm Tosco, her first mate. What be yer name, and how in Hell come ye driftin' to us?" Anticipation lingered in his voice—and in the fingers that flexed around his brass hilt.

Fatigue had not completely robbed Conan of his wits. He made a show of rising to his feet to take a good look at his surroundings. In particular, he studied the ship's helmsman, who stood on the poop deck behind Tosco, manning the till. The helmsman's dusky-hued skin marked him as a Stygian; his leather jerkin and slender dagger bore symbols of Set, the dread serpent god.

Conan groaned inwardly while drawing himself up to his full height. The helmsman might recognize the name Conan—one of Stygia's most infamous pirates. "I am Vraal," he rumbled in rough Argossean. "I am a son of the Border Kingdom—though I know well the code of the sea," he added.

"Vraal, eh? Are ye deserter or slave, then, runnin' from them?" He gestured toward the remote shore, to which many of the Bajkari were swimming.

"Nay, friend Tosco. They ambushed me as I rode through the Mountains of Gold, on my way to sell my sword in Anshan or Aghrapur, wherever it would fetch the highest price. I would as soon pay for my passage by sweat. You seem short of rowers, and if we are waylaid by corsairs, my blade is at your service."

Tosco's grey eyes narrowed to slits, and a frown clouded his sunburned face. "Ha! We be a private merchant in a Stygian priest's hire. Yer bits of bronze and oafish sword-work together would nae be enough to secure ye as much as a place on the thwarts. And we have scant provisions, not for sharin' with the likes o' ye!"

Conan tensed, readying himself for an attack. But he knew that Tosco's gibes were the time-honored Argossean way of testing a stranger's mettle. "Among my bits of bronze," he said, opening his makeshift sack just enough to palm a gold piece, "is a gold dragon." He flipped the heavy coin to Tosco, who deftly caught it. Fingering the thick golden disc, he examined its markings: a Nemedian king's likeness on one side and a royal coat of arms on the other. Grinning, the first mate stuffed it into the pocket of his soiled brown vest. "Bend yer back at the bench. I'll ask the captain if we need another hand. Though yer wits be as slack as yer shoulders are broad, per'aps ye can be trained to row."

Conan suppressed the urge to fling the rude Argossean pig overboard. Scowling, he turned his back to Tosco and moved toward a vacant forward rower's position. Tosco nodded to a short, bald Vendhyan. The little fellow picked up a wooden mallet and sat cross-legged on the poop deck, next to a weatherworn drum. The Vendhyan began pounding his drum to set a pace for the oar strokes.

Irked by Tosco's derisive comments, Conan felt the raw energy of anger revitalizing his weary limbs. He would show this fat sea-cur how to move a boat through be-calmed waters. Forgetting his fatigue, the Cimmerian grit-ted his teeth and sat in the foremost center between the thwarts, gripping an oar in each hand.

Tosco seemed in no hurry to disturb the captain. He

stood on the poop deck like a king on a throne, barking guttural commands to his subjects. "Lay forward! Bend yer backs, dogs—to Stygia, afore our beards turn gray!" he boomed.

He had scarcely ceased his bellowing when Conan began rowing rhythmically. At the bottom of each stroke, the enraged barbarian lowered himself to the deck, then lifted his body for the next pull. Knotted sinews rippled beneath his bronzed skin as the drummer quickened his beats, and the other rowers labored to maintain Conan's arduous pace.

The oars protruded fifteen feet from the sides of the vessel, their wide blades dipping smoothly into the placid sea. Conan did not bother to pace himself; he doubted that he would need to sustain this effort for too long before Tosco accepted him into the crew. And the irascible first mate had not demanded the Cimmerian's weapon or attacked him for the sack of Zariri gold.

Slowly, the *Mistress* gained speed, propelled by Conan's vigorous rowing and the strained efforts of the men behind him. The Cimmerian timed his breathing with practiced skill; he was no stranger to the hard life of an oarsman. Many times had a taskmaster's whip laid open his heaving back while he sat seething, chained to a slaver's thwart, and the memory stoked the coals of his fury. Faster and faster he rowed, until two of his strokes marked a drummer's single beat.

The gasping rowers behind him were robust men, but they could only match half of Conan's mark. As the *Mistress* leapt forward, a gentle breeze stirred across the deck. She cruised west-southwest, within view of Zembabwei's jungle-choked coastline. The Vendhyan pacer's wrists hastened to match Conan's grueling pace, and the drum beats took on a feverish pitch. A wooden crack sounded behind Conan; from the corner of his eye, he saw that an oarsman had collapsed from exhaustion. The Cimmerian's oar smashed into the oarsman's fallen, idling blade.

Tosco, who had kept silent, snorted and spoke to the helmsman in Stygian, lowering his voice—but not low enough to keep his commands from reaching Conan's keen ears. "That insolent cur rows well. He'll fetch a pretty price on the slaver's block in Luxur!"

Conan's blood surged, his face an angry thundercloud. His eyes blazed—fiery blue torches framed by his tousled mane of black hair. Bracing his legs against the deck, he heaved upward and snapped the oars off at the tholepins, raising the spear-length pieces over his head and turning to face Tosco. "Argossean bilge rat! Perhaps you would care to match your sword with these twigs—or is your doglike yapping meant to conceal a feeble bite?"

Roaring, the Argossean whipped the curved three-foot blade from his belt and jumped to the deck between the thwarts, his heavy boots thumping on the hard planking. Racing past the mast and shoving rowers out of his way, he swung his tulwar with brutal ferocity, aiming for Conan's neck.

The Cimmerian smoothly stepped back, blocking the lethal sweep with one oar-shaft and swinging the other with all the force he could muster. It struck Tosco's neck, knocking his head back in the opposite direction. A loud crack sounded beneath the thick flesh of his throat as Tosco's spine snapped like a twig. Twitching, the bulky Argossean stumbled, head wobbling, his right ear lying against his shoulder. Then his eyes rolled upward as his last breath wheezed from his crushed windpipe. He fell over the rail while the panting rowers, drummer, and helmsman froze in amazement.

"You there," Conan pointed to the Stygian helmsman. "Tell the captain that a new first mate is taking Tosco's place. He'll find the going quicker when his ship's run by Conan of Cimmeria—" Belatedly, he bit off the hasty, damning words.

Gasping, the helmsman abandoned the tiller, sliding a slim-bladed throwing dagger from his copper-studded belt.

Conan ducked and rolled between the thwarts, stopping behind the partial cover provided by the ship's single mast and drawing his sword.

The Stygian's well-aimed dagger found a fleshy target, burying inches of steel in Conan's calf. Bending and pulling out the dagger with a grunt, Conan fell to one knee. The knife had sunk into his shin bone. His sword, jarred loose when he struck the deck, clattered beyond his reach.

"Captain!" the frantic Stygian cried, pounding on the hatch to a cabin belowdecks.

Conan planted his back against the mast, readying himself for a last stand. He longed to toss his knife at the Stygian, but it was his only weapon. With it, he could bring down a crewman and grab a better weapon.

The dazed rowers regained their senses, rising stiffly from their benches and surrounding the Cimmerian. They pummeled and kicked him unmercifully, but Conan struck back with blind sweeps of the Stygian knife. Three rowers clutched bleeding wounds and backed away, but the others overwhelmed Conan by sheer numbers. Five men held him down while two others wrenched away his dagger.

Then the captain burst out of his cabin, drawing his double-edged dagger from a high-topped boot and strolling toward the pinned barbarian.

Conan groaned, seeing that the captain was Stygian, taller and swarthier than many of his race. The high, curving collar of his thick leather jerkin protected his neck. His head was shaven at the sides, forming a forward-pointing triangle of raven-black hair that ended above the bridge of his nose. At his sharp command, the rowers backed away—and Conan immediately saw the captain's scar, slanting from his high forehead to the stump of his ear. His bloodshot eyes, the stubble of whiskers on his face, the hasty manner in which he had laced his wine-splashed jerkin—they all hinted that he might have been sleeping off a night of drinking. How else could he have slept through Conan's encounter with Tosco?

He seemed to be fully awake now. Lifting a heavy boot, he kicked Conan in the belly just as the Cimmerian was rising to one knee. Another boot lashed out at Conan's head, burying its hard toe under his jaw and sending a ripple of agony through his skull. Fighting to stay conscious, Conan managed to shake off the blinding pain of the captain's kicks.

The Stygian chuckled, a low, dry laugh that froze Conan's blood, lifting the fog from an old memory. That sneering face was different—aged and scarred—but it was the face of a Stygian admiral he had met years ago. Conan, back in his days of piracy, had put that scar on Khertet's face.

It had been a lucrative raid, surprising the admiral by its very boldness. Too late had Khertet reacted, and his fleet had let the *Tigress* slip through with rich plunder destined for the treasury of the Stygian king and queen. Only Khertet's flagship had caught up with the *Tigress*, but the ferocious defense of the pirates had driven back the admiral.

The Stygian admiral had sunk low indeed, from commanding a fleet of warships to captaining a miserable Vendhyan merchant vessel. Now Conan would bear the brunt of an anger that had doubtless been festering for years.

The Cimmerian tried to rise, but his reserves of strength were drained. All he could do was lie upon the planks while the rowers bound his hands and feet with thick ropes. "Admiral Khertet," he panted, then mouthed a crude oath in Stygian.

"Conan." Khertet spoke the word slowly, rolling it around in his mouth like a bite of bitter food. He fingered his scarred jaw and earlobe, then dug the point of his dagger into the skin above Conan's ear. "After you burned my flagship, the king exiled me, ending my glorious career in Stygia. Since that day, I have prayed to Set for retribution. He has finally answered my prayers." Khertet spat into the prone Cimmerian's face. "Your dying agonies will bring me great pleasure. . . ."

Khertet dug his knife into the flesh of Conan's jaw until blood welled from a deep groove. Laughing cruelly, the red-eyed Stygian slashed the Cimmerian's face, notching Conan's earlobe with a single vicious swipe.

Four
Nightmare at Sea

Khertet surveyed his bloody knife-work while Conan glared at him from the deck, straining against the ropes. The captain had sliced both sides of his face, and slick blood coated his jaw and ears. The Cimmerian had endured the ordeal stoically, although he lacked the energy to resist, even to hurl any oaths at his tormentor.

The Stygian licked Conan's blood from the dagger and spat it into the barbarian's face. Then he took the sack of loot away, peering inside and chuckling.

"This is but a tithe of what I shall have from the king in Luxur. You are fortunate that he has offered a reward to whomever brings you to his feet alive. Killing you would bring me great joy, but I want my command back, and your capture will restore the king's faith in me." His eyes gleamed, and a smile played on his blood-smeared lips. "It is enough for me to know that you will suffer for hours as a serpent of Set eats you alive, digesting you slowly, dissolving the flesh from your bones. You will whimper and beg for death."

Fingering his scar, Khertet bent his face down until Conan smelled his hot, sour breath. "Death will bring you no mercy. Your soul will be banished to our Serpent-God's Hell, doomed to the eternal agony of a thousand unspeakable tortures."

The Cimmerian seethed at his helplessness and ground his teeth, trying to shut off the throbbing pain that permeated his head. Beads of perspiration dripped from his face, dampening his thick mane of blood-matted hair and loosening the dark clots. His blue eyes blazed with the fires of rage, and a measure of his strength returned. "Stygian jackal," he rasped. "Your dogs will not save you when we meet in Hell—where all lackeys of Set are sent as reward for their misbegotten loyalty."

"Empty words, barbarian fool," Khertet said smugly. "In four months, when we reach Luxur, you will beg for my mercy and whine for the privilege of licking bilge-water from my boots. You Cimmerians are stubborn and hardy, and you can survive the voyage with little food and water. Alive you will be when I take you before the king . . . alive, but broken and mewling, a feeble husk of wretchedness." He turned his back and spoke to a white-bearded Vendhyan, who had come through the hatch and quietly watched Khertet's cruelty. "Jhatil! Wash the dog-blood from this oaf's head and bind his wounds. He must suffer but not die—I shall have my command back!"

The aged Vendhyan wordlessly went about his task, pouring stinging salt water over Conan's raw wounds. His inflamed head burned as though thrust into a brazier of coals. He suppressed a grunt of agony while the wrinkled old man knotted a filthy rag over the red furrows that had been dug in his face. The cloth's rough, stiff edge bit into Conan's skin but did not block his vision or gag him. He saw Khertet motioning to two oarsmen.

"Devwir and Matara, take this piece of offal to the cargo hold and bind him to an empty crate. And be sure that you use the stoutest rope aboard; this Cimmerian is more dangerous than he seems. I have seen him in battle,

bleeding from wounds but still fighting like a cornered ti-
ger. Pour a dipperful of water down his throat once a day,
but give him rations only every third day.

"Take shifts standing watch at the door to the hold. I
shall personally check once during every shift, and the
head of any watchmen whom I find sleeping will decorate
the bowsprit. The rest of you dogs, bend your backs and
pray for the trade winds to return. If we reach Luxur in
three months, each of you will be paid double as reward.
Lay out!" he bellowed, swaggering back to the poop deck.
He nodded to the short Vendhyan drummer and barked orders to the Stygian helmsman.

The burly rowers heaved Conan from the blood-
splashed planks and hauled him through the ship's narrow
fore hatch. A small, stout door opened into the cramped
hold. Letting their burden drop to the hard deck, the oarsmen emptied a large, solid crate of its Vendhyan carpets,
which they crammed into the few niches that the hold offered. The Vendhyans were muscular, but their combined
strength was needed to lift and position the empty con-
tainer. Jhatil had followed them through the hatch, carrying a coil of rope that was twice the girth of Conan's
thumb.

The Vendhyans wound the heavy cord around his
already-trussed body, lashing him to the crate with cunning knots that would tighten if Conan struggled. When
they were done, he could barely move his fingers and toes.
They had left his face directly under a narrow iron gate in
the hold's ceiling, which provided meager light and venti-
lation.

Khertet's cruel face looked down at him through the
grate. The Stygian's mocking laughter echoed maddenj-
ingly. Weakened by loss of blood and the constant pangs
from his raw, oozing wounds, the Cimmerian fell into a
sleep of exhaustion.

The full moon hung in the night sky like a giant, dull
pearl, dimly illuminating dense jungle trees and casting

pale light onto the damp, leaf-covered floor. Droplets from recent rainfall shimmered on the dark green foliage.

Conan's sense of smell, which had always been keen, seemed particularly sharp tonight, and his nostrils twitched at musty odors, seeking traces of animal scents.

He moved silently through the trees. There was no path through this primitive landscape, but Conan somehow knew his way through its savage depths. Countless times before, he had tracked quarry through his territory. The sounds, smells, and shapes guided him toward his destination, toward his prey. His belly rumbled, and he craved raw, warm meat, fresh hot blood. The air tingled with the scent of fat, four-legged animals. They had passed recently, leaving their spoor behind them.

A nagging tickle in his brain told him that something was wrong. He was no primitive predator, to track wild game and rend it with his teeth; strange urges filled him. What was he doing in this jungle, naked, without even his sword?

But these thoughts quickly vanished from his brain, and he was again wholly intent on the hunt. His dry throat craved red, rich juices; he longed to sink his sharp teeth into the vitals of a soft animal and tear strips of meat from its corpse. His mind had room for naught else but these bestial cravings. He lived for the hunt . . . all creatures in his leafy realm feared him and his brutish, voracious appetite.

And he relished their fear. Nothing enraged him as much as the rare beast who would fight him, instead of quivering in terror when facing him.

As he crept through the underbrush, his stinking breath rose from his open mouth, filling his nostrils with the stale stench of past feasts. He licked at the corners of his lips, savoring the faint taste of blood from the boar he had slain at midday. He often slept at night, but tonight the full moon filled him with the longing to feed until his bloated belly could hold no more. Even then he would stalk and slay, until that baleful ivory orb sank from the sky.

Ahead lay a clearing in the trees, and the smell of his quarry wafted through the air toward him. Drooling, he smacked his lips and crouched, bending his ears attentively. He sensed the presence of the herd directly ahead. He would spring through the brush and be upon the sleeping animals before they could bolt.

From the crouch, he tensed his powerful leg muscles and leapt through the wall of leaves and moss, extending his hairy, black-nailed hands and baring his crooked yellow fangs. An involuntary growl ripped its way out of his throat, shattering the jungle's silence. He landed atop a sleeping beast that stirred too late to avoid him. His fangs tore through its tough black-and-white striped hide.

Blood jetted from the animal's torn throat; its hooves twitched feebly before it died. The rest of the herd had sprung up, blinking, the moon reflected in a dozen pairs of eyes. They turned to flee.

The sight drove him into a red frenzy. Spraying blood from his mouth, he howled with such savage fury that the herd froze in terror. He slaughtered three more as they cowered and bleated, slashing their throats with his vicious fangs. Then the beasts shook off the paralyzing trance of his cry, and bounded away from him.

He gave chase, filled with the madness that drove him to kill, to spill the blood of anything that breathed. Snarling and panting, he caught up with the herd and dragged down the rearmost beast, rending its hide, ripping its vitals as its still-beating heart pumped gouts of thick, hot blood from its ghastly wound.

Conan's mouth foamed at the sight. Slavering, he stripped hunks of dripping red flesh from the dying beast and crammed them into his mouth, gulping them down without even chewing, tearing meat from the twitching carcass in a gluttonous orgy of frenzied feeding. He lifted his blood-smeared face to the sky, staring at the moon.

It stared back, suddenly taking on the aspect of that Kaklani shaman's wrinkled, tattooed face. The lips were twisted in a mockery of a smile, and the mouth opened, filling the night sky with hollow, diabolical laughter.

Conan woke to the sound of his own shout, instinctively reaching for a sword that was no longer at his side. Perspiration dripped from his every pore. He recalled every detail of the nightmare with hair-raising clarity. His body was damp, but not only from sweat; the coarse ropes had cut into him while he tossed and turned, and blood now spotted them. Pain rose in throbbing waves from the cuts in his face; they itched, but he could not raise a hand to scratch at them. His calf was sore and swollen where the helmsman's knife had pierced it. Conan lay atop the wooden crate, clenching his fists in helpless rage, staring at the ceiling of the cargo hold.

It was night still—he could see the dark sky through the iron gate overhead. The ship's gentle, rolling motion did little to calm him. He seethed, filling his muscles with the strength of rage, and threw his might into one terrific push against the thick ropes.

But the sinews of ten stout men would have failed to break those bonds. Conan relaxed his straining thews and exhaled, groaning exhaustedly. Blood streamed anew from his jaw and rope-cuts, and he gritted his teeth, staring upward through the ceiling grate. Sleep offered him no comfort, for he had no wish to endure another of the strange dreams that had plagued him since the night of the battle.

The night of the red mist.

The dying shaman had summoned some demon to plague his dreams, perhaps to drive him to madness. A hundred haunting tales sprang into his mind, stories of slain men whose spirits rose to seek vengeance. A shiver lifted the damp, short hairs on the back of Conan's neck. His deeply rooted dread of magic and the supernatural whispered dark suggestions to him as he lay in the ship's makeshift brig, gazing at the ceiling.

Then he drew in a sharp breath. Through the grate, the moon rose into view, freezing the blood in his veins. Unable to close his reddened eyes, he stared upward at it. It was but a tiny sliver away from waxing full. The carnage from his dream filled his mind's eye, and he wondered what unspeakable fate a full moon might portend.

Conan turned his head sideways, refusing to let these omens daunt him. What he needed was a plan to escape the hold. If he could but retrieve his blade, he would teach that Stygian dog Khertet a hard lesson about vengeance.

He strained to hear the sounds around him, and the murmuring of voices filtered down. The cloth bandage and the clots of blood muffled some sounds, but he could still hear the creak of the ship's timbers and the gentle slap of waves against her hull. The night watch abovedecks presumably consisted of two men; he could hear two distinct voices, but their exact words were unclear. From outside the door to the cargo hold, he heard a strange, wheezing rasp, which he listened to for a while before realizing that the guard posted there was snoring.

Conan thought about escape—the prospects were not encouraging.

Khertet apparently had no intention of ever loosening the ropes. Conan would lie here, trapped for months, wasting away. The Cimmerian knew the limits of his endurance—with scant rations and a dipperful of water every day, his strength would ebb in less than a week. On many past occasions—during arduous desert treks and other hard times—he had lasted longer, but he could feel that his loss of blood had already drained precious vitality.

The Stygian ex-admiral wanted to keep him alive and deliver him as a prize to the serpent-worshipping scum in Luxur; Crom knew what horrors awaited him in the snake pits of that accursed city. Conan would have to find a way out soon. Once weakened from starvation, he would truly be at Khertet's mercy.

He berated himself again for the ill decision that had involved him in the war between the Kaklanis and Zariris. Mercenary service could be lucrative, but choosing the wrong employer could prove fatal . . . as it had for

Conan's men. The Cimmerian should not have accepted
the Zariri sheikh's offer at face value. In the future—if he
indeed had much of a future left—he vowed to be wiser in
weighing risk against reward. Conan's recent experiences
as a soldier of fortune had yielded meager profits. He had
too often left the battlefield with more scars on his body
than gold in his coin purse.

A faint but noticeable brightening of the cargo hold's interior alerted Conan to the approach of dawn. Then he
heard a rustle that seemed to come from somewhere directly beside his head. He craned his neck to see what it
was and felt a sharp, fresh burst of pain from his left ear.

Conan heard the sound of tearing cloth and again felt a
sharp twinge. Turning, he saw a long, thick, pink tail lying
on the crate next to his head. A plump grey-brown rat was
attached to the tail. From its sharpened teeth dangled a
fleshy strip from Conan's earlobe. Flecks of blood—his
own—stained its crooked snout, and lumpy grey lesions
spotted its sickly fur. Its tiny red eyes regarded the barbarian with indifference as it boldly munched on its early
morning meal.

Conan growled.

The huge, repulsive rodent ignored him.

Enraged by its effrontery, Conan bared his teeth and
lunged for its finger-thick outstretched tail. Seizing it between his teeth, the Cimmerian whipped his head around,
smashing the surprised rat against the crate's hard wood
slats. It struggled, clawing at his face, scratching and biting at an open wound.

Conan's teeth dug in, almost severing the rat's tail.

After a few more blows, the rat ceased its struggles and
lay still. Conan released his grip on its tail, at the same
time releasing his worries about his imprisonment and the
shaman's insidious curse. Injured and bound he might be,
but while he lived he was not beaten. Small as it was, his
victory over the scrounging rat had lifted his spirits. Whatever fate awaited him, he would meet it face-to-face and
fight back with the gifts that his god Crom gave all

Cimmerians—the will and the strength to strive and to slay.

Grinning, Conan spat a scrap of tail out at the rat and looked up at the grate in the ceiling. He racked his brain for a plan of escape as the morning sun's rays filled the cramped cargo hold with warm, golden light.

Although he could not be certain, Conan believed that midday had arrived. The sun was not yet in view, but the ship's sail might be blocking it. A gentle breeze sifted through the overhead grate, growing into a full-fledged wind—enough to fill the sail.

Conan heard Khertet's voice booming orders to hoist the sail. Judging from the sounds of the wind and the wave, the ship was making reasonable headway.

A pleasant breeze reached into the hold, flushing out the stench of bilgewater and rat filth that permeated the stale air. The door to the hold remained shut until well after the raising of the sails, when three armed men brought food and water to the Cimmerian.

He gulped it down, a few pitiful swallows, but he had expected no more. Jhatil replaced the stained, crusty bandage with a fresh strip of cloth, wiping matted blood from the rat's bite. The old Vendhyan took away the vermin corpse, glancing at the Cimmerian curiously and shaking his head. He left without uttering even one word.

Later, Khertet peered down through the grate and hurled a few insults at the surly Cimmerian, who responded in kind. Conan heard little else from above until late that afternoon.

Recognizing the helmsman's voice and Khertet's, the Cimmerian strained to hear their conversation. They obligingly raised their voices, apparently arguing.

"I command this ship, Chadim. You would dare question my change of course?" The insulting tone was unmistakably Khertet's.

"No, honorable one! I—I realize your need for haste, and the heading you order would indeed save many weeks.

But most merchants now avoid the course you suggest."
Chadim spoke defensively, and a tremor in his voice suggested nervousness.

"I am not like most merchants. I do not fear such superstitious tales. I have heard the rumors, but they are only
the lies of drunken fools, spoken to gullible slackwits like
you to procure free ale. You spend too much time in lowly
wharf taverns. Hah! I have heard a thousand similar yarns,
and they impress only weaklings and cowards."

Chadim paused before responding. "Of course you are
right, Admiral."

"Enough of this—man your tiller and round to. We shall
pass through Nehebku's Noose before sunrise tomorrow."

The thump of Khertet's boots faded aftward.

Chadim exchanged a few words with the crew, but the
Cimmerian could not make these out. He lay upon the uncomfortable wood of the crate, wondering about the
"Noose" that Khertet had mentioned. Unlike Khertet,
Conan believed most sailor's tales of sea dangers. He had
found elements of truth in most more often than not. It
was tales of treasure that he doubted.

While he pondered this mystery, the setting sun withdrew its light from the cargo hold. Conan tried to stay alert
but found himself drifting in and out of a light doze. The
constant, pounding throb from his ears and wounded calf
finally wore him down. Eventually, his head drooped back
against the top of the crate and his leaden eyelids closed.
Moments later, he was snoring noisily, too tired to care
about Khertet's "Noose" or the violent jungle dreams.

When he woke up, the hold was as dark as a Stygian
tomb. He peered through the grate, squinting, but he could
see only the inky blackness of a cloudy night sky. Abovedecks, footfalls thudded against thick planking. The night
watchmen were faithfully making their rounds.

Conan's head ached miserably, and he could not concentrate through the fog of pain that seemed to enfold his
whole body. He shivered in spite of the muggy heat that

permeated the hold, and thick beads of sweat ran from his brow, soaking the rags around his head and stinging his wounds. He recognized the signs of fever and knew he was in for a long, restless night. At least no other rats had troubled him thus far.

Warm wind circulated through the grate, providing breathable air but doing little to ease his fever. The *Mistress* was again moving swiftly, if the rapidly slapping waves and creaking timbers were any indication. Little wonder that Khertet had insisted on this change of course. As a former admiral, he must have accumulated a wealth of information about the winds and currents of the waters near to his native Stygia.

A familiar rasping sounded beyond the cargo hold's door; Conan knew well the scrape of steel against whetstone. The sentry was sharpening his sword, a common enough way to avoid nodding off during long stretches of quiet guard duty. Sighing, Conan ground his teeth together, trying vainly to shut out the increasingly painful headache.

Pallid light suddenly diffused the hold, causing Conan to stare through the grate at the sky. Like heavy curtains, the thick clouds had parted, unveiling the full moon. Its dull glow, more sallow than white, drew him in, transfixing his eyes. His gaze as vacuous and unblinking as those of a lotus dreamer's, Conan watched in fascination as the moon grew, filling his entire field of vision like a bloated, pulsating orb.

The loud rush of wind filled his throbbing ears, but he felt no air stirring his body. Grunting apprehensively, he squeezed his eyelids shut, but the image of that bright sphere had been indelibly etched into his brain. His hands began to tremble, and a violent shiver rippled through his body from head to toe. Squirming and twisting as much as the ropes would permit, Conan lifted his head and stared down at his trapped limbs, certain that a nasty fever was burning through him.

The heavy cords seemed to tighten around him, digging into him until blood welled anew from dozens of abraded cuts. Another tremor shook him, and his skin began to itch, as if a thousand ants were crawling over him.

In the dim moonlight, he watched in horrified fascination as thick white hair began to sprout from his sweat-drenched skin. It sprang out, creeping over him and tickling his flesh until he writhed and thrashed, forcing the rope deeper into his arms, legs, and torso. Only then did the awful realization strike him—his body was swelling, his limbs distorting and expanding far beyond their normal size and shape.

His nose twitched uncontrollably at the scent of his own sweat. He detected a hundred other odors in the air, in the hold, and above, through the ceiling grate.

The scent of prey.

Conan shivered.

His hands, which he could bend only at the wrists, seemed to burn as if dipped in oil and set aflame. They had been tied against his hips, and he could feel . . . and hear . . . the fingers growing, elongating with a popping and stretching of bones and ligaments. Likewise, his feet began to curl, warping themselves into large, misshapen hands. The toes grew into long fingers with hairy white knuckles.

Conan opened his mouth to bellow, but all that came out was a rattling gargle. He felt intense pressure against his nose and forehead, as though something swelled inside his skull and sought egress through his face. He ran his tongue across unnaturally sharp teeth, and his jaw thrust itself forward, jutting against the taut skin of his face with a sound like wet leather being stretched and scraped.

A surge of pain knocked the breath out of him, and he arched his back, watching his already-massive chest enlarge. Invisible hands pulled at his ribs, bending them outward with agonizing slowness, until Conan thought he could bear the torment no longer.

A tortured howl finally burst out of his throat, his voice more animal than human. Bucking and heaving, Conan strained against his bonds with his furry white limbs, grunting, flexing, until the wood beneath him splintered. The Cimmerian slid from beneath the ropes and rolled onto the floor of the hold, feeling the circulation return to his misshapen, furry limbs.

He pressed his palms against the sides of his head, lifting his eyes to the glowering yellowish moon, snarling and growling in low, brutish tones.

His memory seemed strangely distant; he reached deep to recall where he had heard those sounds before. If only he could remember! His mind slipped away, and he fought to hold it, to remember who he was. He pounded his massive fists against a sturdy crate, reducing it to a pile of splinters.

Finally, he grasped the time and place of his guttural snarls. Years ago, in the dank, primeval jungles of the Black Kingdoms, he had faced a creature who made the same sounds . . . a hideous grey ape. That carnivorous abomination had torn apart half a dozen sturdy Bamula warriors before Conan and the rest of the Bamula hunting party brought it down. The ape, bleeding and bristling with spears, had wounded three more men before falling.

Conan felt the memory slip away, like water trickling between his fingers, and it was gone . . . all the remembrances of his life as the human, Conan, fled from his lumpy, shrunken brain.

All that remained was raw, unquenched fury.

He needed to kill, to sink his fangs and claws into soft flesh, to rip and shred limbs of anything living, to crack bones and suck the marrow from their jagged ends.

He felt no pain from the wounds on the sides of his head or from his punctured leg. His nose twitched, again catching the sweet scent of warm blood nearby. So keen had his senses become that through the thick wood of the cargo hold's door, he could hear the beating of a heart.

Prey.

He charged at the barrier that separated him from his quarry. His burly shoulder crashed into it, cracking the dense boards and wrenching iron nails from the crosspieces. The door blew off its hinges, slamming the astonished guard against the opposite wall and crushing him like a bug. Conan tossed aside the wooden wreckage and wrapped his hand around the stunned guard's neck, lifting him into the air and squeezing until the man's eyes bulged and burst from their sockets.

Conan casually tore the corpse into two bloody halves, flinging the head and torso away and cramming the man's soft vitals into his slavering mouth.

As the grisly feast continued, shouts from above mingled with the rasp of drawn swords and the thump of booted feet, running toward the hold. Conan's predatory instincts registered all these noises, and he let the guard's gutted carcass plop to the deck. Leaping straight for the hold's doorway, he rushed toward those sounds, knowing that it was more of the weak, pink-skinned beasts that were coming. He would kill them all and grind their bones between his teeth.

He stopped at the stairs leading up to the deck. Bending his knees, he flexed calf muscles that were as thick as a strong man's thighs. Before the sailors reached the top of the short staircase, Conan sprang upward, landing upon the deck with a thump that made the planks shudder under his weight.

A searing light stabbed through his eyes, piercing his brain like a spear. Conan looked up into the black-blue night sky and saw the cause of his pain, the orb that burned him with pale fire. He would quench the flames of his agony with blood from the bodies of these puny, soft creatures who approached him. There were many of them, enough to drench that orb's baleful glow in a river of blood.

Five rowers brandished their blades, surrounding him. Their arms rippled with muscle from years of hard labor at the bench. Vendhyans did not use slaves for rowing; only staunch, robust men with combat skills that had ended many a pirate's career. But even a hardened rogue would have trembled at the sight of the blood-besmeared ape who towered before them. Only their numbers lent them courage, and they struck as one.

Cutlasses whistled through empty air. Conan bounded backward with catlike agility, confounding his would-be slayers. His elongated arms outreached their blades, and he seized the closest rower by his sword arm, wrenching the limb from its socket and hurling the still-twitching appendange into the sea. The dismembered man fell forward, toward Conan, clutching at the spewing socket and screaming like a doomed soul in Hell.

Paling at the grisly ferocity of the ape's attack, the others nonetheless surged forward, trying to drive Conan into the *Mistress*'s narrow bow. Wrapping his claws around the prone rower's ankles, Conan lifted the screeching man and swung him in an arc before the others could stay their sword cuts.

Conan's human shield absorbed the rowers' blows, and the force of his swing knocked two onto the deck while stripping the others' weapons from their hands. Roaring, Conan bludgeoned a prone man with the flopping, blood-spewing corpse, and charged between the two unarmed men.

Other rowers were arriving, pouring from the forecastle, while behind them, the hatch to the officer's quarters banged open. Conan would have recognized the men who dashed out as Jhatil, Chadim, and Khertet—but to the ape they were all naught but fodder. Khertet shouted orders, but all Conan heard were a jumble of sounds, strange mouthings with less meaning than the squawking of birds or the chattering of monkeys.

The disarmed rowers scrambled for their blades, but Conan tore one apart before the man could retrieve his fallen cutlass. The other managed to jab his point into Conan's side before he, too, was held fast in the ape's lethal grip. His arms were pulled from his body, their ragged stumps jetting blood.

The foremost rank of rowers stepped forward, jamming the ship's deck from starboard to port. Eager to strike a

blow for their fallen fellows, they swallowed their fear and
shock, following Khertet's shouted commands, trying to
keep to the rail and looking for an opening. These men
fought more shrewdly, aiming cuts and slashes at Conan's
flailing arms. But again the cunning ape used the bodies of
the fallen, this time as gory missiles.

The deck afforded the rowers no easy means to duck the
hail of severed limbs and mangled torsos that Conan was
hurling. But from the safety of the poop deck, Chadim
tossed knives at the hairy, blood-smeared juggernaut. With
each throw, a hilt jutted from the ape's hide, but the beast
did not so much as flinch. The knives were naught but the
stings of steel bees; his vitals were untouched by Chadim's
short blades.

A few rowers slipped in puddles of ghastly slime that
gushed or oozed from the ruptured bodies of the slain.
Conan pounced upon the fallen, rending their limbs and
cracking their bones, tossing their pulped cadavers overboard with wanton frenzy. Bravely, the crew surrounded
the gore-stained ape and hewed wildly at hide as tough as
a leather jerkin. A few drew blood—thick, reddish-black
ichor that welled sluggishly from deep stab wounds.

These blows served only to pump Conan's savage ape
brain full of murderous hysteria. He ran amok into their
ranks, heedless of their slashing swords, biting huge
chunks of flesh from their unarmored bodies and slitting
their throats with the deadly swipe of his cruel claws. Pitted against an unstoppable storm of talons and teeth, the
crew finally lost their nerve and fell back. Of the score of
men who had stood against the ape, only three officers and
five rowers still breathed.

Khertet thundered in frustration, desperately trying to
rally his beleaguered men.

Five
Nehebku's Noose

The few surviving crewmen turned their cutlasses to the lines of the *Mistress's* single launch, leaping onto it as it fell to the water. They seized the oars and bent their backs, rowing like men possessed. Cursing, the Stygian captain looked up fearfully at the rampaging ape and promptly threw himself through the hatch to the officer's quarters with Chadim and Jhatil at his heels. They had barely slammed the hatch's cross bar into place before Conan reached the stout wooden portal.

This door was more secure than the cargo hold's, for it had been built to keep previous loot—and the officers' skins—safe from pirate assaults. Working with the furious speed borne of fear, the three men wedged every heavy object that they could find against the hatch. They piled up barrels, built makeshift braces of a few spare oars, and hammered spikes into the timbers for reinforcement. The Vendhyan custom of keeping tools in the officer's storage proved its worth, although no mariner could have imagined this emergency.

Roaring with the furor of a dozen tempests, Conan pounded on the hatch until the wood shivered in its heavy frame. But the thick hinge-bolts held, and the hatch withstood the abuse of the ape's bludgeoning fists. By design, the hatch lay at an angle. Its size and position prevented Conan from throwing his shoulder against the wood, as he had done with the cargo hold's door.

Panting, Conan stepped back from the hatch, smacking his lips at the visceral stench that was rising from the ship. He vented his ire upon the human wreckage littering the *Mistress's* gruesome deck. The moon loomed nearer the water, as if bearing witness to the atrocious scene: the grunting ape, gorging itself upon the glistening innards of victims.

Eating until his belly could hold no more, the sated beast loped across the planks toward the mast. Settling against it with a moist, booming belch, he felt his gaze drawn again to the moon. It had sunk below the water, as if swallowed by the sea.

Its glow had receded. He smacked his lips and sighed, sliding down the mast until his buttocks rested upon the deck. When the last sliver of the moon disappeared, Conan's eyelids grew heavy. The red tide of blood had extinguished the unbearable burning of the disc that dominated the night sky.

Conan's head drooped until his chin slumped against his massive chest, and sleep overcame him.

In the officer's quarters, Khertet paced restlessly, his lips drawn back in a ferocious scowl.

Chadim wiped his damp forehead on the sleeve of his tunic. The moist heat of night filled the cabin, and the air was stale and oppressive. "From which of Sebeq's seven abysses did that hairy fiend crawl? By Asura, I have never seen a beast so thirsty for blood!"

Khertet ignored the Vendhyan helmsman, lifting his gaze from the deck only to glance at the barricaded door.

He had not spoken since the pounding on the door had ceased.

Groaning, Jhatil rubbed the back of his neck and scratched his wispy gray beard. "Aye," he said, nodding to Chadim. "Truly it is a demon, but worse than any issue from Sebeq's vile wombs. You were right, Chadim, we should never have set a course through these waters. Nehebku's Noose has snared us!"

"Silence, old fool," Khertet snapped. "You city-bred Vendhyans have never seen the jungle apes of Zembab-wei; I have, though never have I seen one so vicious. That ape is no minion of Nehebku's—it is some deviltry of Conan's. I should have slit the Cimmerian pig's throat when I had the chance."

Chadim's eyes flashed as Khertet spoke. "You are un-wise to discount Nehebku, Stygian. When she last fed, Jhatil's grandfather was but a stripling. Our loremasters say that she awakens every three generations, preying upon creatures of the deep and even rising to the surface to seize unwary vessels. She has taken many forms in her long and terrible reign of this region's waters. This shaggy man-beast is surely another of her incarnations."

"And the blood," Jhatil added, nodding. "That 'ape' has strewn a fresh trail of meat that the most sluggish of sea beasts would find impossible to resist."

Chadim chewed his lower lip. "Did you see the full moon tonight? It marks the beginning of the Month of the Fish, midway through the Year of the Serpent. Yama's star is in the House of Abwharim—"

Khertet interrupted, rolling his eyes upward. "Pah! Only fools or madmen let the night skies decide their fate. I know not how, but the Cimmerian has once again slain my crew and stolen my vessel. By the fangs of Set, I would wish that your Nehebku were real, if she would come and slay the barbarian. Doubtless he stands above us, laughing from the tiller, steering the *Mistress* to some pirate cove."

The three men lapsed into glum silence, staring deject-edly at the walls of their self-made prison. Then Khertet's brow furrowed, and Chadim tilted his head sideways, as if straining to hear a distant sound.

Jhatil, balancing atop a barrel, pressed his ear to the top of the hatch.

WHUMP!

The *Mistress* lurched violently, as if slapped by a giant hand. Jhatil's arms whirled in the air, then he lost his balance and fell to the deck, narrowly rolling away from a toppling barrel.

Khertet, whose sea legs were not so easily upset, stood gaping incredulously as the *Mistress* shuddered, listing and reeling as if rammed full bore by a Turanian war galley. The Stygian's dusky face paled.

"Nehebku," Chadim whispered, his eyes wide, mouth agape. He flung himself to the deck, covering his head with his arms and sobbing in sheer terror.

A thunderous crash jolted Conan from his deep repose. Rising slowly to his feet, he shook an unusual fog of slumber from his brain. He was instantly aware that something was wrong, for he seldom slept so heavily. Even the faint light of the coming dawn had failed to awaken him.

He braced himself against the mast. As his vision cleared, the carnage surrounding him came into focus. He stared at the blood-soaked deck and the shredded heaps of entrails and bones, almost gagging at the putrid, nose-shriveling reek that wafted up his nostrils. And although the haze of sleep lingered in his mind, his body tingled with energy, more vitality than he had felt in days.

But how had he escaped from the cargo hold?

He lifted his hands to the sides of his head, and an icy finger brushed his spine. Where there had been ghastly cuts, his fingers traced nearly healed skin. It was as if the slashes had been made days ago. Conan's flesh crawled in suspicion of this miracle; he wondered if he were dreaming. He accepted the boon with hesitant cheer, for he had an instinctive dread of events that were stained even faintly with the ink of sorcery. The calf-wound he had taken from Chadim's knife had also vanished, leaving not even the pink line of a scar. The only marks on his body were faint abrasions crisscrossing his arms, legs, and chest.

"Crom," he muttered. "What sorcery is this?" Racking his hazy memory, he struggled to recall the events that had brought him here. He remembered drifting into sleep last night . . .

Then the images flashed into his mind, like scenes from a half-remembered nightmare. His transformation—and the butchery that had followed. Reeling from the repugnant memories of his macabre feast, he forced down his rising gorge.

But Conan pushed aside these disturbing, shadowy recollections. He had little time to dwell upon the atrocities that he had committed while transformed, for the *Mistress* had begun to list. The wind was still pushing her through the water on a meandering course. He had thought the crash that awakened him had been the *Mistress* striking a reef, but near her stern, he saw a churning, boiling eddy. It was nothing natural, that whirlpool, a thing unlike any he had ever seen in all his years at sea. His flesh crawled in spite of the heat, and a feeling of dread rippled through his bones.

Staring at the whirlpool, he watched it bubble and foam until steam rose from the water in thick, translucent vapors. The *Mistress*, caught in the swirling current, slowly circled around the eddy's widening perimeter.

Without so much as a warning splash, a scaly, red leviathan reared its head from the center of the boiling region. Barnacles and sea scum sprouted from its bumpy, dull skin. Its immense skull reminded Conan of a serpent's save for the rows of pulsating gills on its neck and the pair of eyes each as large as Conan's head. Those dreadful orbs bulged from its misshapen skull like noxious, pinkish-yellow boils. Its tail was nowhere in sight; doubtless it lay deep below the maelstrom.

Opening its fanged mouth wide enough to swallow three men, the behemoth's head lunged straight for the *Mistress*.

Conan froze, transfixed by the unspeakable, ageless malice that glistened in those veined eyes. It was as if the bowels of the deepest Hell had opened, spewing out the most fearsome serpent-devil ever spawned.

As its dripping snout thrust toward him, Conan could see splintered pieces of the keel, impaled on the sea beast's fangs. The Cimmerian immediately deduced the reason for the *Mistress*'s laboring: the monster's jaw had ripped through wood as thick as a man's waist, tearing out a chunk of timber large enough to gut the *Mistress*.

A blast of steam hissed through the serpent's yawning orifice, reddening Conan's skin and searing his eyes. He shielded his face with his arm and broke the paralyzing effect of the thing's insidious eyes.

The Cimmerian sprang sideways, his heels brushing against the beast's sweltering skin. Its rapierlike fangs missed him by a handspan, closing instead upon the base of the mast. The thick wooden shaft broke like a twig, thumping against the rail. Conan rolled out of its way, ducking under the sweep of the crimson-skinned head.

Undaunted, the barbarian grabbed the largest cutlass within reach, prying away a disembodied hand that still gripped the hilt. Grimly, he braced himself against the slanting deck, preparing for the serpent's next lunge. He had fought against the children of Set before and knew that a well-placed sword thrust through the tender, vulnerable roof of a snake's mouth might pierce the vile creature's brain. He would need to bury the blade deep, to be certain, and his first attack must succeed, before the whirlpool swallowed the doomed ship and sucked him into its steamy abyss.

The air around him grew unbearably hot, thickening and filling his nose with a rotten, sulfurous stench. The laboring vessel creaked as the water roared and bubbled around it.

Swinging back and around, the beast again thrust its

maw toward Conan, who stood defiantly in its path, his feet planted upon the blood-besmeared deck. Again the serpent's gleaming fangs flashed in the light like ivory daggers in curving racks.

But the Cimmerian was ready. Vaulting forward to meet its diving head, he plunged his blade into the exposed pink flesh of the mouth. A stinging cloud of steam washed over him before he could release his grip on the sword, but he avoided the deadly fangs by diving and rolling onto the deck. The powerful jaws snapped onto naught but air— and a few strands of Conan's flowing black mane.

Reaching for another cutlass, the Cimmerian scrambled to his feet and waited to see if his attack had skewered the thing's brain. Would one thrust be enough? Never had he clashed with so gigantic a serpent!

As the beast pulled its head back toward the center of the eddy, Conan could see the hilt jutting from its mouth, its three-foot blade a meager thorn in that elephantine maw. The *Mistress* continued to spiral and sink; the sea rose to the halfway mark on her broached hull. The desperate Cimmerian knew that time was running out. In another moment he would have to plunge overboard and swim like a man possessed lest the whirlpool suck him into its churning, frothing throat.

He tossed aside the useless cutlass as another plan sprang into his head. Positioning himself amidships and bracing his feet against the starboard thwarts, he waited for the sea giant's next assault. Its head, rocking back on a neck thick enough for a horse to ride on, jumped forward again, intent on devouring its tiny but elusive Cimmerian prey.

Flexing his knees and wrapping his iron-hard arms around the fallen mast, Conan strained to lift it, using legs and arms to wrestle the thick, unwieldy spar into the path of the spike-toothed muzzle. Its weight was easily thrice his own, and he felt his back creak from the burden. The thicker end of the mast had been splintered into a tapering, jagged point, and Conan struggled to lift this end over his head, shifting his grip and unbending his knees. He dragged the pole slightly forward, bracing the far end against the deck as if setting a titan's spear against a charge.

The serpent, with eerie cunning, seemed to be aware of Conan's defiant effort. It twisted its snout away, trying to check its swift forward motion. But the *Mistress* was moving, too, as Conan had foreseen.

"Eat this, by Crom!" he bellowed, swinging the wide, hardwood beam straight for the brutish skull. Corded muscles rippled from his forearms and knotted in this shoulders, bulging from the strain. The beast's dodging head slammed into the broken mast, but the jagged base missed its mouth by a sword-length. It plunged into the glowering pink eye with a sickening wet smack, lancing the bulging orb in a gout of yellow spew.

Driven by the force of the serpent's lunge, the mast gouged out the eye and plowed into the thing's thick brainpan. Gobs of pungent pink slime gushed from the gaping socket, spraying the mast with an ooze so rancid that its smell made Conan's eyes water. The gelatinous eye slipped from the end of the mast and flopped to the deck with a greasy splat.

Hissing out a foul gasp of scalding breath, the impaled creature slid down the mast and crashed onto the deck, convulsing. Thrashing weakly, the serpent tugged to free its head, but the mast's yardarm had caught on the rowers' bench, trapping the beast. Spouting puffs of steam mixed with its own vital fluids. The jaws flexed one final time, heaving up a viscous mound of sludge before slumping at the feet of its slayer.

Panting, Conan stepped back, light-headed from his exertions. He looked out over the bow, along the serpent's body, toward the whirlpool. The eddy was slowing, receding. But the *Mistress* continued spinning toward the gurgling center of the maelstrom—from where the now-motionless body of the serpent had emerged. Conan wondered where its tail might be; the thing had been at least thrice the length of the ship.

Other snakes he had slain had whipped their bodies about in their death throes, but this brute had kept its end submerged throughout the battle. Perhaps it was anchored deep in the bowels of a reef or even the floor of the ocean.

But he had no time to ponder this further, thinking instead of how to escape from the sinking *Mistress*. The ship's only launch had been taken, so Conan set to the task of hastily slapping together a crude raft. He dragged up the cargo hold's door, noting with alarm that the hold wallowed in water. Lashing wood from a crate to the door with a length of hawser, he fashioned a makeshift and far from seaworthy craft. He hoped it would hold together long enough to bear him to an island, if not to the southern coast.

He left a length of rope ties to the crude craft, lowering it into the water. If only he could find some supplies ... he eyed the hold wistfully, knowing that the time for foraging was well past. Lack of water would slim his chances of survival ... with even a small barrel, he could last for weeks.

Swearing, he raced for the hatch to the officer's quarters, where the food and water would be found. Perhaps the galley would not be as flooded as the cargo hold had been.

As Conan neared the hatch, a muffled shout reached his ears. Startled, he paused and pressed his restored ear against the wood. From within, he heard a familiar voice.

"Cower here if you wish and drown like rats! Set take both of you dogs!" Khertet's loud curse boomed through the door.

"Nehebku will strip your insolent flesh and crack your bones, Stygian whoreson!" Chadim yelled back, his voice tight with panic.

Jhatil's strained tones cut short any reply that Khertet might have made. "Enough, both of you! The water rises to our knees already, and you waste precious time. Perhaps

Nehebku's gullet is too full of ape-meat to worry with
morsels like us. Better to risk whatever awaits us above
than to spend out last breath trading insults."

A vague memory returned to Conan, of chasing prey
into a hold and being unable to pursue them further. Conan
heard the sounds of frantic scraping and hammering from
the other side of the door, noticing for the first time that
the hard wood bore wide, shallow dents, in the shapes of
massive fists. He put his hands against them, noting with
awe that his alter ego's bestial paws were twice the size of
his own. The door must have been barricaded against him.

Abandoning any hope of recovering a barrel of water,
Conan quickly surveyed the fallen, retrieving the best
sword he could find. Before he could return to his makeshift raft, the closed hatch burst open. Khertet emerged,
his dusky face flushed as he saw the Cimmerian awaiting
him. He lifted his thin-bladed sword, a master armorer's
work forged of unbreakable Akbitanan steel.

Six
Steel Vengeance

"You!" Khertet screamed at Conan. "Barbarian dog, I'll—" he stepped back, gaping at the slain serpent. The beast's gory head lolled on the besmeared foredeck, its single eye frozen in a death-stare.

As the two men faced each other, the ailing ship continued to spin slowly, so that Khertet now stood between Conan and the raft. Conan's blood seethed with red-hot fury. "Stygian scum—join your crew in Hell!" Leaping with the speed of a panther, Conan lifted his blade, aiming a slash at Khertet's swarthy neck.

The wily Stygian regained his composure just in time to raise his blade, parrying Conan's lunge. He whirled and countered with a thrust of his own, nicking the Cimmerian's forearm.

Ignoring the dripping wound, the barbarian aimed another brutal swipe at Khertet. There was no time for prolonged swordplay, and Conan knew that Khertet's weapon—forged from metal as resilient as it was rare—was both stronger and lighter than his own. He would of necessity have to beat Khertet by brute force. Knotted muscle and iron-hard sinew propelled a slash that the Stygian parried by sheer reflex, sparks flying from both weapons at the impact.

Conan's blade shattered. "Crom's teeth!" he swore, tossing aside the broken cutlass.

Laughing, Khertet stepped toward his opponent for a killing blow. But the *Mistress*, continuing to sink, shifted and threw her captain off balance. Khertet stumbled forward and pitched to the deck. His sword clattered to the planks, well beyond the reach of his frantically grasping fingers. The Stygian's laugh turned to a groan of pain as his leg twisted under him. He fumbled at his belt for his dagger.

Chadim rushed out from belowdecks, dagger in hand. Jhatil ran up behind him, cutlass upraised, moving so fast that he nearly stumbled into Chadim.

Conan wrenched a cutlass from the hand of a dead sailor. Balancing it carefully, he hurled it at Chadim, whose arm was drawn back to throw his own knife. The cutlass struck the Vendhyan in the breast, slipping between his ribs and passing through his body. Its bloody point jutted out between Chadim's shoulder blades, slashing Jhatil's neck. Chadim fell backward, his heart pierced. Pinned beneath him, Jhatil drowned in the blood that spewed from his own slit throat.

Khertet held his dagger low for a disemboweling thrust. Conan dived for the captain's dropped sword, seizing its slippery hilt as the Stygian's dagger-thrust grazed his side. Conan shot out his free hand, grabbing Khertet's wrist and twisting it until he heard the snapping of bones. The dagger spun from the Stygian's nerveless fingers, and Conan shoved Khertet toward the rail.

But the stubborn Stygian scooped up a dead rower's cutlass. Wielding it in his good hand, he charged at the Cimmerian. "Scum!" he panted, approaching warily in an expert swordsman's stance. "With this base blade shall I send you to Hell!" He lunged with blinding speed.

Conan swept his arms back over his right shoulder, wielding the Stygian's blade in a two-handed grip. Twisting to avoid Khertet's point, he swung the thin blade in a wide arc, driving the sharpened edge through skull and jawbone. Wrenching the weapon from Khertet's cloven neck, Conan leapt to the deck of the raft while the twitching corpse fell over the rail and into the swirling sea.

The Cimmerian coiled the mooring-rope and took up an oar, hoping to escape from the whirlpool that churned around him. Although the swirling of the water had slowed somewhat since the sea-beast's death, Conan could feel the unnatural warmth of the roiling ocean; it lapped hungrily at his raft. Rowing with deep, powerful strokes, he gradually moved away from the ship of death. He glanced over a laboring shoulder at the doomed *Mistress*. Her bellyful of water had dragged her down, dislodging the floating mast from its deck. The serpent's carcass sank quietly into a briny grave.

Sweat poured down Conan's back. The water had warmed his raft, and the sun blazed down from a cloudless sky. Conan felt precious moisture drain from his body, but he was powerless to stop it. When he had put enough distance between himself and the *Mistress*, he lifted his oar from the water to conserve strength. He was not yet weary, but his pulse was racing and his heart pounded more rapidly than it should from the exertion of rowing.

He did not dwell upon his lack of provisions. In his travels, he had crossed deserts on foot and endured day after day of thirst and starvation. While his raft drifted, he was struck by the similarity between the southern sea and the eastern desert. Vast wastelands they were, ruled by the same king. From his lofty throne, the baleful sun reigned supreme over these two wildernesses, demanding a tribute of sweat from those who dared enter. Even the ruthless kings of Stygia or Turan could show more compassion that the cruel sun.

Conan was concerned less about sustenance than about the mystery of his recent transformation. As much as the sun beat upon him, Conan dreaded more the coming of the moon. Would the shaman's curse strike him again? Its effects troubled even the battle-hardened Cimmerian. He felt no pity for his dead captors. What irked him was the loss of control—no, the loss of his very identity. On the ship, Conan of Cimmeria had ceased to exist. He had become a mindless carnivore.

The thought of eating man-flesh twisted his belly into knots. Once, he had tangled with the cannibals of Darfar, in the lawless city of Zamboula. Those dark-hearted dogs were the scourge of the southern lands, and it sat ill with Conan to share anything in common with them. But the curse had helped him to escape imprisonment and avoid a grisly fate in Luxur. He had beaten the sea serpent, and he would find some way of overcoming the shaman's hideous spell.

He wrung the sweat from his matted hair, feeling a sudden dizziness. Closing his eyes, he settled onto his raft. There was barely enough room on its hard, uneven surface to accommodate his sizable frame. The dull ache in his forearm reminded him of the nick he had taken in the brief fight with Khertet, and he glanced at the red-rimmed wound.

The dagger's cut was narrow, not even as wide as his thumb, but an angry purple swelling had risen from the wound's edges. He recognized all too clearly the signs of poison—a paralyzing stain with a hue characteristic of the Purple Lotus. He should have known that Khertet, in true Stygian fashion, would envenom his dagger. Cimmerians had no need to resort to such base tactics, relying upon their strength and savagery. Conan deemed poison unmanly.

At least the venom was acting slowly, not impeding his escape.

Willing himself to remain conscious, Conan forced his body to move. He dipped the blade into the sea to cleanse it, knowing that its metal was more resistant to rust than baser steel. Washed of its stains, his sword gleamed in the sun. Gritting his teeth, he made three deep slashes across his forearm, then plunged it into the water. He felt the sting of salt burning the lotus from the cuts. When the sensation abated, he drew out his arm and shook it, sucking at the wound and spitting until he no longer tasted the poison's bitter residue.

No venom remained at the surface of the slash, but his rowing efforts had circulated the accursed stuff into the rest of his body. He fought it with fading willpower, eventually slumping back to the raft. Staring upward, he saw that clouds had begun to gather overhead, dark and brooding. Wind gusted across the raft, cooling him off.

Conan fought to concentrate, recognizing the signs of the impending storm. With ebbing strength, he tied the raft's heavy mooring-rope around his waist, lashing himself to the craft lest he become separated from it. He worked his sword-point into the wood, sinking it as far in as he could. He knew he would be in for a rough time, but he did not despair. Tropical storms were wont to end as quickly as they began; he had weathered plenty of them on land and sea.

He struggled to stay alert but could not overcome the powerful taint of the Purple Lotus. While the sky darkened, he slipped into a torpid slumber.

Conan awakened, feeling warm sand against his skin. Bright sun made him squint. Blinking, he stared at the narrow stretch of beach separating him from the sea. His back felt stiff, and stout ropes still bound him to a thick board from his raft—the only board in sight. He surmised that while he slept, a storm had smashed his frail craft and washed him ashore.

He had slept off the numbing effects of the poison, and the arm cut was scabbed over. Aside from a parched throat and a gnawing hunger in his belly, he felt better than he had in days. He did not remember any strange dreams, and best of all, he had reached land. Even his sword, still driven into the board, had traveled to the beach with him.

The salt water had not treated its edge too kindly, but he would have time to tend it later.

He scanned the beach for landmarks, but the lay of this place kindled no flame of familiarity in his memory. Sparkling blue water melded with the finely powdered coral of the beach, stretching as far as he could see to either side. Behind him, the beach gave way to tall, leafy plants. Above these towered fan-leafed palm trees, their gently sloping trunks swaying in the pleasant midday breeze.

Of man or beast Conan saw no signs. He tugged at the cord securing his waist and legs to the sturdy timber from the raft, but the knots had tightened and would yield only to the edge of his sword. Cutting himself free, he stretched until the circulation returned to his limbs. He wanted to explore the area for clues to his whereabouts, but first he would seek food and water.

He moved toward a short palm and climbed it with ease, clinging to the trunk beneath the fronds and knocking loose a bunch of coconuts. Scanning the area from his improved vantage point, he saw that he had landed upon the tip of a thin, crescent-shaped island. The beach filled the interior of the crescent, partially shielded from the sea by the curving points that formed a bay.

The verdant island seemed devoid of settlers, but he could not be certain without exploring the other side. He could see what appeared to be a large clearing at the crescent's far tip. It did not look like beach, for its floor was of a grayish-white color.

Deciding to investigate this clearing, Conan slid down the tree and feasted upon the fruit from the palm. With a bellyful of sweet and chewy meats, he felt ready to survey his surroundings.

He had lost the last remnants of his garments on the night of his transformation, but he gave his appearance only a moment's consideration. Modesty was not one of his stronger instincts. Like a naked savage from a primitive jungle tribe, he prowled the shoreline, gripping his sword and looking for any signs of inhabitants, human or otherwise. The coast bore some resemblance to Zembabwei, but the latter's water was not so blue, its sand not so pristine. And Conan heard only the soft rustle of huge leaves and the surf's gentle susurrations.

Where were the sea birds? The beach wore silence like a mask, as if concealing something beneath its scenic flora and rose-tinted sand. Conan tensed; the absence of any normal jungle noises set his nerves on edge.

From the sinking sun's position, Conan judged that he traveled west, following the interior curve of the crescent. No tracks disturbed the virgin sand, and the plethora of sea creatures that clogged most shores seemed absent from this island. From his perch in the palm tree, the isle had not seemed large. In spite of this, he had reached only the halfway mark between the crescent's curving points. Quickening his pace, he hastened toward the clearing he had marked earlier.

Gradually, the beach's color dulled, its fine, pale pink sand mingling with duller granules of white and grey. When the clearing came into view, he stared at it, noting that stones of irregular sizes and shapes formed a wide, uneven mound. No palms or grass grew among the stones, and a narrow border of sand ringed the clearing.

But more interesting by far was a discernible, apparently man-made path which led to the mound. Eager to investigate, Conan ran toward the low hillock of stones.

Before he reached it, he stopped to examine a large stone, partially buried in the center of the wide, sandy path. Brushing the grit from its round surface, he uncovered it and took an involuntary step backward. "Crom!" he gasped, his flesh crawling.

What he had uncovered was not stone, but the top of a grotesquely misshapen skull.

Its breadth was twice that of Conan's head. A lumpy, bony ridge ran along it, and he kicked away more sand to reveal eye sockets the size of eggs staring hollowly at him. The sockets were on nearly opposite sides of the skull. Conan saw no ear holes or nostril slits, and the sloping forehead tapered into a bony snout, ending in a broken horned bill. He slid his sword's point into an eye socket, lifting the surprisingly light skull for closer examination. Rows of jagged teeth jutted from the insides of the thick gray bill, curving back slightly.

The skull bespoke an unnatural breed of bird. From the cruelly sharp fangs of its beak, Conan could easily see that the creature had been no plant eater. He wondered what had become of the rest of the skeleton.

Frowning, Conan let the bony abomination slide from his sword. Then he chopped at it to prevent the lifeless eyes from staring up at him. At first, his sword glanced from the bony ridge, but a second powerful stroke crushed through its pate, shattering the skull and ending its eerie gaze. Conan strode past it and soon reached the clearing. He drew in a breath, muttering in revulsion at what he saw ahead.

Lying atop the sand, jumbled in piles that rose as high as Conan's waist, were vast mounds of bleached skulls. They stretched all the way to the shoreline, like a bony gray carpet. The tide lapped at them, shifting the skulls at the edges of the piles, imbuing them with eerie movement. Most were as large as the one Conan had first discovered, but others were bigger.

Nowhere did Conan see any rib, leg, or arm bones . . . only disembodied skulls.

Morbid curiosity prompted him to sift through a pile with the point of his sword, looking for any clues to the nature of these dead creatures. At the bottoms of the mounds, the bones seemed older and more brittle. Some had begin to crumble from the slight weight of the skulls above them. Tiny shards, perhaps centuries old, formed a gruesome beach of death upon the tip of the macabre isle.

Movement on the horizon caught Conan's eye. Astonished, he watched as a small fleet of strange boats appeared, moving swiftly toward the island. He counted eight vessels, each bearing four men—no, the one in the rear carried only two. Shielding his eyes with his hand, he peered at the boats until he could see the rowers.

They were men, but unlike any he had seen before. Bright designs covered their olive-skinned, heavyset bodies. They rowed with mighty strokes that would have satisfied the harshest pacer. In spite of their swift progress across the water, the boats looked awkward. Their rowers sat atop a thick, central beam, doubtless carved from a palm tree. Curving crosspieces, like wooden arms, held smaller trunks that paralleled the larger body and provided stability. Each boat's four oarsmen gripped one oar and rowed a single stroke on alternating sides.

Conan reckoned that the efficient but simple design of the craft rendered it suitable only for short voyages as it seemed to be impossible to control in rough waters. Perhaps they had come from a nearby island, or even the mainland—this crescent-shaped isle seemed too deserted to be their home. Although they appeared to carry no weapons of any kind, the Cimmerian did not consider them harmless. Primitive, cannibalistic cults who worshiped ancient gods of evil were not uncommon in the lands of the South. Slipping hastily into the dense foliage, Conan's pulse quickened as he watched their approach.

A few men glanced backward as they rowed. When they drew nearer to the isle, Conan saw that their eyes were actually turned skyward. Lifting his gaze, the Cimmerian uttered a startled grunt.

Swooping from the azure sky and diving toward the frantic rowers, a flock of birds flapped into view. Yet something seemed wrong about their appearance. The afternoon sun shone directly into Conan's eyes; perhaps the light was affecting his vision. At such a distance Conan could not be certain, but his squinting stare beheld vulture-like creatures ... enormous birds larger than men.

Seven
The Shore of Skulls

When the swiftly moving boats neared the shoreline, the men used their oars for poles to propel their vessels toward the beach. From his hidden place among the leafy brush, Conan watched the colorfully painted oarsmen leap from their sitting positions and drag their boats ashore.

The faces of the men bore some resemblance to those of natives from Old Zembabwei. Their wide noses flattened across their faces, nostrils flaring above thick lips, and jutting ridges of bone shadowed their eyes. But even the war chiefs of Zembabwei were not as tall and stocky as the olive-skinned strangers. The shortest of these men dwarfed Conan; he doubted that his head would reach their shoulders. Their waists were nearly as thick as his chest. They wore no garments, not even a simple breechclout. Prominent navels, half as long as Conan's thumb, jutted from bellies that were large but not paunchy. Each of the men's shaved heads bore a single lock of hair. The younger ones had shorter locks with a single knot; the older men sported several knots.

The tallest, most elaborately decorated man reached the beach first. His long white hair was tightly twisted into a rope of twelve knots each a full handspan apart. Deep lines furrowed his brow, and a jagged scar ran from his neck to his waist. A string of lambent shells—blue, violet, green, and red—circled his short, thick neck, scintillating in the afternoon sunlight.

While the other men dragged their boats onto the skull-laden sand, he turned to face them. Raising his arms to the sky, he opened his hands and uttered a strange, deep cry. Conan had never heard such a sound issue from a human throat. The fierce, guttural echoes stirred coals of a battle fire that smoldered in the Cimmerian's breast. He watched, eyes narrowing, while the men mimicked that gesture and cry, lowering their knees to the sand while the imposing, white-haired giant addressed them.

But one man—an unsmiling youth—did not kneel. His sculpted muscles rippled beneath yellow triangles that adorned his chest, arms, and legs. Locks of hair grew from behind each of his ears, braided together behind his neck in apparent indifference to the custom of the others. Ignoring this youth, the old man began talking.

Conan had expected the language of these men to be guttural, like that of Zembabwei. To his surprise, the tongue was a bizarre mix of two familiar dialects. Zembabwan names for places and things mingled with other, distinctly Vendhyan words. The Cimmerian's brow furrowed in concentration as he struggled to comprehend.

"Mighty Ganaks," the white-haired man began, in tones that rumbled like low thunder. He instantly commanded the attention of the others. Not one man fidgeted or averted his eyes from that solemn old face. Only the youth showed indifference, standing behind the others with his huge hands resting on his hips.

The Cimmerian shook his head in wonder. Why did they not take refuge from the winged pursuers or at least seek a more strategic defensive position?

The old Ganak continued. "This day you have fought

well. You have sent many Kezati to the gray lands. But many remain—too many, perhaps." He paused, lowering his arms to his sides. "The fathers of our fathers stood upon these sacred shores, and the fathers of their fathers. Tales of their bravery are told by the bones of our ancient enemies." He swept his arm sideways, indicating the skull heaps. "It is our birthright to honor their memory. We are few, but we are strong!" He made a fist and shook it toward the approaching aerial horde.

"Many among you have fathered sons and daughters. Today, some among us may pass into Muhingo's lands of gray. But our tribe will live on ... if we drive back the winged ones. Let us turn the shores red with the blood of the Kezati!"

"Muhingo, Muhingo ..." the men chanted, and they began to sway. Behind them, the winged predators closed the distance to the shore, close enough for Conan to hear the rhythmic beat of their wings. The skies were thick with them. Only the impassive youth turned his head to look at them.

"Strike for your ancestors!" the speaker bellowed, raising his hands and clenching them into fists.

"Muhingo ..."

"Strike for your women!" He beat his upraised fists together in the air above his head.

"Muhingo ..." Their voices rose, feverish, and they echoed his gesture with their fists. But the yellow-painted warrior did not join the chant.

"Strike for your sons and daughters!"

"Muhingo!" Twenty-nine voices thundered as one, and the strange oath rang out across the skull-covered beach. For a moment, the noise drowned out the flapping of the Kezati army.

Conan watched from the brush, fascinated. These Ganaks were either brave or foolish, to face their winged foes bare-handed. Then he observed that some of them did indeed have weapons: the oars. At one end, each oar had been notched and fitted with a pointed shell. Lifting the sharp ends of these sturdy implements, the warriors braced themselves to meet the wave of winged doom.

The huge birds flew close enough for the Cimmerian to see their cruel features. Their faces and necks were leathery and wrinkled, like those of vultures. The skulls littering the beach were certainly from creatures such as these. Feathers in hues of black, red, and dark amber covered their bodies. Each of their stubby legs ended in five curving, many-jointed talons that were as long as a man's fingers. Inexplicably, their eyes looked human.

The piercing shrieks of their attack assailed Conan's ears, like the wailing of a hundred wretches dying upon torturers' racks. Fiercely hooked beaks, crimson as dried blood, dominated their cruel faces. The shrill cries, the cruel faces, and the misshapen heads—Conan knew these to be distinctive features of vultures. But these devil-birds apparently preyed not on carrion, but on the living.

Extending their talons and screaming with murderous fury, the first wave of Kezati descended. The vultures were somewhat smaller than their prey, but they seemed to outnumber the stout Ganaks by at least ten to one. They flew straight at the upraised oars, as if heedless of the danger of the shell tips.

Conan could not sit idly by while these brave warriors faced that macabre onslaught. He was no whelp, to cower in the bushes while a desperate battle was fought. The Ganaks were not kindred of his, and he owed them no debt, but they were men with families. If he simply watched them die, their blood would be as much upon his hands as upon the talons of the Kezati. Compelled by his barbaric code of honor, the Cimmerian decided to join the apparently hopeless battle against the hideous vultures.

Though Conan's upraised sword was somewhat tarnished by days of immersion in the brine, his vigor was not. Leaping from the brush like a jungle cat, Conan joined the melee.

He crossed the clearing, nearly reaching the shore before the olive-skinned warriors took notice of him. Their eyes widened, but they had no opportunity to react. Conan arrived as the Kezati struck.

The Ganaks moved with speed astonishing for men of their bulk. Those without oars ducked, avoiding the sweeping talons and grasping the legs of their attackers, fingers locking in iron grips. The lighter vulture beasts were unable to break loose. Dragged down, they thrashed and kicked, their beaks darting toward the faces of their captors, stabbing and tearing at olive-hued flesh.

A husky Ganak, standing at Conan's right, faced two attackers. The man's oar impaled one, but he failed to swerve from the path of the other. The Kezati sank its terrible talons into the warrior's eyes and face, peeling flesh from skull, tearing eyes from their sockets, and driving the stricken man to the ground. Once downed, the blinded warrior groped helplessly before the Kezati buried its beak into the Ganak's round belly. In a single, vicious jerk, the fanged bill disemboweled its victim, ripping out a dripping mass of vitals.

Enraged by this butchery, Conan lunged toward the blood-spattered Kezati, swinging his sword in a brutal overhead sweep. The sharp-edged steel bit into the beast's torso, sundering it into tumbling halves.

The gutted Ganak, who, incredibly, still breathed, looked up into Conan's eyes, smiling weakly before slumping to the sand. Conan glanced at the man's ravaged belly, torn open to the spine. He would slay ten Kezatis in payment for that fallen warrior's demise.

Diving talons and slashing beaks filled the air around his head, giving him ample chance to attain his mark. His flashing blade clove a neck, adding a leathery head to the heap at his feet. Then the Kezati wave veered skyward, preparing for another assault.

During this pause, the Ganaks again set the blades of their oars against the ground—all but the white-haired man, whose face paled as he stared at Conan. The others nervously averted their eyes from the Cimmerian, as if they feared to look him in the face. "Kulunga . . . " the giant warrior whispered, then Conan saw that the scarred man's gaze was directed at his *sword*, not at him. Blood from Kezatis, thin and purple, trickled from its gleaming point.

Conan was about to speak, but the shrieks of the swooping Kezati would have drowned his words. The Cimmerian readied his sword for the second wave of airborne warriors. He counted five fallen Ganaks, but smiled grimly at the tally of nearly thirty dead Kezati. Those spear-oars had taken their toll. Even so, thirty was but a tithe of that hook-billed army's number. Determined to account for more of the vile things, Conan flexed his arms, poising his legs to respond more swiftly this time. A few paces away, the Ganak speaker lifted a dead man's oar from the ground and raised it to meet the screaming Kezati.

Conan looked into the rounded, red eyes of a vulture-beast before shearing the creature asunder. Three others plunged simultaneously toward him, talons extended like small daggers, beaks open to strike. The Cimmerian tried to spring away from two while slashing at the third, but his ankle turned on a skull beneath his foot. Stumbling, he smote blindly with his sword, stopping only one of the Kezati. The untouched pair screeched triumphantly, their beaks stretching toward Conan's unprotected flesh.

The Cimmerian heard a swish in the air behind him, and the white-haired Ganak's oar swept into the path of the Kezati attackers. It batted one aside, striking the other's wing and snapping bone. Wielding the oar like a quarter-staff, the Ganak lashed out with the flattened end and hit one Kezati hard enough to crack its thick skull. The other, unable to fly, screamed and folded its wings. Bending its legs, it sprang toward the prone Cimmerian. Conan thrust his sword into its path, spearing it through the belly. He rolled to his feet and finished it off with a single thrust, before feeling something sharp graze the skin on the back of his neck. A sharp pain knifed through his scalp as a Kezati tore a lock of his hair from his head. He heard the sharp clack of a beak behind him.

Whirling around, he swung his sword and blocked the slashing attack. His steel splintered the hardened beak and sheared off the top of the fleshy skull. But more of the things fell toward him from the sky, like a rain of red-feathered demons from Hell's foulest storm clouds. Conan hacked at one beast and swiveled to face another.

He suspected that the attacks from behind were deliberate tactics. Devious minds lurked behind those vulturelike faces. The things kept Conan shifting and spinning constantly. Two or three of them would converge on him, forcing him to move quickly or catch a beak in the back of his neck. And always another deadly wave hovered near, driving him away from the heaps of bones toward the water's edge.

A few paces from him, the long-haired Ganak deftly whirled an oar, knocking Kezati to the ground and spearing those who arose too slowly. The Cimmerian could afford no glance toward any of the other Ganaks, for the relentless hail of stabbing beaks and slashing talons demanded his full attention. Blood welled from a score of nicks and scratches on his face, arms, and shoulders, mingling with sweat that dripped from every pore of his skin. He could feel himself tiring. The energy from his coconut feast ebbed from his heaving, panting body—a little more with every drop of blood and sweat. But the Cimmerian had vitality equal to that of a wild beast. He fought on, willing his muscles to wield his blade and hew feathered necks.

Conan changed his tactics and began backing toward the Ganak warrior. As if guessing his intent, the beasts impeded his progress every step of the way. But the Ganak had also begun moving toward Conan, and the two finally met. They fought back to back until the shimmering horizon began swallowing the sun. As the darkness of the coming night stained the azure sky, the feathered army broke off its attack. Then, spiraling upward into the deep blue-violet sky, they screeched and swooped down again.

The brief pause drained Conan. He struggled to keep

himself on his feet, bracing wearily for another exchange. His hilt felt like a huge, slippery boulder, impossible to grip. By sheer willpower, he forced his fingers around its blood-slicked surface. As the Kezati raced toward him, he drew in a deep breath.

But the winged beasts simply snatched up the bodies of the fallen Ganaks. Veering skyward, they vanished in the direction of the setting sun. As the incessant cries of the Kezati faded in the distance, a comfortable mantle of silence settled about the beach. The only sounds were the groans of the wounded and dying and the breaths of his own laboring lungs.

All about him lay the mangled forms of vanquished Kezati piled nine or ten deep in every direction. The tall Ganak had fought to the end, and he turned to face the Cimmerian. Lowering his right knee to the carpet of scarlet-feathered corpses, he spoke in a dry, cracked voice—a servitor kneeling before a king.

Conan swayed, puzzled by this sight. The man's words were a muddle to his weary brain. Blood and sweat blurred his vision, and his sword slipped from nerveless fingers as the Cimmerian toppled toward the suppliant old Ganak.

"Kulunga!" the Ganak cried in surprise, reaching out his arms to break Conan's fall. He caught Conan under the arms and lifted him, looking into the Cimmerian's half-lidded eyes. But the bone-weary barbarian simply hung there, not looking back. Grunting, the tall Ganak dragged Conan away from the pile of dead Kezati and laid him upon the beach, splashing water onto his face.

"You are a fool, Jukona." The man who spoke laughed, wiping at the blood that covered his yellow triangles. He struck his oar deep into the beach of bone and walked toward the white-haired Ganak.

Jukona drew himself up to his full height and crossed his arms, gripping bulging biceps in his hands. "Mock me if you must, Ngomba. But mock him"—he gestured toward Conan—"and the *Ghanuta* will be fought when we return to Ganaku." He smiled thinly, but his eyes were black glaciers of gleaming ice.

Shrugging, Ngomba returned the smile and bowed. "That is not Kulunga, old one. Kulunga is a whisper who lives on the lips and in the ears of dreamers and fools. And I am neither of these." He sighed and wiped the blood and sweat from his face, looking at the handful of slashed, weary Ganaks limping away from the battlefield. Including Ngomba and Jukona, only seven of thirty men remained.

Jukona spoke again, but a tremor of doubt had crept into his voice. "If he is not Kulunga, then Kulunga sent him. He carried the *atnalga* in battle. It is strange that he is so small. But by Muhingo, never has one warrior—not even you, Ngomba—slain so many Kezati!"

Ngomba scowled. "The night is young."

Jukona's brow furrowed as he looked at Conan. "We cannot leave him here. The Kezati gatherers will return for their own carrion at sunrise. We must take the stranger to Ganaku."

Ngomba shrugged. "If you deem it necessary. We have work to do before they return. We must tear off the heads, so that the spirits of their dead will not haunt this place."

Nodding, Jukona gestured toward a few of the Ganak warriors. "I will tend to the stranger. There will be a great feast when we return! By Muhingo, we have driven them away! They will not dare to return for many moons. We may never again see the shores of bone!"

"I hope you are right, old one," said Ngomba. "But there were so many of them left, more than in the tales of my grandfather. You are a stone, Jukona, if tonight you can sink in the waters of sleep. I shall drift with open eyes, floating on waves of doubt."

A frown flickered across Jukona's lips, but he did not reply to the younger Ganak.

Five Ganaks joined the two at the water's edge, silently awaiting Jukona's instructions. Nasty gashes, torn flesh, and bleeding scalps were the only injuries visible among them. The Kezatis had borne away the more seriously hurt warriors. Jukona and Ngomba seemed least affected by the grueling battle that raged from midday to sunset. The others shuffled along with flat expressions; losing so many of their kin had robbed the joy from their victory.

Following Jukona's orders, they placed Conan in the center of a palm boat. "I shall row in front," he told them. "Pomja, you must hold him in place. Bunoab, you will row behind Pomja."

Ngomba stared at the ground, where Conan's sword lay. He bent, reaching for its stained hilt.

"Ngomba, no!" Jukona shouted, leaping toward the young Ganak.

"Why?" Ngomba asked, pausing. His fingers hovered near the weapon, but he did not grasp it.

"Only Kulunga or his chosen one may touch the *atnalga*. Will you bring the anger of Muhingo upon us? Leave it, I say!"

Ngomba shook his head, seizing the sword's grip with fingers so large and powerful they could have fit a hilt twice its girth. Jukona flinched, raising a hand to his ashen face. The eyes of five Ganaks widened. Gibbering, the men flung themselves to the sand. Ngomba clumsily held the sword, shifting it in his hand. "What did you say, Jukona?" he snorted. "Only Kulunga or his chosen one?"

Jukona stared incredulously.

Raising the stained blade high above his head, Ngomba pointed it away from the vanishing sun. "To the boats! I, Kulunga's chosen one, shall lead you home." His tone was mocking, but brooked no defiance.

The Ganaks rose and made ready their vessels. "What of him?" pleaded Jukona, nodding toward Conan's slumped form.

Before answering, Ngomba pressed his thick lips together in contemplation. His dark eyes glowered at the Cimmerian. "He remains here. Take him out! Kulunga will save him . . . if he is worthy. Let him lie."

Jukona clenched his teeth tightly, but he made no objection. Lifting Conan out of the boat, the Ganak lugged him to a nearby palm tree and set him against its trunk. When Ngomba was looking elsewhere, he scratched something in the sand beside the Cimmerian. Then he rose and joined the other warriors.

There were more boats than there were able-bodied oarsmen. One vessel was dragged into the brush and spare oars were piled next to it. "We shall return to retrieve it and the boat sticks," Ngomba said unnecessarily, as if he enjoyed hearing himself give a command.

Each Ganak pushed a boat into the tide, paddling in the direction opposite the setting sun. Ngomba led, followed by Jukona, Bunoab, Pomja, and the others. When the water was deep enough to row, they each straddled their boat's central trunk, which served as the rower's bench. Rowing slowly, they began putting distance between themselves and the bloody beach of skulls. As the last rays of sunlight sparkled on the crimson sand, the Ganaks vanished into the darkening eastern horizon.

Eight
Into the Jungle

When Conan's eyes opened, he wondered if the battle with the Kezati had been a strange dream. But in the dawn's brightness, he saw scarlet proof that the melee had been no phantom spawn of his slumbering mind. He remembered collapsing in front of the old man ... where were the Ganaks? They must have laid him here, beneath the tree.

A night of sleep without dreams had restored some of his vigor. The recent memory of his transformation summoned crimson ghosts that haunted him. Something was wrong with him still, for these bouts of deep sleep were unnatural. Even after an arduous battle, his repose should be as light as a panther's. He longed to discover the nature of the blasted shaman's curse—or more importantly, to reverse its effects. To that end, he had made little progress.

His hand reached instinctively for his sword, but the weapon was nowhere in sight. Irked, he stood and scanned the beach to see if the Ganaks lay nearby, perhaps slumbering. Eerie silence pressed upon him, and Conan's instincts told him he was again alone on the isle. Rising, he took a step but quickly leaped backward. He had nearly planted his foot on a drawing in the sand.

Large footprints nearby told him that one of the Ganaks had hastily sketched the marks. An arrow pointed away from a lopsided crescent, obviously the island. A series of symbols, meaningless to him, followed a line from the point of the arrow to what Conan assumed to be another island, this one much larger than the crescent. Small circles spotted the perimeter of the island. Near its center, the anonymous artist had traced the outline of his sword.

"Belial's beard!" he swore, kicking at the sand beside the crude map and nearly erasing the marks. Those Ganaks had a fine way of showing their appreciation for his part in their battle. No doubt the curving symbols offered an explanation, but to the Cimmerian they were as enigmatic as the spell-runes of Khitan wizards. Frustrated, he studied them for a span, as if the passage of time would imbue them with meaning.

Growing restless, he gave up and walked toward the beach. The morning sun revealed tracks. Following them into the brush, he saw the stack of oars and the single boat. Perhaps they meant for him to row himself to that island . . . maybe they had seen others like him— Kulunga?—who came from that island. Whatever their reasons for abandoning him, his course was clear.

Climbing a nearby tree, he knocked more coconuts from it, wolfing down their meats and guzzling their milk before pulling the boat to the shore. Before leaving, he memorized the map, hoping the large island was not too distant.

The Ganak boat's design was a model of simple efficiency, albeit suited for a larger oarsman. The Cimmerian had broken a length from the end of the oar, making it easier to wield. Rhythmic, alternating strokes carried him across the gentle waves until the beach was but a white dot in the horizon. It was then that a perturbing thought surfaced, upsetting his rowing beat. What had become of the vultures' bodies? He could not recall seeing them, only their heads, strewn in disorderly heaps across the beach. Had the Ganaks decapitated every one and tossed the headless corpses into the sea? Conan had traveled the length and breadth of many lands, encountering all manner of outlandish and repugnant customs. From what little he knew of the Ganaks, he already considered them among the oddest.

Shaking his head and trying not to dwell upon the memory of those disembodied dead, he bent his back to the oar. Eager to be away from the isle of skulls, he rowed with fervent strokes, muscles bulging and rippling under his sun-bronzed skin.

Before the sun reached its apex, his destination loomed large before him. Grateful for the short and uneventful voyage, he eased his rowing and stretched, studying the approaching coastline. His elation at reaching land banished the fatigue from his arms and back.

This island looked more promising than the last. Dark green jungle choked most of the sloping shore, thickening to a dense, leafy wall in the island's center. A few quick strokes brought him closer to the bright white beach. Gulls and crabs wandered idly amid green weeds and pink shells. The murmur of the surf and the songs of sea birds mixed with the gentle splash of Conan's rowing. This island presented a wholesome and natural aspect, more to Conan's liking than the brooding malevolence of silent beach he had put behind him.

Certainly this place dwarfed that strange isle. At first it had not seemed so large, but as Conan came closer, its depth became more apparent. He estimated it to be six, perhaps seven times the size of the crescent island, and the jungle stretched back as far as he could see. The beach sloped slightly upward, giving way to man-high brush that in turn became increasingly thick with fronds and vine-layered trees. Many of the latter rose to impressive heights, as tall as any Conan had seen in Kush—or even along the forbidding banks of the Zarkheba River, where no humans had dwelt since Atlantis sank.

Indeed, this island had the same primordial sense that permeated the lands south of Kush. Conan doubted that any cartographer's quill had ever sketched this shoreline.

Guiding the boat toward the exact spot indicated on the Ganak's map, Conan watched the beach for any signs of life. Aside from long-legged birds and scuttling crabs, he saw no evidence of habitation. The jungle probably concealed creatures of all sorts, and Conan refused to give up hope that this place might provide clues to where the mainland lay. The Ganak had drawn that map for a reason, which the Cimmerian intended to know.

He poled his boat to the beach, sliding off the trunk when the water was only chest deep. He relished the feel of rock and sand beneath his feet. The placid bay teemed with tiny striped fish, darting from his intrusive approach. Casting a wary eye into the clear waters, he looked for dangers lurking nearby. When he stepped on a large rock, he felt a sudden rush of water past his legs and instantly pulled himself up, clinging to the boat.

What he had trod upon was no rock, but the shell of an enormous clam, so huge it could have easily swallowed him from the waist down. Its thick, rough jaws, blending in with the sand and rocks, had fooled even his discerning gaze. Luckily, their sudden movement had forced a current of water past his ankles, alerting him just in time. He had never seen a clam of such incredible proportions. Apparently it possessed an appetite to match its size. He quickly leapt back onto the boat, remaining there for the brief trip to the shore.

He sorely missed his sword. Bereft of blade or even garments, he was armed only with his instincts and wits. These weapons had won many battles for him in the past, and they would deliver him from his present predicament. Muttering a curse, he reminded himself to keep his senses sharp, lest this island become his tomb.

While pulling the boat ashore, he warily eyed the waving emerald jungle. Its sun-splashed fronds rustled gently in the warm sea breeze, beckoning him to enter and seek shade from the hot sun. Conan ignored their summons, leaving his boat upon the short, sloping hill of sand that led to the trees. The oar he kept. Stick-fighting was an eastern art, not one that suited him, and pole weapons were of limited use in close combat. Even so, the oar's sharp end might prove useful.

Conan scanned the beach for any signs of recent passage. He saw none, but the jungle seemed to thin out in the spot indicated on the Ganak's crude map. Visualizing the symbols in that drawing, he recalled one: a circle with a distinctive mark in the center, drawn at the edge of the beach. Perhaps it meant danger, a warning about the huge clam. Frowning, Conan tried to recall the other dozen or so symbols like it that had been sprinkled throughout the map.

As the Cimmerian moved toward the place where the jungle thinned, he noted that the fine white sand became more soft and moist, and its color deepened from brilliant white to a yellowish ivory. Thin shoots of grass sprang up and thickened, carpeting the soggy ground. In spite of the soft breeze, a sweet odor of swamp rot tainted the air here.

A spear-cast away lay seven Ganak boats. Conan moved toward them, crossing what had become ankle-deep muck. Thick clouds of blue-black flies buzzed about the tree boats, apparently attracted by thick patches of blood that stained the wood. The Kezati had left their mark upon the Ganak survivors, it seemed.

Standing in the marsh, Conan scratched the stubble on his chin, wondering what direction the Ganaks had traveled after leaving their boats here. Farther inland, the marsh became a dense swamp of reeds and vines, melding with the jungle. The Cimmerian's tracking skills were formidable, but not even a Pictish scout could follow a trail through that morass of sludge-spawned flora.

Frustrated, Conan stubbornly examined the boats and the ground for even the slightest clue to where the Ganaks had gone. There had to be a village nearby. If so, it would likely be a goodly distance from this stinking fen. His questing eyes found not one footprint marking the spongy ground. Conan noticed that where he stepped, the loamy beach rose slowly and filled with water, wiping away signs of his passage.

Swatting a bloated blood-fly that had landed upon his calf, Conan glimpsed a bright object near one of the boats. A shell, from the necklace of the old Ganak! He picked it up, marveling at how smooth and bright it was. This bauble would fetch a pretty price in the marketplaces of land-locked cities.

He wondered if it had fallen by chance or by design. Assuming the latter, he closed his hand around the conical red piece, trudging in the direction indicated by the shell's tapered end.

He found another shell thirty paces away, this one a shiny purple wedge, wreathed in swirls of dark red. So the old one *had* marked the way. A faint smile lifted the corners of his mouth as he followed a path that straddled swamp and jungle, weaving through the thickening fronds until they obscured the sea.

The cawing of birds and the buzzing of insects filled his ears. Swarming flies and whining mosquitoes followed him, biting and stinging. Irked, he listened intently for sounds that might warn him of other, more dangerous denizens of this primal forest. He heard no chattering of monkeys, no animal squeals, no predatory growls. The absence of these noises did little to relax him. Where birds lived, predators lurked. He took care to sidestep snakes that lay in the leafy residue, and he avoided a few hanging vines with curious attributes—such as eyes and scales.

Thickets of brush rose from the damp soil in a thousand shades of green. Leaves, the color of emeralds on black velvet, gave way to fronds of luminous, yellowish lime. Flowers of countless shapes and colors grew everywhere, and Conan took pains to avoid their petals when possible. The Cimmerian knew that a blossom's beauty oft veiled lethal venom. Their fragrances ranged from the lightest of perfumes to the most bitter pungency. He took pains to breathe none of them too deeply. Many bore fruit. He quelled the urge to pluck these.

Slowing to accommodate shady surroundings, Conan glanced upward. His smile slipped away, replaced by a scowl. The breeze had become a wind, and dense clouds swept across the darkening sky. Moments later, the storm thundered and howled through the trees, unleashing rain that pelted the Cimmerian's skin with stinging force. "Crom's teeth!" he swore upward at the offending clouds before darting under the broad, moss-covered limb of a monstrous tree.

Shielded from the squall, he watched with dismay as the shallow water rose above his ankles, stirring up mud and silt. This irksome torrent would mask the shell trail. Glumly shaking his rain-soaked head, the Cimmerian slumped against the tree's cushioned bark. At least the downpour kept the swarming insects at bay.

Gripping a small pile of shells in one hand and the oar in the other, Conan leaned against the tree and waited for the tempest to end.

Nine
The Outcast

Behold Kulunga's chosen one!" proclaimed Ngomba, waving his sword before a throng of wide-eyed Ganaks. The proud, muscle-bound warrior stood atop a mound of sun-baked mud, upraised blade sparkling in the golden beams of the morning sun. Behind him, the jungle rose in the distance like a waving wall of green. Thickets of tall reeds surrounded a dirt mound in the center of a clearing where the Ganaks had gathered around Ngomba. The area marked the edge of the village of Ganaku, raised many generations before by Ngomba's ancestors.

At the foot of the mound, five proud but weary Ganak warriors faced the crowd of men, women, and children. Scores of tall, dusky-skinned Ganaks listened to Ngomba's words, their children fidgeting at their feet. Farther back, twenty-one old men sat on long benches—simple logs that formed the triangular perimeter of a crude amphitheater.

These old men sat without moving, as wooden as the benches beneath them. Their wizened faces were without expression; their lips neither frowned nor smiled. Dark eyes gleamed like black pearls, focused on Ngomba. Most of the elders wore skirts of white and gray shells, cunningly strung to form a heavy, flexible fabric. Tinted patterns covered their bodies in designs similar to Ngomba's but faded from yellow to hues of orange or amber. Many of the men bore no embellishments at all. But painted or not, all the aged men had long locks of white or gray hair that brushed the damp ground behind the log bench.

Ngomba spoke again. "Jukona, will you answer my challenge? Or do you concede to the chosen one?" he asked, sneering at the older Ganak. Jukona stood outside of the triangle, hands upon his hips.

Drawing himself up to his full height, Jukona answered in a resonant voice that boomed in every listener's ears. "You are *not* the chosen one. You have stolen the *atnalga* from Kulunga's chosen one, and you are unfit to be warrior-leader."

A murmur rippled through the crowd.

Jukona waited for the whispering to subside, then folded his arms across his massive chest, gazing sternly at the challenger. "I am ready for the *Ghanuta*. Are you?"

The warriors at the foot of the mound whispered excitedly to one another, and the women hushed their restless children. Then all attention shifted from Jukona to a huge elder who rose from one of the log benches. *"No!"* he boomed, his voice even louder than Jukona's.

Silence engulfed the crowd; even the children stopped fidgeting. The elder's massive frame was equal in height to Jukona's but even more bulky. His skirt of shiny black shells clacked softly as he rose, and an ebony necklace rested upon his broad chest. His braid of hair swayed in the morning breeze like a thick length of silvery rope.

"There will be no *Ghanuta*. Three times has Jukona proven his worth, and he has led the warriors to victory. Ngomba, you must lay down the weapon. It was not yours to take. The one who fought beside you is a Ganak friend by his deeds; you were wrong to abandon him.

"We have heard enough, Ngomba. Now you must step down. Holding the *atnalga* does not make you the chosen one. If you are he who will deliver us from our ancient enemy, then you would be a poor choice for warrior-leader."

Nonplused, Ngomba lowered the sword but stayed atop the mound. Clenching his teeth, he drove the blade into the hard-packed mud, burying it so deeply that its curving quillons touched the soil. "I obey your words, Y'Taba Spirit-Leader."

The immense Ganak moved toward the mound, and the crowd parted before him. "You are young, Ngomba, and you know little of the legend of Kulunga. Even Jukona may have forgotten much about the chosen one of Muhingo." He pointed at the young warrior. "Ngomba, step down from the place of speaking, that I may share the tale with all here."

Y'Taba waited until the young warrior joined the others. Then the elder slowly ascended the hillock. With the craft of an expert storyteller, he let his eyes wander all over the crowd. Casting his deep voice like a net, he captured the attention of the assembly. "In ages long past, our first ancestors fought among themselves when their warrior-leader perished. Many warriors died, for none could agree on a choice for the next warrior-leader." Y'Taba's eyes misted, as if he were mourning those long-dead Ganaks.

"Then Muhingo War God, who receives the slain in his land of clouds, came to Ganaku. And he cried, for brothers killed brothers and sisters killed sisters, and tears of blood fell from the eyes of Muhingo, which is why the soil of our land is red. Then he told the Y'Taba to bring all Ganaks who still lived to the place of gathering—where we stand today.

"But Y'Taba's heart was heavy, for he found only one warrior alive, a wise man named Kulunga. Most of our people had been slain; only the very young and very old had survived that foolish war. Muhingo asked Kulunga why he had not fought with his brothers. The wise warrior answered: 'Our winged enemies approach, Muhingo War

God. I see them coming from afar, and if we fight each other, they will surely destroy us."

"The people saw that he spoke truly, for the Kezati horde loomed near the shores of our land. The people trembled, for certain death approached, borne on the wings of the evil ones. They begged Muhingo for mercy and pleaded for his protection. And he said: 'Muhingo cannot save you from the children of his evil brother Ezat. Your folly has doomed you ... unless Kulunga can drive away these winged bringers of death. Your heart is true, Kulunga. Will you stand before them?'

"Kulunga accepted the challenge laid before him, and Muhingo was pleased. From stones possessed of strange spirits, he molded a mighty weapon: the *atnalga*. And he gave it to Kulunga, who stood fast upon this ground while the Kezati attacked. On that great day, one man saved all Ganaks, for our enemies could not withstand the *atnalga*. Kulunga then became warrior-leader. Before he passed into the lands of gray, his wisdom gave us the *Ghanuta*, by which all warrior-leaders are chosen. And Muhingo himself took up Kulunga and the *atnalga*, telling the Y'Taba that if the Ganaks again faced the doom of the Kezati, Kulunga would choose one warrior and bequeath to him the *atnalga*."

Y'Taba smiled. "That day is not today, for Jukona and our warriors have driven back the children of Ezat. And this"—he raised the blade skyward—"this is not molded as the weapon described in our legends. It is too straight, though its color and composition seem similar. This is not the *atnalga*. We must find the *njeni* and return—" A sudden commotion interrupted Y'Taba. The shell-clad elder turned, staring. From the tall reeds nearby, a small band of Ganak women came running.

Though not quite as tall as the warriors, these twenty-odd Ganaks moved with the bearing of fighters. Solid muscles layered their large-boned frames, and in spite of their size, they ran with the lithe grace of gazelles. They bore crude dagger-shaped shells, thrust into their snakeskin girdles, and each carried a shell-tipped spear. Every woman had one long, black braid, curling down the left side of her head, falling past her shoulders. The sweat of exertion gleamed on their olive-hued skin and bare, firm breasts. Spiral designs, blended in subtle hues of green and yellow, adorned their smooth skin from head to toe.

One woman among them wore a necklace that resembled Jukona's. Its string was fashioned from tightly woven strands of hair. Snake fangs dangled from it, spaced between small iridescent shells. This young woman was shorter than the others by a good measure, and her body was smaller but more muscular. All the Ganaks were dark-eyed, but Sajara's eyes sparkled like aquamarine jewels, her flawless face setting her apart from the others like an exotic orchid in a thicket of rushes.

She approached the elder, who stood on the mound with hands resting on his hips. He regarded her with a slightly troubled expression.

"Your pardon, Y'Taba Spirit-Leader," she began, scarcely winded from the exertion of running.

"You bring urgent news, Sajara?" His steely tone promised a rebuke for an unjustified interruption.

"A stranger has come to Ganaku," she blurted. "Not Ganak. Short and pale-skinned, with eyes as blue as the sea, and hair here and here . . ." she patted her hands on the front, sides, and back of her bare scalp.

"A man?" Y'Taba asked.

She grinned; the other women giggled. "Yes, but without marks—he bears no colors honoring his ancestors." The corners of her mouth turned down, changing her smile into a concerned frown. "And, Spirit-Leader—we saw him cross into the Deadlands!"

Y'Taba stiffened, his eyes widening. A gasp rippled through the Ganaks. The elders stirred from their benches, murmuring and shaking their heads. "Then he is lost. Ngomba, do you see now the evil that you have done this day? From your hands drips the blood of our friend. And

Jukona, as warrior-leader, it was within your power to prevent this from coming to pass."

Jukona hung his head. "But, Spirit-Leader, I showed the stranger the way back and dropped shells to guide him . . ." he stopped, mortified by Y'Taba's steely gaze. "Spirit-Leader, I curse my folly. But he may be alive. He is mighty for one of small stature. The Deadlands may claim my life if the gods wish it to be so. I go there now, to seek out this warrior who fought alongside me upon the shore of bones." Exhaling deeply, the huge Ganak warrior balled his hands into fists and crossed them over his burly chest. Bowing low, he began backing away from Y'Taba.

Ngomba simply scowled, clamping his lips together. Sajara stared at them in confusion, her mouth framing a question.

Y'Taba ignored her. "Jukona Warrior-Leader, your folly I can forgive, for your heart is true. May Muhingo guide you back from the Deadlands. But Ngomba," he stared at the tight-lipped youth, who met his gaze without flinching. "Ngomba, what am I to do with you? You are the mighty tree that bears bitter fruit. We have bitten deeply of it, and now we spit it out. Go! Take a tree boat and leave Ganaku. May Ataba, who sees into the hearts of men, judge you with mercy when you meet him."

Sighing, Y'Taba turned his back to the frowning young warrior. The elders, even those bearing triangular marks like Ngomba's, rose from the bench and mimicked Y'Taba's gesture. The Ganaks stared at the outcast, some coldly, others with pity. Ngomba's face became wooden. Without retorting, he walked stiffly away from the other warriors, toward the perimeter of the gathering place.

"Ngomba . . ." Sajara's sympathetic voice trailed off, but he turned slowly to face her. Their eyes met, and she bit her lip before lowering her gaze from his face.

She did not see the single tear that rolled down Ngomba's cheek, vanishing into the damp red clay at his feet. He hissed between his teeth. "Fools! You think we drove back the Kezati? For generations we have met them on the shore of bones so that they would not trouble us here. Hundreds of Kezatis remain—too many! Soon they will come and drench the village in Ganak blood." He shook a tightly clenched fist at Y'Taba's back. "One day you will regret this, old fool . . . a day that draws nearer and nearer."

His tone wavered, and his eyes shifted to the hilt that jutted from the mound. Running and leaping onto the hillock before anyone could react, he wrenched it from the ground and bounded away, plowing through the crowd, scattering women and children. He jumped over a log-bench at the perimeter of the gathering place, vaulting across a narrow stream and running toward the trees. As he reached the edge of the jungle, he muttered a parting comment, beyond earshot of the Ganaks. "*I* shall seek the unwelcome stranger in the Deadlands. He is responsible for lulling my people into this deception of safety."

Ngomba tightened his grip around the hilt and stared at his face, reflected in the gleaming blade. "Without this weapon he is nothing. If I find him first, I shall send him to the gods and let *them* decide his fate." He tensed, thick cords of muscle bulging from his arms and legs as he stepped into the thickset fronds, vanishing from the sight of the villagers.

Jabbering loudly, the Ganak throng milled about, turning toward Y'Taba. The gentle afternoon breeze had turned into a brisk wind, and clouds rolled across the sky, obscuring the sun. "Pay him no heed," the elder said to the expectant crowd, his voice suddenly weary. "This gathering is over. A feast of victory awaits us! Sajara, we go to join your hunters under the roof of celebration and explain what transpired while you were away."

The rainsquall began in earnest as he spoke, pelting the crowd with wind-driven droplets. Y'Taba stood atop the mound, heedless of the rain. He watched his people seek shelter under the reed-thatched roofs of their simple wattle huts. Many Ganaks hurried under a low structure that was supported by erratically spaced trees. Unlike other huts, it was fashioned not of reeds but some other material, smooth and ivory-colored, stained in places, its smooth surface torn here and there. Beneath it, large stones served as tables, heaped high with multicolored fruit, shell bowls brimming with fruit juices, and flat shells containing fish of varying sizes and shapes.

The spirit-leader put his arm around Sajara's shoulders and led her to join the other Ganaks. He took a long last look over his shoulder, toward the reeds where Ngomba had departed with the stranger's weapon.

Rain poured onto Conan, washing away his last sliver of patience. The trees offered little protection from the downpour, and the Cimmerian was loathe to while away the daylight here. Better to pass the night on the beach than in this noisome stretch of swarming and slithering jungle. He would walk for a while in the general direction of the shell-trail and turn back if he found no signs of a Ganak settlement. Perhaps he would even find some safe food to satisfy his gnawing hunger.

He had never cared much for these sweltering, insect-infested places anyway. More than ever he longed to leave this isle and find his way to the mainland—where he could seek a cure for the thrice-blasted shaman's curse. Never in his mercenary days could he recall such a run of ill luck. He felt naked without his sword. A three-foot blade of sharpened steel was a great comfort in times like these, and it was especially irritating to have lost as fine a weapon as the sword he'd taken from Khertet. Conan knew, however, that he would fight with his bare hands if need be. Flexing his fingers, he shook off his gloomy thoughts and concentrated on his surroundings.

The rain drove away the stinging flies and mosquitoes, and it would mask his scent from any jungle predators. That much was in his favor.

He crept through the foliage, sidestepping a dozing viper whose coiled trunk was thicker than Conan's thigh. The dense vegetation gradually thickened, pressing in on him, until finally he could go no farther. Realizing the futility of finding a settlement in this leaf-choked place, he turned back.

Hastening as much as he dared, Conan retraced his footsteps. The rain slackened, stopping abruptly. Dim light filtered through the thick leaves overhead; doubtless the clouds had broken. The Cimmerian took a step, then frowned. Ahead and to the right, he saw a trail through the jungle—a barely discernible trail that a casual glance might have missed. Conan's keen eyes observed its regular lines and even width, partially obscured by the brush but unmistakably cleared by human hands.

The path looked ill-tended; tall foliage had sprung up to fill it, but no trees rooted themselves amid its width. Scratching at the stubble on his chin, Conan felt annoyed that he had missed it earlier; doubtless that accursed rain had obscured it somehow.

He turned onto it without hesitation, hoping that it would lead him to the Ganaks or at least to a place where he could pass the night. Placing speed ahead of caution, he walked the twisting track, eventually losing his sense of direction. The trees that flanked it towered higher and higher, and he judged that the snakelike path was taking him deep into the jungle.

Swarming, stinging bugs surrounded him in a buzzing cloud. Serpents infested the floor of the jungle, reminding him of the unpleasant fate Khertet had planned for him in Stygia. Fortunately, these fork-tongued creatures apparently sought other prey. He gave them a wide berth and none molested him. Birds chattered in the trees, and he welcomed their voices. Some dove into the jungle from their high perches, snatching up small snakes in their beaks and taking them elsewhere to feast.

Conan was tempted to feed as they did, but he would only eat snake meat as a last resort. He had noted a greenish-brown fruit that hung from thick vines overhead, which he could reach with a jump. As he considered this, a big, broad-winged bird neatly plucked an apple-sized piece of this fruit from a low vine, perching on a nearby limb to pick at its meat. Conan decided he would try a bite. Birds often naturally avoided poison.

A running leap gave him the loft he needed, and he pulled one of the lumpy-skinned fruits from that same vine. It tasted strange, vaguely like an unripened coconut, but his famished belly welcomed even its bitter meat, pulpy seeds, and thick milk. The peel or shell he discarded. Feeling no ache in his guts, he choked down a few more of the things while hastening along the path. He frowned, noting a lessening of the light that filtered down to him through the layers of leaves above. He must be past the center of the island by now, after hours of walking. Vines had begun to clog the trail. There were more fruits here but fewer birds.

He rounded a sharp bend, encountering a drooping, vine-choked thicket that blocked his way. The fruits, somewhat larger on these stalks, clustered thickly. He kicked them to knock them aside and several burst open . . . spewing forth hundreds of tiny, wriggling spiders.

The pale green hatchlings spilled out in glistening clumps, some falling onto him in thick, squirming blobs. He leaped forward in revulsion, wiping their pulpy green bodies from his skin and nearly doubling over in nausea—he had eaten three of those spider eggs! Leaning against the mossy trunk of a thick tree, he retched violently, looking up just in time to catch a slight, rapid movement, at the edge of his vision.

Directly overhead, from the thick limb of a tree, an immense, ocherous spider dangled. It was easily twice Conan's size. Dull green hair sprouted from its bulbous, bloated body and long, spiny legs. Its crimson eyes burned with the malevolence of a creature who bent its cunning to a single, bestial purpose . . . sucking the life from any warm-blooded prey within reach of its flexing, dripping mandibles.

"Baal and Pteor!" Conan swore. What foul hell-furnace had belched up this freakish monstrosity? Crouching, he sprang away from those cruel pincers before they dropped onto him. As if anticipating his leap, the hideous beast spread its forelegs, unfolding a net woven from pearly strands.

Conan's jump carried him right into it.

Instantly swathed in thick, sticky webs, he twisted in midleap, narrowly avoiding the pouncing spider. Once again he bemoaned his lack of a sword. The enormous arachnid spun to face him, its bulky body heaving as it lurched for its struggling prey. The Cimmerian thrashed and kicked, but the clinging strands held him more securely than steel chains. Straining until veins pulsed red at his temples and blood pounded hotly in his head, Conan tore free his arms.

The spider's mandibles snapped shut, clamping his waist in a grip that wrenched the very breath from Conan's lungs. Gasping and kicking, he watched in horror as its hollow-pointed teeth dribbled milky yellow slime into dozens of puncture wounds. How long did he have before that venom struck him down?

No—he refused to die in the belly of this beast!

Infuriated, the Cimmerian shot out his hands, seizing a mandible in each of his mighty fists and pulling with every muscle his corded arms could bring to bear. Conan's chest heaved, his sinews bulging like rope beneath his sweat-drenched skin.

A dull throb spread through his abdomen, numbing him as insidious poison coursed through his web-bound body. He felt the agonizing pressure of the jagged jaws, locked around his lower ribs, squeezing with force that threatened to crack his bones and crush his vitals.

The gasping Cimmerian gathered the shreds of strength that lingered in his limbs, forcing his brawny arms to work. Slowly, torturously, the pincers pulled away from his ravaged sides. With a heave that tightened his muscles into quivering knots, he jerked the poison-smeared mandibles apart, forcing them backward.

A bestial cry burst from Conan's foam-flecked lips as he

wrenched the pincers asunder, splitting the misshapen head into slime-spewing halves and ripping the jaws from its torn ruin. He shucked them at the thing's convulsing body.

"Crawl back to Hell!" he panted, watching sludge ooze from the spider as its legs thrashed in a macabre dance of death. Squeals and hisses issued from its torn maw like the shrieks of a devilish choir.

Staggering, Conan overbalanced and toppled to the path. With his numb, aching arms, he dragged himself toward a tree, spending the last of his power to prop himself up against its trunk.

He sank against the moss-covered bark, exhausted. He could not stop his pounding heart from pumping the spider's virulent poisons deeper into his vitals. Moments later, Conan's chin dropped to his heaving chest. His eyes glazed over as dusk wrapped the dense jungle in a shroud of indigo.

Ten
Prowlers on the Path

As dawn broke, the morning sun's rays turned the jungle's dew-covered leaves into a glittering sea of emeralds. Jukona scarcely noticed the beauty of his surroundings; to him, the jungle was a hostile land of death, fraught with peril at every step. The elders told of a time long ago, beyond the memory of even Y'Taba's great-grandfather . . . an age when the Ganaks had actually lived in the Deadlands.

Jukona had always doubted this tale. The Deadlands were said to teem with creatures so strange, so vile, that only the most evil of gods could have brought them into being. As Jukona crept more deeply into the jungle, he wondered if even the evil gods had forsaken the Deadlands.

His ancestral marks—painted with the milk of *vanukla* fruits—kept away most of the insects. Their warding powers seemed unaffected by the jungle. He had stepped on a well-concealed snake, and the sting of its teeth lingered in his foot. The elders told tales of long-toothed serpents whose bite brought death, but Jukona's attacker did not have the curving fangs described in those stories. He slowed his progress to a crawl, carefully scanning the ground for other slithering creatures.

The Ganak women were better suited to tracking, but Jukona would not ask Sajara—his daughter—to enter the Deadlands. The women were hunters and watchers, at least those women unable to bear children or unwilling to join with a mate. They were not warriors. Only in ancient times, when the winged children of Ezat invaded Ganaku for food, had the women been compelled to fight.

Jukona shuddered at the thought of a Kezati horde descending onto his village. He hoped he would never see such an event come to pass. The Ganak people depended on their warriors to protect the very young and the very old. In a few years, another forty or fifty boys would reach the age of induction and set their feet upon the warrior's path. Until then, Jukona and his seven warriors would be all that stood between the Kezati and the tribe.

Ngomba had been right about one thing: the recent attack on the Kezati had taken a severe toll. Jukona had led two hundred men in the invasion of the Stone Isle, where the winged ones nested in dark caves. Only thirty warriors survived that savage battle, rowing like the wind to meet the final wave of Kezati on the shore of bones. Thirty would not have been enough, but the gods had sent the pale-skinned stranger and his mighty weapon.

Confused by Ngomba's speech, Jukona had left the stranger to the mercy of the gods. He should have known that Ngomba's claim was false, that the weapon was not the *atnalga*, but his wisdom failed him when Ngomba seized the small warrior's weapon. Jukona was pleased that the stranger had found the secret marks in the sand and followed them to Ganaku.

To the Deadlands.

Thickets of trees and towering leafy plants separated the Ganak village from the jungle, where the Deadlands lay brooding. Not even the hunters and watchers dared enter the dark heart of the island, which had spawned the most nightmarish legends ever told by the elders. For generations, the Deadlands had swallowed the few Ganaks who dared enter. Some of the bravest and strongest had disappeared there.

Jukona knew the way; his grandfather had told him how to find the old path. Thus far, the way had been as described. Near the edge of the village, alongside the river, grew a tree of three trunks. Starting beside the tree, he had walked directly toward the afternoon sun, counting thirty paces of three steps each. Now he could see the path.

Choked with short fronds and young trees, the way to the Deadlands revealed itself in the fading sunlight. Here, near the outer edge of the jungle, the trees did not press close as in the Deadlands. Drawing a deep breath and exhaling slowly, Jukona set his feet upon the winding way that he hoped would lead him to the stranger. His eyes scoured the leaf-littered sward for any signs of passage, even the slightest trace of a footstep.

Enormous insect clouds clustered around him, sometimes probing his flesh before the *vanukla*'s scent turned them away. The birds here were larger than those who dwelt near the village, and their beaks and hooked talons likened them to the Kezati.

The sight of these winged predators instinctively stirred hatred inside him. If he had brought his boat stick with him, he might have chanced a few blows at these small brothers of his enemies. Unfortunately, the boat sticks were too long and clumsy to wield in the confines of this jungle. A hunter's spike, like those carried by the women, would have served him better. Warriors never carried the spikes, which were of no use against the long reach and diving attacks of the Kezati.

A rustle in the trees nearby froze Jukona's legs. He swiveled toward the source, straining to see if something lurked there. Crouching, he crept toward the sound. Despite his girth, Jukona moved with the stealth instinctive among men weaned in wild lands. He thought he heard the rustle again, but the wind gods had begun to murmur, and their breath stirred the trees. Reaching the coppice beside the path, he studied the ground. His patient sweep of the jungle floor revealed thick-bladed grasses that marked a suspicious patch.

A patch shaped like a large foot.

He searched for other signs of passage, wondering who—or what—had passed by him. The stranger's feet had not been so large, not as he could recall. Jukona fidgeted with his lock of white hair, staring at the silent trees. A hundred tales of foul beasts, flesh-eating demons, and fierce monsters rose in his mind, and he broke into a chilling sweat. Did creatures from the Deadlands prowl this path, seeking victims?

Jukona swallowed the knot of fear in his throat and stood, throwing back his shoulders. He would not abandon the stranger. Not again. He was warrior-leader of the Ganaks, and he would face whatever trials the gods had in store for him. With muscles tensed, Jukona forged ahead, ignoring the increasing winds and the rain that had begun to fall.

When the wind gods argued among themselves, their mothers shed tears that drove away the insects and brought cool relief from the sun. Jukona welcomed the soft rain. Its waters would wash away his scent while its sounds hid his footfalls from the ears of stalking predators. In their tales of the Deadlands, the elders had spoken of monsters who struck without warning—who could tear a warrior in half before he even heard them attack.

He quickened his pace, the elders' voices still echoing in his mind and weighing heavily upon his spirit.

Through slitted eyes, Ngomba watched Jukona. He had followed the warrior-leader through the jungle, relying on Jukona to show him the way to the Deadlands. Ngomba had nearly given himself away a few moments ago; he would not step so clumsily again. Jukona was old, but the passage of years had not dulled his hearing.

The young warrior distanced himself from the path, lowering his head. He kept one eye on Jukona and the

other on the jungle, watching for the children of
Damballah. The bite of the evil god's serpents brought
death. Sometimes one made its way into the village, killing a Ganak before its presence was detected. Ngomba
was not as clumsy as Jukona. That old white-haired fool
had blundered not too long ago, stepping onto a serpent
and suffering an ankle bite for his carelessness. Jukona
was fortunate that the serpent had not been a venomous
child of the evil god.

Ngomba moved with powerful but stealthy strides, easily matching Jukona's timid pace. He did not believe the
wild fables of the Deadlands. The elders were full of such
dreams and told them only to frighten children. Stinging
serpents were the real menace here. Many times he had
considered a foray into the Deadlands, but he had never
found cause to risk the serpents—until now.

When he found the stranger, he would challenge
him—if the stranger still lived—and make the weapon his
own by right of victory. Jukona would find the body and
lay the blame upon the beasts of the Deadlands. The
Ganak needed the stranger's weapon; it was their only
hope against the doom that would soon come, borne on the
wings of Ezat's ravening children.

Ngomba's people had cast him out, but he would not
abandon them. He would wait for the day of redemption.
On that day, he—Ngomba—would save the Ganaks from
the folly of Y'Taba and Jukona. They would welcome him
back. Sajara would become his mate, and he would become spirit-leader. The Ganaks would flourish under his
strong leadership, and their children would not need to
fear the Kezati.

Ngomba's eyes burned with the fire of his pride as he
stalked Jukona, every silent step bringing him closer to his
destiny.

Conan woke up in Hell, dead from the spider's bite. He
lay in the torture pit of some nameless fiend, trussed in unyielding bonds while a thousand invisible imps jabbed at

his flesh with fiery needles. He moaned in the darkness, struggling to move, but his leaden limbs refused to obey.

His eyelids lifted, and he realized the cloying blackness surrounding him was merely the jungle at night. Conan's eyes rapidly adjusted to the sparse light from pale moonbeams, filtering through the treetops. The searing pain in his sides issued from the deep grooves dug by the spider's viselike jaws. Conan could barely feel his fingers and toes. His legs and arms might as well have been sticks, carved to resemble human limbs.

A few feet away lay the spider's carcass, fouling the air with a reek as potent as a sea of festering sewage. A trail of greasy, congealed muck glistened in the faint light, spreading from its halved head to where it had crawled to die.

Nauseated by the unholy stench, the Cimmerian made a vain effort to rise. A dull ache had begun throbbing in his legs, spreading slowly to his sides. Perhaps the spider's venom was slowly releasing its grip on his muscles. He hoped it would ebb quickly. Lying motionless against the tree, he was easy prey for anything that happened along the path.

He lay there sweating, listening to the leaves rustle in the wind. In the silence of the jungle, even his breathing seemed loud. As time passed, he managed to loosen his jaw and even crane his neck to peer at his dark surroundings. Glad to avert his eyes from the spider, he scanned the shadowy trees for any signs of movement, but the jungle seemed to be slumbering.

The moon's light was unsettling, and he wondered if the shaman's curse would at any moment seize him. How satisfied that old Kaklani shaman would have been, had he known that his dying spell dealt Conan a blow far worse than any sword stroke. From beyond the grave, that shaman held Conan's mind and body in invisible chains.

As a youth Conan had endured the bonds of slavery, when the Hyrkanians had captured him. He had become the property of his cruel masters, and for too long he had suffered the agony of captivity. Of all the villainous scum Conan had known in his life, none were more despicable than slavers. They had driven him to near madness, until he had attempted an escape that no sane man would have considered. He remembered the exultation of the day when his arms had torn loose the chains of his bondage—chains that had, ironically, served as weapons to slay his captors and win his freedom.

The shaman's spell-fetters would not break so easily. Experience, however, had taught Conan that one mage could undo the work of another. He hated the idea of seeking help from a spellcaster, but for now he could see no other option.

When the paralysis ebbed from his limbs, the moon's light had faded. Conan worked himself free of the webbing, pleasantly surprised to find that its stretchy strands had weakened. Freeing his legs, he rose. A tree lent him support until his balance returned.

Conan resumed his course, following his path. He often looked up, to see if any other spiders lurked overhead, ready to drop their insidious webs upon him. The path veered left, and Conan's foot landed squarely on a fallen tree limb. His ankle twisted, and he fell sideways, caught off balance.

Rolling on the sward, he came face to face with a large human skull. In the shifting shadows of the jungle, its gaping mouth seemed to move, and its eye sockets stared at him, resentful of his intrusion.

Cracked bones lay in a scattered heap nearby.

Conan propped himself up on his elbows, his eyes narrowing. A waist-high pile of skeletons—Ganak, judging from their size—blocked the path.

He picked up a loose rib and examined it curiously, squinting and running his fingers along a peculiar series of deep grooves in the bone. He recognized immediately the work of the spider's deadly mandibles. But the sheer size of the bone pile whispered to him, suggesting that no single spider could account for so many large, strong victims.

The thought made his flesh crawl. Conan did not fear any man or beast that could be slain by steel. With his bare hands, he had overcome one of these things. But weakened as he was, still foggy from the venom, he had no wish to face what could well be a score of those crawling creatures.

His ankle was sore but serviceable. He backed up, moving with a silence that would have shamed a stalking panther. Leaves about him rustled softly, freezing him in place. A bright moonbeam sliced through the dense fronds overhead, casting light upon the ghastly mound of skeletons.

Furtive movement above the mound caught Conan's eye. Behind him, through the veil of jungle sounds, he heard a hiss. To his left, a tree limb creaked, as if bending under the strain of a great weight.

Conan flexed his knees, crouching. His only warning was a faint rush of air on a huge leaf that waved a few feet above his head.

Springing to his right, he landed on his right shoulder, rolling. Gooey strands of web clung to his left ankle, stretching until they snapped. A green, bulbous object thumped onto the path, scurrying toward him even as it landed. The bones clattered as something large dropped onto them, scattering the pile.

By the time Conan climbed to his feet, the path was alive with wriggling, hissing horrors. As if drawn by his scent, they moved ponderously toward him, their shiny eyes brimming with malice. More spiders dropped from the trees, spiny legs flexing, obscene bodies bobbing up and down as they lumbered toward their prey.

He shuddered in revulsion, standing fast to face their charge. The sight of that slavering hell-horde would have made the most stout-hearted Æsir berserker soil his own breeches. Conan had slain many monstrosities in his travels and battled beasts that crawled from Hell's darkest crevices, but these creatures made his blood curdle like no others had. He was in no condition to take on a whole army of the things. Cursing, Conan half-ran, half-walked through the trees, their branches whipping at his naked flesh, raising welts as he plunged into the murky depths of the jungle. He loathed spiders almost as much as he loathed spellcasters.

Only when he reached a tightly packed row of trees did he slow down. His pursuers' bulk kept them from catching up; their rustling and wheezing had faded to far-off whispers. But they showed no signs of abandoning their prey. They tracked him with the relentless precision of Picts on a blood trail.

The chase had fully awakened Conan's limbs. He ignored the hot throb in his sides, concentrating on his search for a gap in the barrier of trunks and limbs.

He heard the click of mandibles as the spiders approached him.

Conan clenched his teeth in frustration. The trees formed a wall that began curving out, forcing him back toward the path. Jammed together, the thick trunks grew so closely that he could not force himself through them.

The trees offered no refuge. These spiders had demonstrated their climbing skills, and Conan did not delude himself with false hopes of escape. Their webs would catch him, and they would drag him down, tearing his flesh, crushing his bones in their jaws.

He would not become another skeletal trophy in their ivory mound of death. Panting, growling with the fury of a cornered lion, he turned to circle around them and escape.

With his back to the wall of trees, he spent a few precious seconds choosing the direction in which he would charge. He could slay one or two of them, perhaps more if he kept beyond reach of their deadly jaws.

Uncannily, his eight-legged enemies had organized their attack with the precision of a Turanian general. The smaller, more mobile spiders scurried through the forest, flanking him. The foliage directly ahead rustled with the sounds of approaching predators.

They formed a living web. Escape was impossible.

Clenching his fists, Conan braced himself for the onslaught.

Eleven
Treason and Terror

Jukona paused, wiping sweat from his forehead. Nightfall had made the path difficult to follow. His progress was painfully slow, and the tense trek was wearing him down.

But the sweat on his furrowed brow came not from exertion; it rose from the sense of being watched. The denizens of the Deadlands lurked all around him. The snakes were the least bothersome, for they could be sidestepped. He had clumsily trod upon one earlier, receiving a stinging bite for his carelessness. The serpent's teeth had sharpened his senses. Since then, he had remained vigilant. When the green, net-throwing beasts had approached, he had been prepared.

Tales told by his grandfather had warned him of their insidious tactics. To ward them off, he carried a sack of their eggs, which the beasts laid in clusters, covering their jellylike spawn with a thin, leathery shell. They seemed to value the safety of their unborn, for they would not attack one who toted an egg. Jukona did not know why such creatures would care about their spawn, but the minds of the *anansi* were unfathomable.

They permitted him to pass, although he could still feel their eyes on him, burning with the hatred they harbored for all warm-blooded beasts—especially the two-legged variety.

He wondered how the stranger had avoided them. Perhaps he also carried a talisman. But Jukona was concerned; he had heard a commotion farther ahead, before the moon goddess had begun her descent from the sky.

He took a few steps forward, peering down the shadowy path. He stopped to stare at a huge object, huddled on the path a few paces away.

His eyes widened and he sucked in his breath.

Before him lay the maimed carcass of a net beast.

Slain by the stranger . . . or by something far worse, something that might lurk ahead?

In the distance, thrashing sounds broke the night's silence. Creatures were stirring, moving through the dense vegetation. A loud, bestial cry ripped through the jungle, startling Jukona. He recognized the sound: the cry of war, made by the stranger on the shore of bone when the Kezati attacked.

He hastened toward it, wondering what monsters beset the warrior who had fought so bravely against the Kezati. Even though the warrior was not a Ganak, Jukona would gladly die to save him.

Bolting through the brush, Jukona tripped over the outstretched foot of Ngomba. Jukona fell heavily, gasping as the wind was knocked from his lungs. Eyes flashing, the yellow-painted warrior raised his weapon to smite Jukona. He swung it with enough force to fell a tree.

As the glittering blade descended toward the prone Ganak's neck, its hilt twisted in Ngomba's grip. The flat of the blade struck the base of Jukona's skull, driving his face into the ground. Ngomba stepped away, watching the old warrior roll onto his back, groaning. Jukona lifted his chin, his bewildered gaze meeting the fierce eyes of his assailant. Blood trickled from one ear, seeping into the ground.

"You should have listened to me, Warrior-Leader," he whispered. "You have brought this doom upon yourself. Better that you died before leading our people down the path of death."

Ngomba jabbed his thumb with the sharp point of his weapon, then stuck the weapon into the dirt. He smeared his finger with blood and painted three simple symbols upon Jukona's brow, warrior marks that would permit Jukona's soul to pass freely into the gray lands of Muhingo.

He had been reluctant to strike Jukona, but the old warrior could not be allowed to save the intruder. Ngomba listened with satisfaction to the rustling and thrashing sounds of the net beasts as they hunted the doomed stranger.

Ngomba bent to pick up the egg sack that had kept him safe from the web-throwing beasts. He felt more certain than ever that his actions tonight were justified. After all, the war gods had delivered Jukona before the fool's overconfidence could doom the Ganaks. And the dark gods had sent their children, the Deadland beasts, to slay the stranger. Clearly, Ngomba was favored equally by all the gods, light and dark.

He strode down the path that would take him home. It was time for him to return, to tell his people what had transpired, to fulfil his destiny.

He had taken only a few steps when faint sounds reached his keen ears. Listening intently, he heard the flapping of wings, a sound he knew all too well. It came from afar, like distant clouds that foretold the coming of a cruel storm.

As he had feared, the Kezati were approaching. But they had come so soon, before he was ready! From the sound, there were many more than even he would have expected—a hundred, maybe more.

Their wings beat slowly; the long flight must have made them weary. But Ngomba guessed they would reach the village before dawn, attacking while his people were recovering from their feast of victory.

He cursed the foolishness of Y'Taba and Jukona. Their false assurances might yet be the death of the Ganak people . . . and the death of his beloved Sajara. An image of her rose vividly in his mind's eye. He pictured her, torn to pieces by stabbing beaks and slashing talons. It must not come to pass! His blood boiled, hotter than the sun god's fiery breath. He tightened his grip on the new weapon. With it, he could save her.

He sprinted madly down the path, his mind awhirl. His people had cast him out, but they needed his help. They must not die from the wrongful decrees of Y'Taba. Ngomba would show them that their spirit-leader had acted foolishly, convince them that he was the chosen one. When he drove away the Kezati, they would acknowledge his claims. They would honor him, demand that he be chosen as the new warrior-leader.

Then Sajara would become his mate.

Jukona had forbidden their joining. Sajara was his only daughter, and he had never liked Ngomba. But the old fool was gone. And Y'Taba would gladly give Sajara to one who saved the Ganak people from the winged ones—he would have no choice but to obey the demands of the chosen one.

Ngomba's legs pumped furiously, his muscles burning from his pounding strides. He threw aside all caution; no serpent or Deadland beast could stop the chosen one from fulfilling his destiny.

"Sajara!" he cried fiercely, raising the weapon as he ran, his heart hammering in his chest.

Conan backed against a sturdy tree to keep the pack of bloated spiders from surrounding him. He extended his arms, hands ready to seize the first beast who struck. Though he was unarmed, he would sell his life dearly before they dragged him down.

A rustling in the trees overhead warned him of an attack

from above. "Crom's teeth!" he bellowed, diving aside as the thing smacked wetly to the ground where he had stood. A low tree limb nearly knocked him senseless.

His ill-aimed jump landed him on the pulpy back of another spider. Its hide was thick enough to support him. Hissing, it heaved upward, dislodging Conan.

All around him, menacing shadows closed in, a clicking hairy mob of malignance. Their cloying reek filled the night air, putrid as the devil's breath. Hundreds of evil, unseen eyes stared at him with such hateful intensity that he felt their presence, their *touch*, upon his naked flesh.

Sharp mandibles brushed his calf, and his outstretched arms touched a pudgy, bristling body.

Deeply inhaling fouled air, he bent his knees and sprang straight up, reaching for a tree limb above him. The fingers of his right hand curled around the top. Flexing his arm, he hauled himself onto the smooth branch, the spiders' dripping jaws clacking shut on empty air below him.

The hideous green horde began swarming up the tree in pursuit, incredibly agile for creatures of their size. Cursing, Conan balanced himself on the slippery limb, which shook and swayed. He looked up, seeking other branches to climb, but none were in reach.

The moon's light had nearly vanished, but enough remained for him to scan his surroundings. The wall of trees seemed to extend forever upward, as impassable as ever. Jutting tree branches were tangled and twisted together in wooden embraces.

Conan observed that the trunks tapered gradually, and he immediately devised a plan. Leaping as high as he could, he threw his arms around the trunk and began climbing.

Mere paces below him, the shadowy hunters chased Conan. Their limbs, as if coated with invisible glue, clung to the slippery wood.

Conan's fingers grappled the moist bark, his nails digging in, his legs wrapping around the tree.

Frothing jaws lunged toward his ankle, splattering his toes with gooey droplets.

Conan clung to the tree, pulling himself up by his hands, the nail of his middle finger peeling back. He ignored the burst of pain, wrenching his foot away from the spider below. He let go of the trunk, wedging his hands back-to-back between the tree he had climbed and the tree to his right. He swung to the right, supported only by the pressure his palms exerted on the two trees.

Shoulder muscles flexing, he hurled all of his upper body strength into his hands, desperately trying to pull apart the two trees. If he could spread them just a little, enough for him to slip through, they would snap shut behind him and cut off pursuit.

Straining, his muscles trembling, he pitted his considerable might against the unyielding bulk of wood. His chest heaved as he drew in deep breaths, his body feeling every ache from the hardships of the past few days. The trees bent slightly, giving an inch or two but no more.

An explosion of hot pain burst from his calf as the spider below him sank its jaws into his flesh.

Exhaling with a bestial roar, Conan's thews swelled, the bones of his arms grinding in their sockets from the strain. The trees bent apart, giving in to the incredible pressure. Conan pulled himself through, feeling the agonizing scrape of mandibles as they slid down his calf, stripping the flesh to his ankle.

The creature lunged through the gap, relentlessly pursuing Conan, its bulbous eyes agleam with dark fury, its dripping mouth agape with hunger. In the pale moonlight, blood from Conan's leg glistened wetly on its snapping jaws.

Then he was through, past the wall of wood. He let the trees snap back onto the thing's hideous head. It burst like a hairy black grape crushed between powerful fingers, spraying viscous brain-jelly in all directions.

Gasping, Conan plummeted to the ground, unable to maintain his grip. He rolled instinctively as he fell, and the muddy loam softened the impact. On the other side of the makeshift barrier, his pursuers wheezed in agitation, frustrated by the unexpected escape of their prey.

Conan scanned his new surroundings. Strangely, the trees ended abruptly where he had pushed past them. He lay in a vast clearing.

Numb from traces of spider venom absorbed, he leaned against a tree, panting. He scrubbed the wound with a handful of watery mud, barely able to make his muscles perform this simple chore. His arms hung loosely as if attached to his shoulders only by a thread. Flashes of red blurred his vision, making him dizzy. But the pain kept him conscious until he could steel himself.

When his vision returned, he stared ahead, eyes widening in amazement. He looked upon the high, slightly rounded wall of an immense castle. Its gargantuan dimension matched the mightiest of Aquilonian fortresses; indeed, it was of sufficient size to encircle a whole village.

Had the fall addled his wits, or was it some trick of the night's shadows? The sky had begun to color with the deep blue of dawn, further improving visibility. Closing his eyes, he breathed deeply, shaking his head to clear it. When he looked again, the structure was still there. Its wall loomed over him like a massive tombstone, silent and grim, a stone sentinel guarding the bones of whatever lay within.

Mesmerized, he lay unmoving, listening to the fading squeals of his would-be devourers, who were doubtless retreating to their leafy lairs. Whether they had given up the chase or were simply hiding from the light of morning, Conan knew not. He was simply thankful to have escaped.

As he gawked at the stone edifice, the first rays of sunlight touched the tops of the trees, dispelling the castle's eerie, brooding aspect. Conan yawned, weary from the last night's desperate flight through the forest. His arms had never known the throbbing ache he now felt. But he noticed these ailments with detachment. The bizarre wonder before him dominated his thoughts.

The sky had brightened, enabling Conan to note the wall's state of advanced decay. Its massive bricks sagged as if weary from centuries of standing. Cracks permeated its surface like wrinkles on an aged face.

He tilted his head to study the battlements. There, remnants of decorative stone sprouted crookedly like broken stumps of teeth in an expansive jaw. A crumbling minaret towered beyond the wall, its tapering spire worn to a nub.

Conan saw no means of entry. The castle, though crack-ridden and apparently untended, appeared impenetrable. Its appearance was altogether forbidding, but Conan felt its irresistible lure. Its very existence on this forsaken, primitive island presented an intriguing mystery. What hands had shaped it, and where had the stone come from? Why had the jungle not overtaken it?

A new observation brought a scowl to Conan's face. Where the wall of trees ended, the clearing contained no vines, no leaves, and not one blade of grass. In a circle that radiated from the round-walled castle, Conan saw no trace of anything green or living. Even insects shunned this place. The utter absence of life suggested a number of unpleasant possibilities.

But he longed to know what lay inside its walls. Favoring his sore calf, he walked in a slow circle, staying near the trees. The curving wall contained thousands of close-fitting, dark brown blocks. Conan judged that any one of these might equal him in weight. He marveled at the craftmanship, wondering how many backs had bent to the task of building this hulking structure. Was it the work of whip-driven slaves ... or had free hands labored to construct a haven for their families?

On the other side of the clearing, Conan found an oval-shaped portal where a gate might once have hung. "Ymir's beard," he whispered, his eyes widening as they traveled upward.

From top to bottom, a horrific bas-relief image of a naked woman covered the wall. Sitting cross-legged, she leered at Conan, her lips twisted in a snarl. Tusks curved upward from her open mouth; long, ragged locks radiated like sunbursts from her face. She wore a necklace of skulls, bracelets of snakes, a belt of severed limbs, and tiny arms looped through her pierced lobes—arms attached to children's corpses.

Ten arms sprouted from her bare, huge-breasted torso. In one claw-like hand she gripped a wide-bladed scimitar; from another long-nailed hand dangled a severed, blood-dripping head. The arched doorway gaped open below her navel, a repugnant and lewd invitation.

Conan remembered seeing a likeness of this freakish female, but he did not recall exactly where or when he had looked upon it. He sifted through the nooks and crannies of his memory, but failed to dredge up anything but a vague sense of familiarity. The sculpted effigy radiated cosmic hatred, a malovence that would have frozen the very bowels of many stout-hearted men. Conan shuddered.

Light from the rising sun sparkled in the sculpted eye sockets. Each had been fitted with an oval-shaped ruby the size of a hen's egg. In his thieving days, Conan would have immediately climbed to those glittering sockets and pried out the rich prizes therein.

But experience had tempered his youthful rashness. He resisted the impulse to seize those huge gemstones—at least for now. The taint of ancient, unspeakable evil fouled the very air, and a horrible death might await a would-be thief. In spite of the morning's warmth, a chill crept down Conan's spine. He tried to turn away, but icy fingers of fear wrapped around his brain, freezing his soul. In that face—no, in the *eyes*—lurked the black void of chaos.

Those repellent but entrancing eyes pulled him in. The pain faded from his body as his limbs went slack. The damp, musty scent of the clearing became but a vague memory. He could not feel the sun on his flesh. His feet no longer touched the muddy ground; his lungs no longer breathed air.

He was floating in a boundless realm. Two scarlet suns glared down at him like the eyes of a baleful god. Their distant glow was the only source of illumination. Darkness, thick and tangible, pushed against him, filling his nostrils and mouth as if he were submerged in deep, black water.

He had no strength to resist. He was suffocating, unable to hold his breath, unable to pull his eyes away from the hypnotic crimson light.

The twin orbs vanished.

For a moment, his mind went black; all around him was a murky gray void. Then painful brightness burst upon his numbed brain, and he was back in the clearing. He shut his eyes, raising his hand to his brow to shade his face. He coughed, jarring his lungs into motion. Drawing in shallow breaths, he waited for his eyes to adjust to the light of the morning sun.

Jukona stood between him and the malefic effigy.

Conan took a clumsy step backward. "Crom," he gasped, eyeing the huge Ganak warrior with suspicion, his hand instinctively reaching for a sword that was not there.

The tall Ganak dropped a round object onto the ground. Palms facing up, he spread out his arms. "Peace, stranger, I, Jukona, am the Ganak warrior-leader. I would be your friend."

Conan's brow furrowed in concentration, but the Ganak language was not difficult for him to manage. He rasped a surly response. "Conan of Cimmeria. And I would not befriend a man who takes my sword and turns his back upon me after I aid him in battle!"

Sighing heavily, Jukona hung his head. "I did not wish to go without you. Ngomba demanded that you be left behind. He claimed your *atnalga* ... if that is what you mean by 'sword'? I believed he was Kulunga's chosen one, whose words must be obeyed. But he did not forbid me to show you the way to Ganaku. Before we rowed away from the shore of bones, I marked path-symbols upon the ground beside you. When the seekers brought news of your arrival at Ganaku, I came here in search of you. Ngomba attacked me with your weapon, near the path of the net-beasts, and left me for dead."

"Net-beasts?"

"The elders call them *anansi*," Jukona offered, rubbing at the lump on his head.

"Had you not found me when you did . . ." Conan shuddered, thinking again of the ruby orbs that had held him in thrall. He noticed that Jukona stood interposed between himself and the hideous stone image. He pointed to it. "Who in Zandru's Nine Hells is that she-devil?"

Jukona blinked, his face blank with confusion. "I have never seen it before, but I sense its presence of evil. The Deadlands teem with dangers to the body and the soul. I am glad that your cry for help awakened me from my stupor." He rubbed at the back of his head, wincing.

Conan frowned. "I remember no such cry for help."

"I believe that your spirit was being drawn from your body. Perhaps you could not hear your own voice. You resisted for a while, long enough for me to follow your trail and climb between those trees over there. As I ran to you, I *saw* your spirit, floating up to those eyes in the wall, rising from your body . . ." He paused, shuddering, as if reluctant to say more.

"How did you find me?"

"I lay on the ground over there." He pointed far away to the other side of the clearing. "Past the trees. Your howl stirred me. You made the same sound on the shore of bones when we fought the Kezati. I saw the dead net-beast caught between the trees and guessed that you had ventured into the dark heart of the Deadlands."

"Aptly named," Conan said, shuddering at the vivid memory of his narrow escape. His eyes narrowed. "Yet these blasted spiders did not attack you."

" 'Spiders'? It is a strange word. But no, the elders say that net-beasts will not strike one who bears a egg, a sack of their unborn spawn." Crouching, he picked up the dull, leathery object as he spoke. "We are safe from them for awhile. It is said that the sun god's face burns their eyes, but when he sleeps, they will come again. And they will hunt any time if they hunger. We must go to the village now, for the net-beasts are the least of the perils lurking in the Deadlands. The elders whisper all manner of dark tales about Deadlands, but never have I heard of this wall that devours souls."

Conan grimaced. "Gladly will I depart from this thrice-accursed jungle. Look not into the eyes of the she-devil, whatever you do. When we leave, I would as soon seek Ngomba and show him the error of crossing a Cimmerian! And with my sword in hand, we would not need to fear the denizens of this hell-jungle."

" 'Sword.' " Jukona shook his head and stared at Conan's long mane of hair. "Conan of Cimmeria. Your words and ways are strange. And yet . . . at heart I believe you to be a warrior like me and a man of honor. Did the gods send you to us?"

Conan broke into a laugh that pained his bruised ribs. "If so, they were gods who wished to make a cruel jest at my expense! Nay, Jukona, my poor judgment and ill luck brought me here, naught else. I came from a land far north of here, across the southern sea and farther north yet. No Cimmerian has ever journeyed so far from the dreary valleys and dark woods that my kin call home."

"A land . . . across the sea? The elders say that the sea is without end. The gods created only three lands: Ganaku and Zati, and between them, Arawu, where we fight the Kezati."

"Those giant vultures? By Crom, never have I seen such creatures, not in all my years of wandering." He turned, averting his eyes from the insidious image, and began walking to the trees at the edge of the clearing. "There are dozens of known lands in the world, and more are thought to exist, as yet undiscovered. I have roamed from the Pictish coast to the Hyrkanian steppes and beyond. I have encountered people of all races, but none quite like you or your enemies. But the world teems with so many men and monsters that no one man may know of them all." He raised an eyebrow, struck again by Jukona's height. Conan was taller than most men. It was a peculiar feeling, having to look *up* to see another man's face. "You seem as strange to me as I must seem to you."

Jukona followed Conan, stopping at the foot of the two gore-smeared trees. The Ganak handed the egg sack to Conan and hauled himself up the trunks, bending them apart with what seemed to be minimal effort. Jukona's arms looked like bundles of rope, as thick as the Cimmerian's muscular calves. While Conan climbed through the gap, avoiding the crushed spider's oozings, he realized that subduing Ngomba would be no easy task. In hand-to-hand combat, the Ganak would tear him apart. Conan hoped that Ngomba would rely on his stolen blade. These people seemed ignorant of swords. Steel was a powerful servant only when wielded by one who possessed the skill to master it.

Holding apart the trees, Jukona lifted his legs, leaping feet-first through the opening. Thick branches snapped together behind him.

When they reached the ground, Jukona plunged into a dense thicket, following a trail of trampled and bent leaves that led to where he had been waylaid. "I do not have the skill of a seeker or gatherer, but if the gods favor us with a few signs, we can find Ngomba."

Conan immediately saw a deep footprint, pointing toward the broad trail that he had followed into the jungle. "There," he said, pointing.

"We must be careful," Jukona said, lowering his voice. "Of my warriors, Ngomba is the strongest and most stealthy."

"He even *looks* different. Does he come from another tribe?"

A look of pity crept into Jukona's eyes. "At birth, his mother's life was taken by the gods. We call such children *Mkundo*; our elders raise them, and they must wear the paint that honors the sacrifice made by their mother. Ngomba obeys this tradition, but I think he has never accepted the death of his mother. When he was a boy, he asked many questions about her. It may be that he blames our gods for her death. He does not respect the Y'Taba, and he argues with me and the elders."

"What about his sire? Cimmerians do not tolerate such behavior from their brats. A few belt-lashings on my backside and a buffet or two on the ears taught me to respect my elders."

"His father could not raise him," Jukona said, his voice heavy.

Conan sullenly eyed the wide path, slowly retracing Ngomba's steps. "Then it falls to us to give him a lesson long overdue. But enough! We waste time with this prattle while he gets away."

They fell silent, intent on pursuit. While following the trail, they moved as silently as possible so that Ngomba would not hear them approaching.

At first, they had no problems following Ngomba's route. But eventually Conan needed his tracking skills; the huge spiders had smudged and nearly obliterated all signs of the Ganak's passage. For several hundred paces, he moved on intuition alone, gratified when he again saw a heel mark, then a complete footprint. By noting the depth of the impressions that remained and the distance between them, Conan speculated that Ngomba had been running hard and fast.

What surprised Jukona was the direction of Ngomba's flight. "He ran toward the village," Jukona said slowly, pinching his lip between his teeth. "But Y'Taba banished him; it is impossible for him to return!"

"He may turn from this course, ere he reaches your village. Let us follow and see. We must not let him leave this island."

Jukona muttered a reply which Conan could not quite translate.

They hastened their pace as much as possible. The sun crept across the sky, heating up the jungle. In spite of the thick humidity, Conan's tongue felt as dry as the hide of a

Zamoran desert-lizard. He would gladly have paid a purse-ful of gold for a jack of ale. But the nearest cask was probably a two-week sea voyage from here ... wherever *here* was. That was one of many problems he would have to face later.

He trudged on, keeping one eye on the ground and the other on Jukona. Although the huge warrior had saved him from the soul-stealing she-devil, he had decided not to trust these Ganaks. They had abandoned him once and might do so again. They seemed a superstitious lot, and Conan had never quite understood those who blindly en-trusted their fate to the gods. In Conan's experience, the gods helped only those who helped themselves.

He tried to think of where or when he had seen that she-devil's—or goddess's—likeness. It had been crudely chis-eled into a stone block, smaller, less detailed, he was sure ... the shadowy ghost of that face and ten-armed body rose into his mind. But try as he might, he could not illu-minate that dark corner of his memory.

Frustrated, he turned his thoughts again to the trail. The trees were farther apart, smaller in height and girth. When Conan noted that the footsteps veered sharply off the path, he halted instantly, listening.

A half step behind him, Jukona froze in midstride. He bent down, whispering into Conan's ear and pointing in the direction of the footsteps. "The village lies that way." Smiling grimly, the warrior-leader straightened, peering through the trees. Their trunks were spaced farther apart, but the foliage off the path rose to Conan's waist—midthigh on Jukona. Conan could not easily examine the turf, but he had no need to do so. Ngomba had bolted through the tangle of leafy growth, leaving trampled stalks in his wake.

Conan grudgingly credited the fleeing Ganak for his en-durance. They had been trailing Ngomba since dawn, and the sun had nearly reached its midday mark. There had been no evidence that the rebellious warrior had let his pace slacken. He had run as if chased by every slavering devil from Hell. Conan began to discount the possibility of an ambush. Where could Ngomba have fled, if not to the village?

The jungle eventually thinned and the trees lessened in height and breadth, until the terrain consisted mainly of marshland. Tall reeds rose up to Conan's forehead, but Jukona could see over their yellowish-green tops.

"We are near," Jukona panted. "I see the hill, but—oh, Muhingo, it cannot be! Follow me!" He broke into a run, down the sludgy road of bent and broken reeds. Conan followed, ignoring the complaints of his weary limbs. Swampy muck sucked at their feet as they splashed through the insect-infested bog. Reeds whipped Conan's sunburned flesh, raising dozens of stinging welts.

Although he could not be certain, Conan thought he heard the distant murmur of voices, mingled with what might have been weeping. Perhaps it was just the wind in the reeds. But Jukona also seemed to hear it, for he lifted his head and quickened his stride. Crossing the tall mass of stalks with a burst of speed, they encountered a long, narrow patch of red, sandy mud. Conan slid to a halt, nearly stumbling into a sluggish, meandering stream that blocked their way.

The Ganak village was a few hundred paces beyond the ribbon of murky water. From its center rose a small hill, upon which lay the shredded bodies of several Ganaks. Scattered around the hill were dozens of slain Kezatis.

Twelve
Village of Mystery

No!" Jukona howled like a victim on a torturer's rack, his cry echoing across the village. Fists clenched, the warrior-leader forded the water while Conan stared. He had seen the gloomy aftermath of battle far too often in these past few weeks.

Survivors milled nearby, their faces turned his way. Jukona reached the other side of the water, beckoning impatiently for Conan to follow. As Conan waded through, two Ganaks detached themselves from the group near the mound, hastening toward Jukona and Conan.

"Y'Taba!" Jukona shouted to the approaching Ganaks, then lowered his head to murmur into Conan's ear. "He is called Y'Taba, our spirit-leader. Do not let his age deceive you; his strength matches his wisdom. By your words and deeds he will judge you. Say nothing to offend him or our people."

Conan nodded. "Who is the girl?"

"She is called Sajara, *Ranioba* of our huntresses and

seekers . . . and my daughter." Though subdued, his voice radiated with a father's pride.

Conan barely took notice of Y'Taba, glancing only once at the immense Ganak's skirt of gleaming black shells. His gaze had been captured by the woman Sajara. She was as tall as he, olive-skinned like the other Ganaks, her hair shorn to but a single braid. His mouth went dry at the sight of her compactly muscled body, covered only by a tattered snakeskin girdle. Brightly painted spirals adorned her naked torso. She moved with supple, long-legged strides, her full breasts swaying gently as she walked.

Conan had not so much as *seen* a woman since the night in Jaral's tent . . . some two weeks ago. It seemed like years had passed. He stared at Sajara, his eyes burning fiercely with unabashed appreciation. When she drew closer, he saw that her face was as stunning as her body. Conan could not recall any woman endowed with such exotic beauty. Kings had warred with each other for women less alluring.

Regaining a measure of his composure, Conan realized that he had stopped, letting Jukona get far ahead of him. He hurried across and caught up with the others. When Y'Taba stood before him, he could see the cuts, bruises, and smeared patches of blood upon the old man's body. Red furrows marked his beefy arms and broad chest. Blood had seeped from an ugly slash in his forehead, matting his silvery-white eyebrows with dark stains.

Sajara's wounds were mere nicks and scratches; her face had escaped injury altogether. A knife, the first bladed weapon he had seen among these people, was thrust into her girdle. Thick Kezati blood stained its blade and hilt. He eyed it curiously, noting that its tapering length had been fashioned from a shell, polished and sharpened to a point. A poor weapon against the Kezati, who struck simultaneously with beak and talons.

Sajara ignored Jukona's outstretched arms. "Father," she said coolly.

He opened his mouth to greet her, but instead simply

hugged her. Sajara did not return the embrace, stepping back as soon as she could and returning to Y'Taba's side.

Jukona opened his hands, extending them palm-up to the imposing old Ganak. "Y'Taba Spirit-Leader, I have returned from the Deadlands, and I bring the stranger. He is called Conan. He comes from Cimmeria, a land far away."

"Welcome to Ganaku, Conan of . . . Cimmeria," Y'Taba said, his voice soft and sad. He held out his palms to Conan, who awkwardly mimicked the gesture. "Beside me is Sajara Ranioba, she who is daughter of Jukona."

"Welcome," she said, her voice softening. She made no gesture, so he simply nodded, trying not to stare.

Y'Taba continued. "Your return from the Deadlands is the only glimmer of sun to brighten this day of darkness. We have wronged you, and I ask for forgiveness from you."

Conan shrugged. "*You* have done me no harm. My quarrel is with Ngomba, who took my sword."

Nodding, Jukona interrupted. "We followed Ngomba here, but what happened then? I see, but cannot believe . . . the Kezati dared to attack our village?"

Y'Taba's broad shoulders slumped. "This morning, just before sunrise, they descended from the sky." He paused, his tone becoming bitter. "All but a few of our warriors now rest in the care of Muhingo. May he welcome them, for they fought well. Even so, the spawn of Ezat were many to our few. Were it not for Sajara, her hunters, and the unexpected return of Ngomba, many more of our people would wander in the realm of gray clouds. Not since the days of our first ancestors have the wicked children of Ezat violated our village."

Jukona frowned. "Ngomba must have sensed the coming of the Kezati—how, I do not know. Did the Kezati send him to Muhingo?"

Sajara spoke before Y'Taba could reply. "With the *atnalga*, he killed many Kezati. As they flew, blood dripped from their wounds like red rain. It was a terrible fight. They were as thick as the flies of the swamps, but

Ngomba had the worst of it. Three, sometimes four, flew at him." Admiration was evident in her tone. "For a while, he drove them away ... but there were too many. Even Ngomba could not withstand them all."

Conan listened, fascinated equally by the tale and its teller. Since the battle with the Kezati on the skull-covered beach, he had been curious about the Ganaks and their winged enemies. "Why do these vultures attack you?"

"For food," Y'Taba said. "Their land is barren. Long ago, they stripped from it all things living. The children of Ezat dwell on Zati, a great rock devoid of birds, beasts, and plants. Our enemies cannot dive deep enough to feed upon the fish in the sea, as we do. Once, they preyed upon the beasts of Arawu, which is a small isle that lies between here and Zati. Now Arawu is dying. Only trees and bushes remain; even the birds have been hunted and eaten."

Conan remembered the eerie silence that pervaded that isle, where he had first seen the Ganaks. "The shore of skulls," he muttered.

Y'Taba nodded. "For generations, we have sent our warriors to Arawu to meet the Kezati in battle. If we did not, their hunger would drive them here, to prey upon us and our families ... as they did on this dark day. Not since the time of the first Y'Taba have our enemies invaded our village. We defeat them at Arawu, where they bear away their own dead and feast upon the bodies, though they leave the heads behind."

Conan grunted with revulsion. "But after they devour their kin, how then do they survive?"

"They do not survive ... they all starve after fighting among each other and eating each other. Or so it has been," Y'Taba answered solemnly. "But always, after a generation of peace, they return. We believe that they lay eggs before they die, eggs which bear young only after the passing of many, many moon-cycles. The hatchlings then burst forth, the stronger devouring the weaker. These survivors, who are aggressive and strong, mature quickly and become able to fly. They first seek food at Arawu and consume whatever meager animal life has sprung up since their predecessors' scouring of the place. Many more perish as they quarrel over a plump bird or other choice catch." Y'Taba paused, clearing his throat. "It is then that Ataba, god above gods, sends the dream to me. Ataba warns us of the coming of the Kezati."

Conan, becoming restless, scratched his whiskered chin. "Why do you wait until they can fight? Destroy the eggs!"

Jukona shook his head. "The nests of Zati lie atop a sheer wall of rock, taller than any tree on Ganaku. In the past, some among us tried to reach the nests but failed. Zati is impossible to climb."

Conan had his doubts. He seldom encountered a cliff that he deemed unscalable. As a youth, he had learned to climb by scaling steep hills and slippery, ice-covered mountains in Cimmeria. On this island, the Ganaks would have no means to develop such skills. He wrinkled his brow in puzzlement. "Then who discovered the Kezati eggs?"

"Omjdu, whose mother and father were among our fist ancestors. When the Kezati first met our warriors at Arawu, they captured Omjdu and several others, bearing them back to Zati . . . alive. A few Ganaks ran to the log-boats and gave chase.

"Omjdu, in the grip of a Kezati, was taken to Zati, but before his captor dragged him inside for a feeding, he fought it for a while and broke its neck. Through a hole at the top of Zati, he saw a cavern that bulged with eggs beyond counting. Huge they were, their shells swollen with unborn Kezati. Helpless to intervene, he watched as the other Ganaks were fed to hatchlings. But then more Kezati came for him, and he jumped off the cliffs atop the island. Our warriors found him upon the rocks below, broken and dying. He spoke before passing into the lands of gray, describing what he had seen. The elders still tell Omjdu's tale."

"He was an ancestor of my family," Sajara added proudly.

"You and Jukona are the last of his line," Y'Taba said sorrowfully. He looked at Jukona. "Her brother—your son—met Muhingo today. He lies with the others who fell before the Kezati."

"Pomja," Jukona whispered, his eyes turning toward the slain Ganaks who lay on the mound. Tears welled in his huge eyes and spilled down his stricken face. "Bunoab . . . Sobhuza . . . Rozwi! Ah, what a day of evil this is, by Asusa!"

"We must pray to Asusa for aid, not swear by his name," Y'Taba chided. "Perhaps the gods are angry with us, or they may be at war themselves. If so, now is the time for prayer and also the time for difficult decisions." He straightened. "Sajara, gather the elders. Before the Kezati return, there is much to discuss. We shall speak of many things after I have tended to the hurts of our people. Your huntresses took wounds, but none beyond my skill. However, I fear that Ngomba will live only if the gods grant me the power to heal him."

Scowling, Conan balled his hands into fists. "If he does not return my sword, not even the gods will be able to heal him."

Jukona nodded. "And if he lives, Ngomba must face me. He tried to kill me in the Deadlands. My heart holds no pity for him. His deeds today do not wash from him the red stain of treachery. Do not trust him, Spirit-Leader! The serpent who bites an enemy today may bite a friend tomorrow. And this serpent was ever the mightiest of my warriors—and the most dangerous."

Y'Taba sighed. "Peace, Jukona. Whatever else he is, Ngomba is Ganak, not a beast of scales and cold blood. But we shall speak of this later." He rubbed at a cut above his eye. "Conan of Cimmeria, your weapon will be given back to you. If Ngomba survives, you may punish him for his crime in whatever manner your people would choose. We shall neither interfere nor help you, for this is the way of my people. If he perishes, mighty Ataba will have chosen Ngomba's punishment." Y'Taba looked directly into

Jukona's eyes. "And if our wounded men do not survive, you will become the last Ganak warrior."

The sullen warrior-leader did not reply, his gaze still resting upon fallen comrades.

Y'Taba's voice was slowing with weariness. "Conan of Cimmeria, if you would later join me, I would welcome your company, for I have many questions. Jukona, I must speak with you before we join the elders."

Sajara glared at Jukona, who seemed oblivious to her. "Ngomba saved us today. Will you never see him as a warrior pure in heart and purpose?" She whirled away from him.

Y'Taba sighed. "She speaks truly. Ngomba fought bravely this day. But Sajara, you must see that Jukona also speaks truly, as does the *njeni*, the stranger, Conan of Cimmeria. None of us can trust Ngomba. But we have no more time to speak of this. Before we heal the wounds of heart and soul, there are wounds of flesh and blood to tend. Ngomba and the other warriors need me. Sajara, find the weapon that belongs to Conan of Cimmeria and have it returned to him. Then assemble the elders. Our enemies will return, and we must be prepared for their coming."

Sajara nodded, her temper seeming to cool. "We should meet under the roof of celebration. My huntresses will need time to clear the foul remains from the place of gathering." Her eyes blazed as she looked upon the heaped Kezati carcasses.

Y'Taba began walking toward the village. "No longer will it be called the roof of celebration," he said. "Let all Ganaks call it the roof of sorrow; never again shall our people feast there. Had Ngomba's warning been heeded, we might have better withstood the attack." He moved ahead of the others, mumbling quietly to himself. "Among us, only he knew. I must ponder what has come to pass and seek the meaning."

"I would as soon seek victuals," Conan grumbled. "I am nigh famished, by Crom!" He stared unabashedly at Sajara's voluptuous body as she walked ahead of him. The natural, lithe sway of her hips was more arousing than the practiced movements of an emperor's seraglio-dancer.

Jukona nodded glumly. "You are right, Conan. The mourning must wait. We can eat and drink while Y'Taba hears of our journey in the Deadlands."

"How can you look upon death and yet think of food?" Sajara shook her head in bewilderment. "I shall ask a bearer to bring meat and gourds of *kuomo* to you."

"Two bearers," Jukona advised. "Conan of Cimmeria may look small, but a warrior's appetite always matches his prowess."

Conan grinned, reluctantly shifting his stare from Sajara. He did not wish to earn Jukona's ire by ogling the warrior's daughter. Silently, he observed the devastated villagers as they went about their grim labors. Conan saw only the young and old at work, dragging Kezati corpses toward the swamp near the village's edge. The Ganaks seemed content to let their dead lie upon the mound, gathering flies as they baked in the hot afternoon sun. "You do not bury or burn your slain?" he asked.

Jukona wrinkled his brow. "Bury? Burn? Are these prayers or rituals of your people?"

"Rituals, you might say. In many lands where I have traveled, people dig holes, called graves, for their dead. They cover the bodies with dirt while a priest mumbles or mourners croon a dirge. Stygians have even more elaborate customs, building vast chambers—tombs, or even pyramids—according to the status the deceased held in life. Others dispense with all the bother and set fire to corpses, letting them burn into ash.

"Priest . . . tombs . . . pyramids . . . fire . . . ash." Jukona shook his head. "I understand some of what you say, but not all of your words hold visions for me. Our elders remember all Ganak lore and may know of what you speak. Let me show you my village, that you may learn of my people." He led Conan past a long bench fashioned from a tree. Two other such benches formed a triangle with the mound of the dead rising from its center. "This is the place of gathering, where my people hear the voice of Y'Taba, wisdom of the elders, reports of our *Ranioba*, or other words of importance to all."

Conan nodded, observing that the wooden benches had been smoothed to a polish by generations of observers. He also noticed that the top edges were slightly squared and beveled on the back side. This and something about their curvature made their appearance maddeningly familiar. He doubted that three such trees could have simply grown into such a shape and size. But these Ganaks possessed no evident tools of carpentry. "Where are the benches from?" he asked.

Jukona shrugged. "The elders would know, or Y'Taba. Look over there. That is what once was the roof of celebration, which shaded feasts of victory when our warriors returned from Arawu. Look what the Kezati have done to it, Asusa curse them! Will the goddess fashion another for us, I wonder?"

"Crom, it's—" Conan blurted, staring slack-jawed. From a distance, he had thought it to be a simple roof of dried leaves and branches, crudely propped up by a frame of trees.

The roof consisted of crumbling sailcloth, doubtless the mainsail of some ancient craft. Stained and shredded, its remnants hung like the tatters of a centuries-old burial shroud. The sight of them opened a door in Conan's mind—the benches. Their distinctive shape . . . they were *keels*, salvaged from immense ships. Conan's eyes narrowed as he studied the village, whose origin raised a hundred questions.

"Yes," Jukona nodded, misinterpreting Conan's reaction. "It is ruined." His voice became distant.

"The gods made this for you?"

"For Kulunga, a first ancestor. It was the veil of Jhaora. When Kulunga saved our village from the Kezati, there was a feast of plenty held to honor the gods. But Ezat, angered by the deaths of his children, hurled his tears of bitterness upon Ganaku and put an end to the feasting. So

Jhaora, who hates Ezat more than any of the gods, made a gift of her veil to our first ancestors, protecting them from Ezat's tears."

Conan feigned interest as Jukona continued his tale. Perhaps the warrior-leader did not know the true origin of their roof of celebration. But what if the elders knew secrets of the past and deliberately kept their people ignorant? Conan decided to spare the warrior-leader from further questions for now. But when he spoke with Y'Taba, Conan would demand some real answers.

He needed to leave this strange island and return to the kingdoms of Hyboria, where he could seek a cure to the shaman's curse. The sooner he left, the better. He wanted no more of the strange dreams. Worse yet, the curse might strike him again. If it came upon him at night in the village . . . he would butcher Ganak elders and children. He shuddered, cold sweat suddenly dampening his brow.

Ships had landed here, perhaps centuries ago, and Conan was determined to learn of their origin. Even the mariners of old kept logs or carried maps and charts. If Conan could but find where the mainland lay, half of his problem would be solved.

The other half—*how* to get to the mainland—was another problem entirely.

Thirteen
Song of the Shell-Spirits

Ngomba groaned, struggling to rise from his bed of leaves and marsh grass. His body was a red mass of ravaged flesh. Multihued salves had been applied to the slashes; blood-crusted leaves covered patches on his head and upper body where the Kezati talons had torn away the skin.

Y'Taba stood over the injured Ganak, watching for a short while before deciding what should be done. Ngomba had lost so much blood that his skin was as pale as the stranger's. The *jumbura* and *gurundi* berry-juices, which had considerable healing power, had not closed the deep gashes in Ngomba's body. Y'Taba believed that Ngomba's wounds and his pain were punishment, meted out by the gods for the sins of pride and disobedience.

Ngomba would recover. He might even grow wiser, if he learned any of the harsh lessons taught by the day's events. Y'Taba had watched Ngomba grow up; a stubborn boy with a tongue as sharp as his wit who had never before known defeat. And he had always gotten his way—until Jukona forbade him to join with Sajara.

At first Ngomba had driven himself to win Jukona's favor. Ngomba had ever been larger than Ganaks of his age, but still he pushed his body beyond the limits of endurance. When Jukona told the warriors to circle the village seven times as fast as they could run, Ngomba would circle it ten, twelve, even fourteen times. When the sun dipped from the sky and the other warriors slept in their huts, Ngomba sat at the feet of any elder who would talk to him, drinking lore like *kuomo*.

Ngomba learned patience. He asked Jukona again, this time in proper custom, for permission to become Sajara's mate. She pleaded with Jukona, telling him that she would join only with Ngomba.

Still, Jukona refused to give his consent. On that day, he and Ngomba had become enemies, bitter as the oil of *vanukla* leaves. The young warrior immediately challenged Jukona in the *Ghanuta*. But Y'Taba had forbidden the combat, saying to Ngomba that he must first prove himself in battle with the Kezati. Later, the village's old *Ranioba* named Sajara as her successor. The joining was then impossible; *Raniobas* may not be joined until they have chosen and trained a replacement. And indeed, Sajara had seemed to lose some interest in Ngomba when she became *Ranioba*.

Ngomba finally seemed to give up. He withdrew from the other Ganaks, spending much time by himself. The only enthusiasm he showed was during the warrior exercises, at which he excelled. He became more surly with the passing of every day.

Y'Taba looked down upon the battered, slashed form of his son, a tear wetting his wrinkled cheek. No Ganak knew this hidden truth: their spirit-leader was the father of Ngomba. And Y'Taba would never confess. The gods would damn him for it, he knew. For his silence, Ngomba had suffered as no Ganak should.

His son had been conceived on the very eve that he had

become Y'Taba. He had been weak on that night of madness, and the gods had punished him for it.

The elders said that *kuomo* opened the ears of men to the whispers of Anamobi, Moon Goddess who delighted in the pleasures of the flesh.

The moon goddess need not have whispered to Y'Taba on that night; Nyona *Ranioba's* beauty spoke well enough for itself. He had fallen in love with her, but he was Y'Taba. Spirit-leaders of old who had joined had lost much of their powers to heal—their power to command the spirits in the shells that hung around Y'Taba's neck. And Nyona was *Ranioba*. To seek a joining was to ask her to name a successor and give up her chosen way of life.

After their night together, she vanished into the Deadlands. The face of the moon thinned, vanished, and became full again until the search for Nyona ended. The Deadlands swallowed her up.

When he saw her again, he had become Y'Taba. He had no memory of his former name; it was a shadow, washed from his mind like a footprint in a rainstorm. It had ever been so, since the first Y'Taba. But he would never forget the night of her return. A woman had given birth to a child that day, a child suffering from a wasting disease. Y'Taba, alone with the child, had used every herb, every berry, every prayer at his disposal to heal the child. But the gods had sealed the infant's fate, taking him into the lands of gray.

On that moonless night, Nyona slipped unseen into Y'Taba's hut. In her arms she held an infant boy . . . their son, Ngomba.

She had begged him to give their son to the parents of the dead child, and he had agreed. After a brief, almost bitter embrace, she had taken the body of the other infant and disappeared again. He wondered what had become of Nyona. Had she fallen prey to a beast of the Deadlands, or had she made a secret home in the trees? Sometimes he dreamed that she still lived, still came to the edge of the village and watched him.

Y'Taba covered his face with his sweating palms, his

heart almost bursting from the burden of guilt that lay upon it. That weight had grown heavier with the passing of every day. Had his misdeed brought about the evil that had come to pass? Had the gods waited until now to mete out his punishment? If so, the blood of all Ganaks might stain his soul eternally. He shivered, although his hut was warm. Crouching, he placed his palm upon Ngomba's feverish brow.

"You spoke truly, my son," he whispered. "I am an old fool. May the gods forgive me for my pride and grant me the power to heal you."

Y'Taba closed his eyes and wrapped his fingers around his necklace of ebon shells. During his lifetime, he had seldom called upon the spirits in the shells. They heeded only the spirit-leader's call; their secrets were known only to the Y'Tabas, who passed them down to successors.

Clearing his mind of turbulent thoughts, he inhaled and exhaled in slow, regular intervals. Speaking to the shell-spirits was in some ways like a game played by young Ganaks, in which flat stones were skipped across the waters adjoining the Ganaku beaches. A stone thrown just so would skip many times and travel far if the seas were placid.

Y'Taba, however, was not throwing stones. He was skipping words—his thoughts—across the sea of his mind. Concentrating, he found his inner voice and began whispering to the shell-spirits. His palm pressed against Ngomba's sweat-slicked brow as his grip on the shells tightened. His thoughts skipped and spun outward until they faded into the distance. He listened for a response, for something to reach the ears of his mind.

There! They had heard him. His hand tingled, as if covered with hundreds of biting ants. The feeling traveled along his arm and moved inward, past his skin, until he felt it in his bones. A hum—the song of the shell-spirits—emanated from his fist, deafening him.

Ngomba's mouth opened in a cry that was drowned by the hum. Y'Taba clenched the shells in a grip so fierce that it whitened his knuckles. Sweat streamed down his face and veins pulsed at his temples. The spirits had awakened; their song rang in his ears, unbearably loud, and he fought to keep his eyes closed. The shell-spirits were angry at him for rousing them. The song ended as suddenly as it had begun. They were resisting him; he must try harder.

Heart pounding, pulse racing, he again called out to them with his thoughts. "By the will of Asusa Sun God, come to me—now!" And be bore down again on the shells, so fiercely that one cracked in his palm, its shards digging painfully into his flesh.

The room was plunged into silence, and before him stood the spirits. They appeared as shapes of water, transparent and rippling, and they shimmered like veils of dew in the hut's dim light. Their forms changed constantly: tall, thin spirals; squat, bobbing spheres; and shallow, spinning ovals.

"Long has it been since you last dared to awaken us," they murmured, their voices a distant wail in his mind. "Again we hear your call, if only to honor our promise to Asusa. Speak your purpose for this summons."

"To heal the wounds of Ngomba, who lies here before us. Wash him in your waters of healing and make him well again."

Twisting and churning, the spirits spoke again. "Know that you have broken the trust which binds us to obey you. You have joined with the one called Nyona."

"That was long ago," Y'Taba objected.

"Your voice does not bend us to the will of Asusa. For the sake of Muhingo, who is beloved of Asusa, we shall do the task to which you have set us. Know also that only once more shall we come when called by you, and then only if your summons pleases Muhingo."

They flowed together, forming a wave that swept across Ngomba, leapt into the air, and vanished.

Y'Taba sat heavily, panting. His ears rang and a dull pain throbbed in his bones. He stared at his son, whose wounds were closing, fading before his eyes. Realizing that he was still grasping the shells, he relaxed his grip and eyed his aching palm. Fragments of a crushed shell had lodged into his palm, blood welling up in the tiny punctures and seeping into the cracks of his skin.

Ngomba stirred, looking up at Y'Taba's face through half-closed eyes.

The spirit-leader's voice was a hoarse whisper. "Your body is well. Rest, Ngomba . . . let your spirit heal."

The young Ganak's eyes closed again; his breaths became deep and even, slowing as he drifted back to sleep.

"As for me," Y'Taba said under his breath, "my night will be long." He brushed shell fragments from his hand, wiping off the blood with damp leaves.

He rose slowly, standing tall and squaring his shoulders. His people needed a strong Y'Taba. He must appear confident, not weary or afraid. Stifling a yawn, he walked outside to hear the stranger's tale.

Then Y'Taba would make decisions that would save —or perhaps destroy—the Ganak people.

Jukona shifted on the smooth wood that marked the edge of the place of gathering. A sudden weariness had settled over him.

He and Conan were finishing their tale of escape from the Deadlands. Y'Taba and a small group of elders listened, staring intently. "And when I found Conan, she had nearly drawn the spirit from his body—or was it *spirits*?" Jukona took a long drink from his coconut shell, draining every drop of *kuomo* juice. "Unless some trick of the Deadlands deceived my old eyes. You cast two shadows back there—one in your shape, the other in the shape of . . . something else. How could this be—unless you have two spirits? Or is this the way of people from Cimmeria, Conan?"

Conan's eyes narrowed. *Two* shadows? "Nay. Perhaps it was a tree's shadow, or as you said, some trick of the sun." He took a casual swig of *kuomo*. It was an agreeable, heady drink, its flavor similar to Zembabwan coconut wine.

Jukona rubbed his jaw. "It was taller than any Ganak. Its head was huge and misshapen, and its arms reached nearly to the ground. Its legs were short but thick. It looked more like . . . a beast . . . than a man. I hope never to meet a beast that casts such a shadow." He grabbed another shell, gulping *kuomo*.

Y'Taba's brow wrinkled. "The shadow was no trick of the Deadlands," he said, studying Conan's face. "When I first saw you, Conan of Cimmeria, I saw this beast. It lurked in your eyes, cringing back from the bright face of Asusa Sun God."

Conan scowled, his fingers twitching instinctively toward the hilt of his sword, which had finally been returned to him. This spirit-leader was no hoax; he had somehow discovered the shaman's curse. It was still there, no doubt waiting for the moon to again wax full. Conan's flesh crawled at the memory of the carnage his ape-self had left aboard the *Mistress* . . . slaughter more wanton than a tribe of berserk Æsir.

A thought sparked in Conan's mind, kindling a flame of hope. Earlier today, Y'Taba had spoken of healing the wounded. He was shaman, a spirit-leader. Did he have the power to disenchant the shaman's ape-spell?

"But all men have a beast inside them," Y'Taba continued, and the elders nodded solemnly. "A newborn is more beast than man, but the gods make our spirits stronger than the beast within us. We draw strength from our beasts and wisdom from our gods. It is this balance that separates us from animals—like the Kezati, who are dominated by their beasts. But I will speak more of them later, and we will decide what is to be done.

"You, Conan of Cimmeria, play a part in our decision. Already you have fought alongside our warriors, slaying many Kezati. You owe nothing to us. Yet I ask you, on behalf of my people, to aid us in what may be our only hope of survival." He surveyed the somber faces of the elders, many of whom had locked their gaze on Conan.

Jukona rose suddenly, eyes flashing. "By Asusa, you

would ask this of him? He sides with us once though we are not his kin, turning the tide of a hopeless battle. And we thank him by stealing his weapon and leaving him to die—"

"*You* abandoned him on the shores of bone," Y'Taba glowered. "As warrior-leader, you should have opposed Ngomba."

Jukona reddened; his shoulders slumped. "It is as you say, Y'Taba. But in this you give no choice to Conan, for his is the honor of a warrior. If he declines, you steal his honor. As you said, he owes us nothing." He sighed heavily. "And yet I understand why you ask this of him."

Y'Taba stood. He was even taller than Jukona, and his stern gaze further shortened the warrior-leader. "Conan of Cimmeria, you are by all accounts as mighty a warrior as any Ganak who ever lived. The elders believe that our gods summoned you to save us from doom. But we know not how—or if—we can defeat the Kezati. The clouds of a great storm darken what few days may be left to us. As it was in our past, one warrior may make the difference between the survival . . . or destruction . . . of the Ganak people.

"As spirit-leader, I have knowledge that no other Ganaks possess. Every Y'Taba is entrusted with secrets. Tonight I tell you a tale left untold, unknown even to our elders. In the hope of saving our people, it falls to me to break a vow of secrecy I made long ago, to the Y'Taba before me. He revealed the true nature and origin of the Deadlands but swore me to secrecy.

"But in that dark place lies what may be our only hope of salvation. But what lurks there may be worse than the threat of the Kezati. With your help, Conan of Cimmeria, we may retrieve that which was lost long ago . . . that which has the power to rid us of our enemy—forever."

Conan hunched forward on the bench, his mind awhirl. The Ganak spirit-leader's voice had an entrancing quality to it, compelling him to listen. The eyes of the elders gleamed expectantly under the darkening sky, and Jukona sat motionless, his *kuomo* apparently forgotten. The Cimmerian exhaled, trying to loosen the fingers of the tension that gripped him.

Y'Taba stepped back, fingering his necklace of shells. "Long ago, before the time of our first ancestors, a tribe of giants inhabited Ganaku. Their customs and language were unlike our own. In fact, even their name for our land was different. They called it Rahama. At the center of Rahama was a great pool, enchanted by the gods so that its water spouted upward in a spray that was cool and clear. They called it the fountain of the gods, and all those who drank from it never sickened or grew old.

"In gratitude, the Rahamans built a wall of stone around this fountain. Upon the stones they carved praises and prayers. This pleased the gods, who blessed the Rahamans with many generations of fertility. The Rahamans spread peacefully across the land, provided for by their gods, living without fear of hunger, disease, or enemy. The Kezati never troubled them, and the Deadlands did not exist . . . not yet.

"The Rahamans were masters of stone. They built an outer wall to protect their village from storms that were hurled at Rahama by jealous gods. Soon after the wall's completion, three boats were seen approaching Rahama. Huge they were, many times the size of our log-boats, their construction as strange as the people they conveyed across the sea. These people were small in stature, shorter than even Conan, their skin as pale as *kuomo*. Their leader was called Jhaora, a woman from a land whose name we do not know. The Rahamans welcomed her, and she soon learned the powers of their fountain. Its waters preserved her youth and beauty, which pleased her. But she was not content to share the fountain with the Rahamans.

"On one night of treachery, Jhaora and her people attacked. The sleeping Rahamans were massacred. Only a few dozen escaped; they fled and found shelter in what is now our village. They were joined by some of Jhaora's people, those who refused to take part in the murder of the Rahamans."

Y'Taba paused to sip his *kuomo*. His audience was rapt. Sajara and some of her hunters had gathered behind the elders and were listening intently. Y'Taba raised his voice. "The children of these people were our first ancestors."

A startled murmur rippled along the row of elders. "By Asusa!" and other cries were uttered until the crowd again fell silent.

Y'Taba continued. "Without the fountain, the Rahamans became sick with age and began to die. To worsen matters, Jhaora had turned the wall of praises into a wall of blasphemies. Her people carved the image of their cruel goddess upon the outer wall and blocked all but one of its openings.

"The Rahamans beseeched Jhaora for pity, but she slew any who came within the walls. The Rahamans prayed to their gods, but the only power their gods held was power over the fountain. So they fouled its waters. All who drank from it were transformed into creatures of evil, beasts of hideous aspect who fought among themselves for food or for the joy of killing.

"The water of the fountain seeped into the ground and spread; soon nothing living could grow within the walls, and the evil creatures were forced to dwell in the jungle. The Rahaman gods then tried to restore the fountain. But Jhaora, who was last to transform into a beast, had cried to her goddess of evil for vengeance before she lost forever her womanly form. The goddess fought with the Rahaman gods, a terrible battle joined by the jealous storm gods. In that clash, Jhaora's goddess and the Rahaman gods were destroyed. The fountain ran dry. What became of the twisted creature of evil that was once Jhaora, I do not know."

Conan leaned forward, intrigued. The origin of that immense castle was now clear. But from where had Jhaora come? Which of the seafaring Hyborian races were short *and* pale-skinned? The answer, he felt, was within his reach, if he could hear but one more clue.

"The Rahamans never returned to their village within the walls. Beasts infested the jungle, and the hardships of survival occupied the Rahamans and their children. They began to call themselves 'Ganak,' which means 'born of stone.' But they no longer worked stone as they had, for the people of Jhaora were too small and lacked the craft. It was a time of trials, worsened by the appearance of the Kezati. When they first attacked, their numbers were few. But they returned again and again, their forces growing. The Ganaks prayed to their gods for help. But they lacked hope, for they knew that the Rahaman gods were no more.

"Most of Jhaora's people worshipped a god whom they called Azhura. Their god was neither good nor evil. But Jhaora had forced some of their people to pledge their souls to Khatar, a goddess of death." He pointed to an elder whose body was painted with yellow triangles. "Their descendants—many of you—bear marks of warding to protect your spirits from Khatar. She does not hear prayers unless they are accompanied by the screams of victims who are offered in sacrifice. As for Azhura, he hears only the voices of his priests, none of whom had come to Ganaku. Our ancestors would have perished, were it not for Muhingo War God."

Conan nearly choked on his *kuomo*. Azhura . . . could it be *Asura*, a god of Vendhya? Khatar, though the spirit-leader pronounced it strangely, was surely Katar, an evil goddess of Vendhya. Conan had spent little time in that land. It lay many leagues to the east of Iranistan. Although it extended far into the Southern Ocean, Vendhya lacked abundant seaports. Its ways and peoples were strange. Yet it seemed likely that Jhaora had been Vendhyan. Perhaps Ganaku was one of the Misty Isles, a cluster of small islands off the western coast of Vendhya. If so, Conan reckoned, he had drifted more than five hundred leagues after the sinking of the *Mistress*. He focused his attention back on Y'Taba, hoping to hear more clues.

"He appeared in a dream of a first ancestor who was also the first Y'Taba. Muhingo said that the Kezati were the spawn of his brother, Ezat. He told Y'Taba about Ataba the All-Father and Asusa Sun God, who were strong and good. These gods were sorry that their son, who was evil, had brought harm to the Ganaks. He was forbidden by Ataba to slay any Kezati, but he gave Y'Taba the *kabukruh*." Y'Taba lifted his black shell necklace briefly, letting it fall back onto his chest with a clatter.

"He then said to Y'Taba: 'I name you Y'Taba Spirit-Leader. You must guide your people in the ways of Asusa. In return, I shall make you master of the shell-spirits who dwell within the *kabukruh*. Choose one among your people to become warrior-leader. Command the shell-spirits to protect him. Then send him and his warriors to a place of battle which I shall reveal to you. There your warriors will triumph and the children of Ezat will not come to your village. The shell-spirits have other powers; you may command them to heal the sick and the dying. They will obey you for as long as your people remain true to Asusa, but if . . .' " He paused, stopping himself to clear his throat. " 'If you ever beget a child, your mastery of the spirits will wane and the *kabukruh* will become dust. If you stray from the path of Asusa, the spirits will not obey you.' "

"Have we lost our way then, Y'Taba?" Jukona asked, his forehead wrinkling.

"Perhaps we have. It has happened before—long ago, when the first warrior-leader aged and passed into the lands of gray. Then our warriors fought among themselves until only Kulunga remained, and again Muhingo came to our aid. Since then, the Kezati have never come to Ganaku. It may be that we suffer for the misdeeds of Ngomba."

A wizened Ganak spoke, his voice softened by advanced age. "What of Kulunga and the *atnalga*? Can a chosen one rise again?"

Others nodded in agreement. They looked expectantly at Y'Taba.

"That is why we need the help of Conan," he said solemnly. "When I told you that Muhingo took up Kulunga and the *atnalga*, I repeated a falsehood that every Y'Taba has told. Glad am I to speak the truth, though in doing so I break my vow to the Y'Taba before me." He drew in a deep breath. "Kulunga was *not* taken up. After driving back the Kezati, he journeyed in secret to the Deadlands. Only the Y'Taba knew, and he forbade Kulunga to go. But the chosen one would not obey. He sought the fountain of the gods and spoke of reclaiming the village built by his ancestors. His mother and father were Rahamans, and they instilled in Kulunga a desire to see the walled village. He hoped that with the *atnalga*, he could defeat the creatures of evil that lie in the dark heart of the Deadlands. So Kulunga entered the outer wall . . . and never returned to his people."

"Why was this truth hidden?" A thin-faced elder demanded, his voice shrill and angry.

Y'Taba shook his head. "I know not. But the Y'Taba's people had endured much. He may have deemed it wise to give them hope, knowing that the shell-spirits would again obey him."

Whispers buzzed among the elders, dying down quickly when Conan spoke. "I have heard enough, by Crom! Ask what you would have me do and you will have my answer."

"You have seen the outer wall already," Y'Taba answered coolly. "None here save you and Jukona know where it stands. He is our last warrior, and he must stay here to protect the village if the Kezati strike again. If the shell-spirits still obey me, they will protect him as they have before."

"Then why should I not go?" Jukona jumped up. "Send me! Let Conan guard the village."

Y'Taba shook his head. "Only the chosen one may wield the *atnalga*. It is death for any other warrior who lays a hand upon it. I believe that Muhingo has sent Conan to us. Kulunga's chosen one is Conan of Cimmeria."

Conan emptied his shell of *kuomo* and tossed it aside, rising from the bench. "So you want me to hack my way through the beast-infested Deadlands, enter the devil-haunted walled village, and bring back this *atnalga*. Crom, man, why didn't you just say so! I'll go—but first you must swear by your gods that you will use these shell-spirits to banish the beast that you saw within me."

Y'Taba fingered his necklace of shells. Would this summons please Muhingo? Would the spirits obey him one more time? He did not know, but he knew that he must not waver. He had no choice but to do as Conan demanded. Y'Taba's dark, round eyes met the smoldering blue eyes of the Cimmerian. "I swear by Asusa Sun God and Ataba the All-Father that I shall command the shell-spirits to banish the beast from within you."

"You need not go alone," Sajara said, stepping forward. "I and three of mine will accompany you."

"We may need you," Y'Taba said sternly.

"And if Conan fails, we all may perish," she replied, crossing her arms. "As *Ranioba*, the decision is mine to make, and I have spoken."

Y'Taba sighed. "So be it."

"We leave at dawn," Conan grinned, slapping the hilt of his sword. He eyed Sajara as she gathered her hunters and left. Her size gave her natural beauty an exotic flair that he found more intoxicating than the *kuomo*. And she seemed as strong as she was supple, qualities he admired in a woman. He knew she would prove her worth in the jungle if the accursed spider-beasts or other jungle denizens attacked.

Conan had decided to enter the walled village, with or without the spirit-leader's promise. He reasoned that within the walls he might find Jhaora's ships' logs or charts. With these, he could find his way to the mainland. And the rubies in that wall, if he could devise a scheme to pry them loose, would fetch a handsome price when he returned to civilization. Each of those beauties was easily worth a room full of gold.

Smiling, he walked alongside Jukona and the others to turn in for the night. There was little doubt that his luck was about to change.

Fourteen
The *Vugunda*

In the rising sun, the dense jungle leaves glinted and winked like emeralds, a swaying and shimmering wall of green at the edge of the Ganak village. Conan inhaled the humid, sea-scented air, invigorated after a night of dreamless sleep and a meal of raw, flavorful fish called *panga*. His head suffered none of effects he would have expected from a night of excessive *kuomo* consumption. Aside from a negligible twinge where the spider-beast's mandibles had nearly halved him, Conan felt like a new man.

Y'Taba stood with the elders near the place of gathering. His eyes had a dark, swollen look to them. He apparently had not slept as well as Conan—if indeed he had slept at all.

"This *atnalga* is made of *stone*?" Conan asked skeptically. "Yet it resembles my blade." He shifted his grip on the hilt of his sword, the polished steel flashing in the bright sun.

"No Ganak among us has actually seen the *atnalga*, of

course," Jukona said, approaching Conan and joining the conversation.

Y'Taba rubbed his eyes, blinking to clear them. "Jukona speaks truly, but you should have no difficulty in recognizing the *atnalga*. Our legends describe it in detail. It is said to be the length of a man's arm, the shape of a serpent's fang, and the color of the sea on a day without wind. The stone from which Muhingo molded the *atnalga* was said to have come from afar ... from a place beyond even the lands of gray, where only gods may dwell. And though it be molded from stone, the *atnalga's* edges were said to be sharper than the shell-blades and shell-sticks fashioned by our huntresses."

Conan tried to visualize such a weapon, shaking his head in puzzlement. Never had he seen or heard of such a thing, and he was beginning to question its existence. Storytellers were prone to enhance tales with every new telling. Even sages and learned historians had a way of gilding worthless lore, knowing that history's truth lay silent, buried forever in dusty tombs with the men who had made it. Conan cared not if the *atnalga* was forged from the shinbone of Mitra, so long as he could find it.

Conan turned his head at the sound of a light step behind him. Sajara stood there with three Ganak women, all of whom were smiling. "Crom," he muttered. Their approach had been stealthier than that of a kitten padding across a thick rug. It was as he had thought; Sajara and her band would be welcome companions on this foray.

"So, Conan of Cimmeria, are you ready to face the Deadlands?"

He grinned. "I was ready last night. What took you so long to prepare?"

"We awakened long ago, before the face of Anamobi Moon Goddess dipped from the sky. Avrana, Kanitra, Makiela and I were spearing fish with our shell-sticks, as we often do before the others rise. We must take provisions with us. The beasts and the plants of the Deadlands are not safe to eat."

Conan grunted agreement, remembering his gut-curdling experience with the spider's eggs. He began rubbing himself with a handful of berry pulp given to him by Jukona, wrinkling his nose. "This berry juice reeks like a Zamorian offal-pit."

Jukona grinned. "The berries have no scent; they serve only to give it color. What you smell is fresh droppings from the *tsatsa* bird, which preys on the small creatures in the jungle. The odor is strong enough to drive away the stinger-bugs and winged blood-bugs, whose bites may bring sickness or death. We mix the juice of berries with the droppings so that we may paint our bodies for protection from these bugs. You will soon become accustomed to it."

Casting a dubious eye on his besmeared torso and limbs, Conan shrugged. "Doubtless that same smell attracts other predators who are capable of doing worse than stinging. No matter; if it works, I suppose that I care not how vile its aroma is. What matters is that we be underway. Perhaps we can find the *atnalga* and bring it back to the village by dusk. I would as soon not pass the night in the Deadlands." Agreement to his sentiment was universal.

Jukona turned to Y'Taba. "How is Ngomba this morning?"

"His body has begun to mend. He is ashamed of his treatment of you and Conan, and asked me to wish you safe and swift return from the Deadlands. In truth, he seemed sad that he could not go with you."

Jukona's eyes were downcast; he said nothing.

"We shall return soon," Conan said, dropping the subject of Ngomba. He had not yet forgiven the impetuous Ganak.

After making their farewells, Sajara and Conan followed Makiela, the tallest of the Ganak women, out of the village. Two Ganak hunters walked behind them, shell-sticks in hand. Both women wore crudely wrapped pouches— snakeskin, or possibly eelskin, Conan thought—on their left hips; these contained what few provisions the party needed for their excursion. Makiela moved with panther-like grace, scanning the ground, choosing the path taken by Jukona and Conan the day before.

"Makiela is a huntress without equal," Sajara said proudly.

Nonplussed, Conan watched the tall Ganak critically. "In a land near Cimmeria are a race of people called Picts, born and bred in the forests. A Pictish scout can track a grown snake to its place of spawning. Any woodsman worth his salt could follow the trail that Jukona and I made." Inwardly, however, he had to admit that Makiela moved at least as fast as any Pict he had ever seen, and she was certainly better looking.

Sajara smiled. "In time you will see what I mean, Conan of Cimmeria. You are proud of your people, as we are of ours. But there is much you do not know of our land and our people."

They entered the trees that bordered the village, following Makiela. She never slowed, guiding them decisively, keeping a constant distance a few paces ahead of Conan and Sajara. The others followed behind, walking alongside each other and scanning the trees incessantly. The jungle was quiet this morning; the few serpents they encountered were sluggish or often asleep, and only a few birds were about.

"We will find some eggs of the *anansi* soon and take them with us. The *anansi* do not come to this part of the jungle; the sun is too bright. Where the trees become thick and the path becomes dark, we must tread with care."

"I saw little else before I reached the clearing," Conan said. "Nothing that could stop us from reaching the walled village, at any rate."

"You were fortunate," Sajara replied quickly. "The *anansi* are food for many predators who prowl the region that we seek. It is good that you have your weapon at ready. Our own weapons cannot slay the stalkers of the Deadlands. It is for them we watch, though even Makiela may not detect their presence until it is too late."

"Stalkers?"

"The elders call them *vugunda*. They hunt alone, never in packs like the *anansi*. The *Ranioba* before me once saw two of them fighting each other; the larger—*vugunda* females are much larger than males—tore the limbs from her opponent one by one, eating it alive, saving the head for last." She swallowed nervously. "An elder once saw a stalker that was twice the height of Jukona, with a body as long as a log-boat."

"Such a beast must be easy to see or at the very least too large to surprise its prey," Conan said.

"Not the stalkers. If you watched them hunt, you would believe me. Their bodies are—"

Makiela turned around, scowling. Squinting, she brought a finger to her lips, halting everyone with a raised palm. She swept the jungle with her eyes.

Conan peered into the trees, wondering what she had seen. The vegetation was still thin here, affording little cover. Besides, they had not yet come to the wide pathway that Conan had taken into the Deadlands.

Brow furrowing in annoyance, Makiela lowered her arm and spoke. "I heard a sound behind us." Her voice was as deep as a man's, but its tone was pleasant, almost musical. "It may have been a bird above us or the wind in the trees."

Conan had heard nothing, and in spite of his idle talk with Sajara, he had been watching and listening for signs of anything nearby. But the wind had begun to stir the leaves, and insects swarmed everywhere—a bountiful feast for the small birds that nested in the trees near the Ganak village.

"I can lead if you wish," Conan offered. "I remember the way from here, and as Sajara said, your weapons are of little use against the fiercer denizens of this place."

Makiela laughed. "A man, a stranger, leading the *Ranioba* and her three best huntresses into the Deadlands, as if we were children. I think not, Conan of Cimmeria."

"The decision is mine to make, Makiela," Sajara interjected. "Were he a Ganak, I would agree with you. Our warriors are not as skilled in the ways of the jungle as are we. But Conan has been to the wall of the ancient village; we have not. He has survived the attack of the *anansi*. Let him lead."

Wordlessly, Makiela stepped aside, gesturing for Conan to replace her. "We must find the eggs of the *anansi* soon to be safe from them."

"I saw them near the path," Conan said. "A bird was feeding upon one." He was irked by Makiela's doubts of his ability as a guide and determined to show her and the others what a Cimmerian could do. He had been on his share of jungle expeditions. The terrain and conditions bore almost no similarity to those of his homeland, but Conan adapted readily to any primal environments. Indeed, he felt more at home in a teeming wilderness than a crowded city. In his experience, men were often more devious than any creatures of the wild, and the streets of so-called civilized settlements could be more hazardous to navigate than any jungle.

Whenever men founded cities, they made laws that even strangers passing through were expected to understand and obey. Penalties for infringement were severe; many times had Conan left a city with its guards chasing him for violation of some foolish local rule. But whether it was the hills of Cimmeria, the deserts of Shem, or the jungles of Ganaku, he knew well the simple law of the wilderness: the strong and wary survive, the weak and heedless perish. Conan was a barbarian, and in many ways he was closer kin to beasts than to men.

Quickening his stride, sword in hand, he took the lead. By Crom, he would show this Ganak wench a thing or two about tracking.

The midday sun hung in the air like an immense, white-hot sphere of coal in a vast blue brazier. Its unrelenting heat had turned the jungle into a sweltering green hell.

Sweat poured down Conan's face and gleamed on his bare, powerfully muscled body. Like the women, he was nearly unclothed. Early in the morning, back in the village, he had obtained a long, wide strip of snakeskin and fashioned it into a crude breechclout. This he had done not for modesty's sake, but for practicality. The scaly green-black hide would afford him a means to store his rubies; he would wrap them in a spare piece and tie them with loop-knots around the waist of the breechclout. His simple garment provided a sword-belt of sorts, a feature that could prove to be invaluable later.

Sajara and the others wore snakeskin girdles that offered minimal coverage. They were tied diagonally across the waist, fully exposing the right hip and reaching down to the middle of the left thigh. He could not help but to admire the view. It was a practical enough fashion, affording them freedom of movement and a place for their shell-knives, but little else. They were bare from navel to neck with the exception of Sajara, who wore her necklace of snake fangs. Their fashion was not unlike that of women in Punt and Zembabwei, lands that lay south of Stygia. These savage kingdoms were as densely sworded as Gana-ku, but by Conan's estimation, their climes were milder. This jungle was as sultry as a Turanian steam-bath.

He noticed that the Ganaks were perspiring far less than he; their skin gleamed where his dripped. The paint on his face and chest had begun to run, but their spiraling stripes of green and yellow held fast. Their heads, nearly bare but for their braids, were clearly more comfortable than his thick, black mane. He glanced over his shoulder again, wiping sweat from his eyes. He was struck again by the exotic look of these voluptuous women. It was just as well that he had moved in front of them, where their appearance would not distract him.

"There," he pointed to a cluster of vines that dangled from a nearby tree.

"*Anansi* eggs, at last." Sajara sped up, walking alongside Conan toward the lumpy, dull-colored objects.

Conan recalled that before, while traversing this stretch of jungle, he had seen fewer small birds but noted increasing numbers of the larger, hook-billed variety. The brooding quiet of the place unsettled him, for it usually signified the presence of a predator so nasty that even the swift jungle birds shunned it.

Makiela's troubled expression mirrored Conan's. "The Deadlands are too silent. By Asusa, it is as if the jungle itself awaits us, lurking like a snake in the grass, unmoving, making no sound until it lunges and strikes."

"Aye," Conan muttered. "But this snake will find no mouse in its maw. Any beast who would prey upon us must first deal with my blade."

"And my shell-stick," added Kanitra, one of the hunters who had followed behind them. She watched the leaves with fierce eyes. She gripped her spear, the muscles of her arm flexing.

Makiela climbed nimbly up a vine, pulling several eggs from it. She dropped back to the sward, handing out the lumpy things to the others. She stood warily at Sajara's side, egg in one hand, shell-knife in the other, ready to jab anything that burst from the trees.

Conan noted with approval that the shell-knife had been scraped, apparently against a hard stone, to sharpen its edges. "The pile of bones will lie a few paces ahead, and the vines will become thicker. I care not for this unnatural calm. When I last came this way, there were birds aplenty who feasted on these things." He flipped the *anansi* egg into the air, catching it in his left hand. As he led them along the path, he devoted much of his attention to the limbs above them. "Beware their webs, which they drop before pouncing." He realized that the prospect of facing the loathsome spiders troubled him little, now that he had his sword. Its blade would hew them down like a scythe harvesting wheat. What concerned him more was the beasts the others had mentioned—the stalkers. A predator of immense size with stealth to match it would be formidable. He took comfort in the knowledge that these creatures were at least flesh and blood. The real danger doubtless lurked within the demon-haunted walls of stone, which they neared with every step.

"There are the bones," Sajara said, spotting the pile as they rounded a bend in the path.

"No sign of the *anansi*." Conan scowled. "Never did I think that I would wish to see them again."

Sajara looked at the splintered mound of ivory, replete with decaying skulls. "The remnants of brave Ganaks," she mused. "So many who perished before venturing farther into the Deadlands." She lagged a pace or two behind Conan, solemnly pondering the horrible fate that had befallen those slain Ganaks.

"There is the carcass of the beast I slew," Conan pointed with his sword. Although it was long-dead and rent asunder, the thing looked as vile and venomous as it had in life. It really had been nearly his size.

Sajara stared at Conan. "With your hands, while its jaws closed upon you, you ripped it apart?" She reached out a hand and laid it upon one of his massive biceps, squeezing. "Jukona did not treat you fairly when he said you were as mighty as any Ganak. Few if any of our warriors have strength to match yours, Conan." She left her hand on his arm and walked beside him.

Conan grinned. "Not even Ngomba?"

"Poor Ngomba," she sighed, but did not take away her hand.

There was an awkward silence as they walked, the only sound was that of their breathing and the quiet tread of their bare feet on the damp, leafy ground. Conan wondered if his gibe had offended her.

Presently Sajara spoke again. "He may be able to best you in a contest of strength, but wisdom has eluded him. You have the better of him, Conan, and I am sure that he hates you for it. Did you know that he and I might once have joined as mates?"

Conan raised an eyebrow but made no comment.

"I loved him—I still do—but as a sister loves her brother. Now I would not become his mate, not after all that has happened. His spirit is strong, but his vision of what is right for our people has possessed him. He was not always so grim."

"Grim? Crom, girl, he stole my sword, abandoned me, and later tried to slay your father," Conan interjected.

"Ngomba has ever been one to act out of passion," she said defensively. "He and my father . . . they are both stubborn, and my father can be a fool. Ngomba may have stolen what was yours, but you have it back now. He did it to save us, or at least that is what he would believe. He risked death to defend the villager and would do so again. Of that I am certain. Were it not for the Kezati threat, you and he might have become friends."

"I shall have no *friend* who deserts his comrade," Conan said sullenly. "You have forgiven him for trying to kill your father?"

"Toward Ngomba, my father's heart has hardened like stone. Their wills oppose each other, but they must work together for the good of our people. The elders once told us a story in which two serpents try to devour each other by the tail, but in doing so devour themselves. Jukona and Ngomba are like those serpents. They have each other by the tail, but that is as far as they will go." At that, Sajara lapsed back into silence, letting go of Conan's arm.

"Do the *anansi* not attack when the face of Asusa is in the sky?" Avrana asked, the suddenness of her question and the harshness of her voice startling Conan.

"Asusa's light scarcely pierces this place," Makiela retorted. In truth, as they ventured farther inward, the jungle had darkened considerably. Only a few slivers of blue sky were visible overhead, where a chance parting of leaf and frond permitted them to shine through.

"They were eager enough to gnaw my bones," Conan grumbled, his suspicions roused by the absence of the eight-legged abominations. "With these eggs, would they hide from us out of sight, or simply let us pass unhindered?"

"All we know is that they do not attack one who bears an egg," Sajara said, peering upward.

"The barrier of trees is this way." Conan crouched, examining signs of his earlier passage. He had also found tracks made by either Ngomba, Jukona, or both. Studying the trees around them for signs of ambush, he crept through the foliage, slowing to check every nook of forest for a slavering spider that might be lurking behind leafy cover.

Tension gripped everyone as they crossed the sward, drawing nearer to the place Conan had narrowly escaped. Steadily they moved among the trees, and with every step the trunks grew closer together, their limbs intertwining in thick coils of dark wood. Vines and leaves thickened until the jungle became a cloying, humid mass of vegetation. Visibility worsened, slowing their progress to a crawl.

"It was not packed so closely before," Conan grumbled. "We must have strayed . . . no, here is where Jukona lay senseless. Well, at least those blasted spiders will have trouble moving through here." He walked onward, coming to a place where the clot of flora broke up. "Hah! Over there is where I squeezed through, into the clearing beyond." He gestured toward two trees, at whose trunks were heaped the viscera of the spider crushed between them. "Follow me." He stuffed the *anansi* egg into the pouch that would eventually hold his looted rubies. Avrana and Kanitra placed the remaining eggs into their hip-slung sacks.

Visibility was better without the thick clustering of plants. He took a few steps before stopping in his tracks. Sajara and Makiela froze beside him, drawing in their breath as they caught sight of what lay nearby. It was a dead *anansi*, but one only barely recognizable as such. Its remains were a headless bag of hide, as though someone—or some *thing*—had neatly scooped out its innards. The thing's hairy flesh was not shredded where the neck had been; it was as if a headsman had decapitated the beast with a sharpened axe. "By the bones of Badb, what did *this*?" he murmured.

Sajara bit her lower lip. "I do not know . . . I do not *want* to know. Let us hope that we do not find out."

Avrana poked the flesh with her spear, lifting it up and examining it, her nose wrinkling in disgust. Its spiny legs dangled limply. She let the loose, sagging mass drop back to the sward, wiping her shell-tip on some leaves.

"Aye," Conan nodded. "The sooner we enter the wall and leave this place, the better." Running toward the trees, Conan leaped high, wrapping his hands around a low-hanging limb. He swung himself upward, balancing atop it. A tigerish leap carried him through the air until the gripped a besmeared trunk, the same one he had scaled to escape from the spiders.

Sajara and Makiela did the best they could, although it was evident to Conan that they were unaccustomed to climbing.

Makiela hissed. "There," she said, looking at something directly above her.

Conan followed her gaze upward to a broad, curving limb that intersected with the trunk to which they clung. There the body of another spider dangled, headless, an empty sack of hide. Its legs swayed faintly, the motion so small it was almost imperceptible. But there was no question that the beast was dead.

The Cimmerian looked around for signs of a struggle or smears of ichor on the branches, finding not a trace. In spite of the day's wilting heat, a chill crept along his spine, raising the hairs on the back of his neck. These *anansis* had been masters of the ambush, nimble and many-eyed creatures of cunning.

A fat droplet of fluid splattered into a leaf an arm's length from Conan's face. He sniffed at its faint but foul smell.

Fresh blood from the spider . . . and there was not even a breeze, but the legs had been swaying on the branch.

"Hurry," he called down to the others. He peered into

the leaves around them, his eyes gleaming like blue sapphires in the shadowy jungle, fingers twitching near his sword-hilt.

Avrana and Kanitra handed up their spears and followed, stopping when they were directly below Sajara and Makiela.

Gritting his teeth, Conan began wedging himself through the small gap in the trunks, placing his back against one and pushing outward against the other, flexing his muscles as he strained to spread apart the trees. Sajara grappled one of the trunks, throwing her considerable strength into the effort while Makiela held onto the spears. After an eternity of straining and heaving, wood gave way to bone and sinew.

Makiela jumped through first, diving and rolling on the ground in the clearing beyond the trees. Next, Avrana and Kanitra slipped through the opening and thumped onto the damp soil below.

"Go!" Conan growled between clenched teeth, his arms shaking from the effort of holding apart the trunks.

Sajara pressed her feet against one trunk and her back against the other. When she swung her legs outward and leapt, Conan pushed off against the tree with his hands. They landed side-by-side, rolling to lessen the impact on their joints as Makiela had done. Sajara wound up atop Conan, flashing him a smile before getting to her feet.

Turning, all five of them fell silent, awestruck by the immense stone structure that loomed before them. As if by design, its cracked walls curved in the same line as the trees surrounding the clearing, and their crumbling bricks rose to just below the treetops. From where Conan and the Ganaks stood gaping, the edifice was but a stone's throw away. Conan immediately averted his gaze before remembering that the insidious image had been chiseled into a different section of the wall, an area not visible from where they stood.

"The outer wall," Sajara said reverently. "Built by our

ancestors. It is—ungh!" she groaned as Makiela slammed into her.

Conan roared in surprise. The Ganak hunter must have sensed something a heartbeat before he had. Before Makiela and Sajara hit the ground, the Cimmerian whirled, sword in hand.

As quiet as the rustle of leaves in a breeze, the enormous creature sprang from the tangle of limbs above them, bearing right for Conan. For a moment he thought it was a part of the tree; its shiny body was of similar greenish-brown hue, its abdomen as thick as Conan was tall, tapering to a neck the diameter of a tree trunk. Its four powerful back legs were long and slender, bending behind it as it dived. Translucent green wings beat the air silently, propelling it downward toward its prey.

Outthrust forelegs were folded in a hideous mockery of a suppliant priest praying to his god. Daggerlike spines bristled on these appendages, which opened like a trap as they rushed toward Conan. But more horrifying than these was its head; tapering antennae swept backward, rising between its bulbous eyes. Those multifaceted orbs glimmered wickedly, lusting for the blood of its victim.

"Stalker!" Sajara cried out, rising to one knee and whipping her shell-spike from her girdle.

Kanitra and Avrana tried to set their spears in its path, but the stalker struck more swiftly than a diving hawk. Conan aimed a brutal overhead slash for its head, but the thing's forelegs blocked his blade. Tempered steel rebounded, blocked by armor as hard as adamantine plate. The beast sprang its trap, its forelegs snapping shut before Conan could blink his eyes. But the Cimmerian had flung himself aside as he struck; the spines brushed his shoulder, missing his head. The sound rang in his ear as the air from the impact rushed past him.

The stalker bounded away, wings flexing. Conan was awed by its speed; the thing was the height of a horse and easily twice the length. Head swiveling on its slender neck, the stalker's antennae twitched as it measured the distance between itself and Conan. Like a bolt of lightning it struck again before he regained his balance. Stumbling, Conan cursed defiantly as the thing's forelegs clamped together.

Spines raked his face. Wrenching his head backward, he narrowly evaded the stalker's deadly embrace. But his upraised sword was trapped between those powerful limbs, though he still gripped its hilt. He tugged to free it, but it may as well have been wedged between two millstones.

Kanitra and Avrana had been ready for the stalker's second strike. With fierce cries they jumped toward it, jabbing its swollen abdomen with their spears and ripping them free. Droplets of yellow ooze flew from the shells atop the sticks and dribbled from the stalker's punctured belly.

The creature opened its mouth, issuing a weird wail that no human throat could have mimicked. Its teeth flashed in the sunlight, deadly curving rows that could decapitate a man—or an *anansi*—in a single bite.

Sajara and Makiela flanked the stalker, shell-knives in hand, slashing at the expansive underside.

Beating its wings furiously, the gigantic insect flew into the air, beyond the reach of knife and spear.

Conan felt himself rising into the air, but his weight was slowing the creature's ascent. In the span of a breath, he considered letting go of his sword; mayhap the stalker would let it drop. Then he realized that while those forelegs were closed, the advantage was his. Hanging onto the hilt with one hand, he grasped the stalker's neck.

Laboriously, its huge wings fluttered. It stubbornly held onto Conan's blade, unaware that the weapon was not part of its victim's body. Head turning and lunging, it gnashed its teeth. Unfazed, the Cimmerian maintained his grip— one hand clutching the sword, the other locked behind the stalker's head. He squeezed, bearing down with enough force to crush a man's windpipe, but the stalker's tough neck gave no more than a wooden pole.

From below, Avrana and Kanitra cast their spears. One fleshed Conan's already-raw calf, eliciting a grunt and a curse. The other skewered the stalker's underbelly, passing through it to jut an arm's length from the creature's back. Unfortunately, it missed the madly flexing wings. Ocher slime flowed down the stick, streaming from the wound. The defiant creature flew on, already halfway between the ground and the treetops. Below, Sajara and the others were shrinking from view.

If the stalker set down in the trees from which it had attacked, all Conan had to do was pull the spear from its body and impale the bulbous head. His sword would either stay locked between those forelegs or fall to the sward. The thing could not quite reach him with its teeth, and its wounds would surely slow it down. Grimly, Conan held on. The beast had to land *sometime*.

He was level with the top of the wall now. Though the stalker was flying toward the edge of the clearing, his altitude afforded him a view of what lay beyond that impressive brickwork. Glancing downward, he saw the crumbling ruins of the Rahaman village. Earlier, he had thought the structure to be a castle, but it was clearly more of a shield wall. Oval in shape, its diameter was incredible, larger than the outer walls of many civilized capital cities.

Several buildings seemed to be intact, spared from the elements by the surrounding curtain of stone. At the center of the ruins was the minaret he had seen before. It rose from the scattered cylindrical buildings, narrow but reaching to an incredible height. Conan supposed that it afforded a view of the entire island. Aside from the worn spire, it looked untouched by the decaying effects of time. He guessed that it had been built to enclose the fountain of the gods.

But his time for gawking was up. The stalker showed no signs of landing in the treetops. Mindlessly, it kept drifting upward. It swerved erratically, its back legs beginning to twitch. Shrieking again, it suddenly opened its forelegs, releasing Conan's sword.

He snatched it back immediately, swinging his legs around as if he intended to ride the stalker bareback. Faltering, the stalker groped at him with its spiny appendages but was unable to bring them to bear. Conan slashed at a wing, hoping to force the thing to land.

For a moment, his plan worked. The stalker spiraled away from the trees in a slow descent, unable to control its direction. Then it shuddered, its limbs thrashing spasmodically, its wings no longer beating. It spun toward the treetops before plummeting down.

Conan's string of curses was drowned out by the rush of wind. Thrusting his sword into his belt, he took a deep breath and dived from the dying stalker's back, angling toward the treetops. The limbs and leaves rushed up at him in a speeding blur. He extended his hands, elbows and knees bent, pulse racing. He would have only one chance.

He had seen the trick done once in a Zamoran circus act; the acrobat, a nimble Khitan who leapt from the roof of a tall building, grabbed a series of horizontal poles built especially for the act. By swinging around these poles, he gradually slowed his momentum until he was able to drop from the lowermost pole.

When Conan's fingers closed around the thick branch he had chosen, he realized two things: the Khitan's weight and speed were probably one-third those of his own, and the Khitan had likely practiced the act a hundred times.

Conan's arms were nearly wrenched from their sockets. Forced to release the tree limb, he spun in midair, desperately hoping to catch another branch with his legs. He missed one, which crashed painfully into his side, but another obligingly fitted itself behind his knees. As in the circus act, the impact forced his legs to straighten. He groped frantically, fingers closing around a branch that grew at the wrong angle.

The rest of his breakneck plunge was a leaf-whipping, branch-snapping blur. It was all he could do to protect his skull from being split open. His body was beaten unmercifully by trunk and limb. He finally fell to the ground, groaning like a wretch on a torturer's rack. He wiped at his eyes, his hand coming away red and sticky. Rising on wobbling legs, Conan took a few drunken steps before he could again see clearly.

Sajara and Makiela were running toward him, shouting. That was something; he had somehow managed to fall on the right side of the trees, if nothing else. And his arms and legs seemed workable—nothing broken, though his bones ached in a hundred places. Rubbing at his throbbing skull, Conan grinned weakly at the Ganaks. "These stalkers aren't so bad, by Crom! Methinks the spiders were worse."

Sajara's face was pale. "You Cimmerians must be made of stone!" Her relieved smile quickly turned to a worried frown. "We thought the stalker had slain you even before you fell from its back. But we must go back to the village," Sajara said. "Your wounds need tending." She plucked a broken twig from his cheek.

Conan waved her hand away, shaking leaves from his hair. "Nay, girl! We have no time, and it would tire me less to walk through yon portal than to trudge through the thrice-accursed Deadlands." He staggered forward while they gaped at him. "Blasted beast," he muttered, noticing that the snakeskin loop holding his sword had torn away—and the sword with it. Before he could ask for help finding it, he pitched forward, eyes closed before he thumped to the ground.

"Conan. Conan of Cimmeria."

Sajara's soft voice awakened him. Opening his eyes and stirring, he looked up. Her face was a vision of beauty framed by the moonlit sky, her long braid of hair brushing against his cheek. He wondered if she was appearing to him in a dream. But no, he reasoned, in a dream he would not feel as if a legion of Hyrkanian cavalry had trampled him underfoot. Propping himself up on his elbows, he looked around.

They had carried him inside the structure, that much was certain. His sword, another welcome sight, rested against the nearby brick wall. He resisted an impulse to wrap an arm around Sajara and kiss her. "Where are the others?"

"Asleep," she whispered, gesturing along the wall. "After you fell from the stalker's back, Makiela led them into the jungle to find some *yagneb* leaves and to pick up Kanitra's shell-stick. They found both but were tired from the search."

"*Yagneb* leaves?"

"You must eat them to regain strength. Y'Taba feeds them to us if we are sick or hurt." She produced a handful of them. They were heart-shaped and mottled with sickly-looking white spots. "You were right when you said that we should not return to the village. We must try to find the *atnalga*. How do you feel?"

Conan reckoned that he had suffered through worse than the fall. He was willing to forge on at sunrise. "Some food and water would serve as well as these leaves. I am not sick. I have been sleeping since midday."

"There is a spring not far from here. Before the sky darkened, Makiela saw a bird come from above to drink from its waters."

"The fountain?"

"No, by Asusa! This is but a pool that is clear and cool—much like the one in our village. The *yagneb* leaves are bitter. Water will help you to swallow them."

He would have preferred a few jacks of ale or a pitcher of wine, but he welcomed the prospect of drinking his fill and dunking his head. The Ganaks had no waterskins, and the day had been long and sweaty.

Picking up his sword, Conan walked with Sajara to the spring. It was not far from where he had lain. He noticed that the blood and dirt had already been washed from his face and body, though he must have somehow slept through it. His skull had probably been knocked on the way down.

Kneeling at the spring, he scooped handfuls of water to his mouth until he could hold no more. It was better than ale or wine, after all. He took a bite from one of the leaves. "Pah!" he gagged, spitting the pulpy leaf-chunk onto the ground. An alley rat's rotting carcass would probably have been more palatable. To humor Sajara, he choked down as much as he could, gulping water to rinse the rancid taste from his mouth. Then he dipped his head into the spring and shook it dry, a process that seemed to amuse Sajara.

"Do all Cimmerians have hair like yours?" she asked, fingering her braid.

"Many, but not all. Some crop it shorter." He made a cutting motion, then asked question he had meant to pose earlier. "How do your people shave their heads?"

She blinked, confused. "Shave? I do not understand."

He pointed to her shell-knife. "Do you not have some tool that you use on your head?"

She raised her eyebrows in bafflement, shaking her head. "Our hair grows however it will. We do nothing but twist it as you see."

Conan pursued the matter no further, seating himself crosslegged by the pool and gulping a few more handfuls of water. Sajara lowered herself the ground beside him, and they surveyed the shadowy ruins that sprawled around them. Unblocked by trees or clouds, the moon bathed the ancient village in pale light, shadowing more than it revealed.

Much of the Rahaman stonework was intact. Y'Taba had understated that race's mastery of stone. Rarely had the Cimmerian seen such elaborately sculpted buildings as those in the long-deserted village. The style defied comparison with any that Conan had seen in the lands he had traveled. Brickwork blended fluidly with expanses of smooth, seamless stone in rounded, asymmetrical shapes. The effect differed most from that prevalent in Aquilonia and Nemedia, where evenly spaced columns, arches, and angular features dominated most cities. And yet it was not any more like the architecture of Turan, Iranistan, or Vendhya, which for centuries had favored rounded towers with tapering spires.

He admired the craftsmanship, but its strangeness made him feel unwelcome. He was in a crypt—the final resting place of an ancient people and their gods, who were now but a fading memory. The darkness and desolation lent the place a sinister aspect that would eventually tie his shoulder muscles into knots of tension.

He was surprised to see vines clinging to some of the buildings. A number of strands had taken a liking to the tower in the center. Nothing green seemed to grow in the clearing outside. At first he had thought these vines to be decorative, cunning likenesses carved from the stones. But closer examination proved his assumption wrong. He would examine them more closely in the daylight, and study the buildings themselves for other clues about the Rahamans and Jhaora's people.

Sajara seemed nervous, her eyes constantly flickering from shadow to shadow, her shoulders hunched tensely. "Do you feel it, Conan?"

Hesitating to consider his answer, Conan shifted his position, extending his bruised legs and leaning back on his elbows. "It is only the fading footprint of a past civilization. Some say that such places are haunted by the specters of dwellers long dead, their ghosts forever roaming the ruins. Often that is true, but I have no feel of it here. What do you sense here?"

"Eyes, that hide behind shadows. They glower at us unseen but unwilling to strike, like serpents without fangs who lurk in the bushes. I shall welcome the face of Asusa when he awakens!"

Conan could sympathize with Sajara's discomfort. He would be glad when the sun rose. Yet he was not afraid of the place, just wary. This Rahaman settlement intrigued him. On the morrow he would uncover the secrets of this place and discover what treasures it might hold. The rubies on the outer wall had whetted his appetite for loot. But the thing of most value would be the *atnalga*. It would buy him what a vault of gems could not: freedom from the shaman's curse. In spite of his aches and bruises, Conan was more ready than ever to complete his part of the bargain he had struck with Y'Taba.

Sajara moved closer to him, her smooth skin brushing his arm. "Now you must eat more *yagneb* leaves and rest until sunrise. I do not think that I can sleep among these shadows . . . and if I could, my dreams would be dark and disturbing. I shall watch for anything that stirs and rouse you if there is danger."

"We could pass the night in the clearing. I have had enough rest and can take watch." He squinted at the tall but narrow doorway that led to the clearing outside.

She shook her head. "Another stalker could strike, and even Makiela may not see it in the dark of night. I do not like the feel of this place, but from here we can see a stalker if one should approach. They are too large to enter as we did, and they could only attack from above. The light of Anamobi Moon Goddess is feeble compared to that of Asusa, but it is enough for us to see danger from above." She leaned against him, her body surprisingly soft considering her muscular build.

"You need not watch over me, girl," Conan snorted. "Even if I dozed, my senses would rouse me if something were amiss. And I slumber with sword at hand, ready for anything that may come near. Besides, this *yagneb* of yours is powerful stuff. Already I feel invigorated." In truth, something had begun to restore his vigor. It was either the draughts of fresh water, the leaves . . . or it might have been Sajara's nearness. Her curvaceous body and stunning face were enough to bestir a graybeard from his deathbed. He longed to seize her in his arms and crush her lips to his.

Sajara's breathing had become deep and regular, and Conan grinned. She was sleeping as soundly as a kitten, her head nestled against his shoulder.

He spent the night beside her in a half-doze, listening to her breathe softly. When the moon's reflection faded from the mirrorlike surface of the pool, Conan slipped into a light doze.

Fifteen
Scent of Evil

Yawning, Sajara lifted her head from Conan's shoulder. She squinted from the brightness of the sky, feeling a momentary surge of panic before realizing that she had fallen asleep beside Conan. As far as she could tell, he had not moved from where they had been sitting the night before. His eyes were half-shut, but they snapped open when she stirred as if he had not been sleeping at all. He did not blink as she had; he seemed as alert as he had been when leading them through the Deadlands.

Makiela and the others had not risen. Sajara shifted, feigning sluggishness. She wanted to enjoy this moment of peace before they began their search for the *atnalga*. Asusa's face had only just risen into the sky; of this she was certain for the air still felt cool on her skin. She stretched, looking sideways at him. His eyes were strange, a blue more intense than any she had ever seen. His skin, hair . . . well, nearly *everything* about his appearance was different. But it was his eyes that captured her now, that and the powerful muscles that bulged everywhere on his body. She stood up, stretching her arms and legs.

Conan splashed water on his face, letting some drip onto his shoulders and chest. "How was the night watch?" he asked, grinning.

"I saw nothing but a beast with long hair. He sat by this very pool."

The Cimmerian rose swiftly, lifting his sword from where it had lain. If he felt any soreness from his encounter with the stalker, he did not show it.

They joined the others, for Makiela had stirred, then jumped to her feet at the sound of their voices. They looked as alert as Conan; Kanitra and Avrana stood ready with spears in hand, and Makiela was surveying the sprawling structures around them.

"The sooner we leave, the better," Conan said, inspecting his sword. He was annoyed to note that the stalker's foreleg had put a notch in the otherwise unblemished blade.

Makiela seemed surprised, if not upset, to find that Conan had risen before she had. "The leaves of the *yagneb* have restored you, then?"

Conan made a face. "They may have helped, but I could not finish even one without choking on it."

Avrana smiled, the first time Conan had seen her do so. "What a sight you were atop the stalker, choking it as it bore you into the air. When we found it, I could see that your hand had crushed its throat. By Asusa, the elders will be telling this tale for many generations!"

Of all the Ganaks, only Kanitra seemed withdrawn. She averted her eyes from Conan until he finally spoke directly to her. "It was all I could do to keep my grip on the blasted insect. It was your spears that kept it from getting away."

"Mine nearly pinned you to the stalker," Kanitra said bitterly.

Conan was wondering which of them had made the errant cast. "Do not concern yourself," he said. "Such things happen in the heat of battle, and I bear you no grudge for it."

Her gloomy expression mellowed somewhat. "You are kind, Conan of Cimmeria. My next cast will be true."

He let the matter drop, turning his attention to the layout of the walled village. Its architecture seemed even stranger in the daylight than it had in the moonlight night. Near the spring were several segments of barren ground divided by a pathway fashioned from flat stones. The stone pathway extended in a perfectly straight line from the doorway in the outer wall to the tower in the center. On either side of the pathway, the empty areas extended to the outer wall. Conan surmised that the Rahamans may have used this space to grow crops.

In fact, the soil looked dark and rich, though not a single leaf sprouted from it. He could not fathom how this could be; in these conditions, the ground should have been overrun with vegetation. The gods had indeed forsaken this place, he concluded. Out of curiosity, he pried up one of the slabs of stone that formed the path, tilting it up onto its edge.

In the moist earth beneath it, no worms or beetles wriggled. Crom, the lowliest bugs shunned this ruin! Conan did not doubt that the vile visage of the she-devil, engraved into the brick outside, discouraged all forms of living things from entering. He was already rethinking his plan to pluck the rubies from her eye sockets.

Brushing clumps of loam from the stone's underside, he stared at its surface in fascination.

The Ganak women—save Sajara—took a step backward.

Etched in the rock was a long string of elaborate symbols, spiraling outward from the center of the slab to its elliptical edge. Some of them represented familiar objects: the sun was depicted in the spiral's center; trees appeared at intervals in the string of glyphs; a crescent moon, half-moon, and full moon each appeared once; men and women, depicted as sticklike figures, were easily distinguished from the myriad of mysterious shapes that linked them together.

The style was completely foreign to Conan. It bore no likeness to the cuneiform characters he had seen arranged in neat vertical rows on Khitan scrolls. Nor did it resemble the hieroglyphs of Stygia, the runic inscriptions of past or present Aquilonia, or the crude cave-paintings of the Bear and Wolf Pict clans.

He let the stone drop back into place. Whatever meaning those runes held was submerged in a sea of time.

"Those were praises to the gods of the Rahamans, of which Y'Taba spoke," Sajara concluded.

Conan, recalling the spirit-leader's words, supposed that her assumption was near the mark. Doubtless Jhaora's people had overturned these to hide them. Possibly they had tried to desecrate the works of the Rahaman people. As enigmatic as the etchings were the means by which they had been enscribed. Without metal, which Conan had yet to find here, what methods had the Rahamans employed?

It was a riddle which he had neither the time nor the inclination to solve. Their quest lay before them, not beneath them. Ahead, the desolate patches of dirt gave way to diverse buildings. These appeared to have been fashioned from solid masses of rock, as if immense white or gray boulders had been chiseled and shaped by means as cunning as they were mystifying. Conan had observed earlier that the outer wall was dark-hued, composed of brick, and clearly lacked the resilience of the structures within. This fit Y'Taba's explanation of the village's history.

Makiela pointed to the nearest building, a cylinder of speckled white-gray stone with a domed roof. It lay between them and the tower. "Kulunga may have met his doom inside one of these things. If you wish it, Sajara, we can begin our search there."

"We must start somewhere." A trace of discouragement was evident in Sajara's tone. "There are so many of them . . . may Asusa guide us to what we seek. If he does not, we may pass more than one night within these walls. Had I known what we would encounter, I would have told Y'Taba to wait four or five nights for our return."

They followed the path for a while, stepping off its gradually widening stones only when they neared their destination. When they drew close to the building, Conan saw that its sides had been crudely chipped. More of Jhaora's work, it seemed. The spiral script may once have adorned that cylindrical wall.

Circling, Conan looked for a door but found no way at all to enter. Other than a few coconut-sized chunks of stone that had crumbled away from the roof, the stonework looked quite solid. Lifting the largest rock he could find, Conan pounded on the wall. It gave off a hollow-sounding thud, confirming that this was not simply a monument of some kind. He pressed hard against various sections, hoping to find a secret door of some kind, but his efforts were fruitless.

"Set take these stonemasons," he growled. "If I find a boulder of adequate bulk, I'll make my own doorway!" His voice echoed through the ruins as they moved on, approaching a similar edifice. A series of them rose from the path, their height and diameter varying but the shape remaining fairly consistent. Many of the roofs sloped asymmetrically, as he had noted the night before. Every surface had been defaced in what must have been exhausting efforts of vandalism. Only the topmost decorative embellishments remained intact.

They moved methodically among the odd constructs, eventually reaching the halfway point between the wall and the tall tower. Conan's temper was hotter than the midday sun. Sajara and the others wore expressions of helpless frustration, but they continued to comb the area.

Presently the Cimmerian came across a rock twice the size of his head. "Ha!" he grunted with satisfaction, hefting it. Taking aim on a spot near that from which the stone had fallen, he hurled it, his pent-up fury lending him force that would have rivaled a siege engine's.

The boulder struck with an earsplitting crack, splintering into fist-sized stones. To his red-faced dismay, only a few slivers fell from the sturdy wall. "Crom, Hanuman, and Ishtar!" he bellowed, adding other expressions to a string of curses that would have shriveled the ears of a jaded sailor. The stones rang with names of a dozen pantheons before his tirade trailed off. Sajara and the others merely stared at the shattered rock.

"We have wasted half the day on these thrice-cursed pillars," he muttered. "Methinks your Kulunga would have made straight for the tower, anyway."

"*I* would have led us there long ago," Makiela snorted, giving Sajara an accusatory look. "But *you* decided that the stranger should lead, so I have held my tongue."

"And it wags falsely now, wench!" Conan said hotly. "It was at your suggestion that we start our search among these wretched buildings, not mine. Crom!" he shook his head, his teeth grinding in irritation.

Makiela backhanded him with a blow that would have knocked a pit-fighter on his arse.

Conan, however, possessed considerably more stamina and far better balance than any pit-fighter. He took an awkward step backward, recovering his balance and rubbing at his stinging cheek. He clenched a fist, blue eyes blazing with fury. Conan would have pummeled a man for striking him thusly, but he stayed his hand. Though a barbarian to the core, it was not in Conan to strike a woman.

Of course, Sajara had no way of knowing this. Stepping between them, she shoved Makiela away with a display of incredible strength and speed, sending the taller woman sprawling to the hard pathway. In the same motion, she swung around to face Conan in case he showed the inclination to brawl. "Enough, by Asusa! Are you warrior and huntress, or are you brats whose backsides need a switching? Makiela, we shall never finish our task if you cannot respect Conan. And you," she turned to the Cimmerian, her eyes now sparkling with some amusement, "you must do likewise."

Releasing the air from his lungs, Conan nodded, extending a hand toward Makiela. She looked at it reluctantly, then grabbed it, hoisting herself up. Conan flexed his fingers when she released them, grudgingly impressed by the raw power in her fingers and hands. She could win a king's ransom arm-wrestling challengers in taverns. Women were never favored in such contests, but then no ordinary wench—not even the amazons of the southern jungles—could match the prowess of these Ganak women.

Kanitra and Avrana whispered to each other, chuckling in amusement until Sajara threw them a withering look. With the tension among them easing, the band continued along the path, heading straight for the tower. Sajara walked beside Conan; Makiela trailed a step or two behind, followed in turn by the two spear-bearers.

"You swear by many strange gods, Conan of Cimmeria," Sajara commented.

"Aye, and none of them listen—at least not to me," he said gruffly. "Of course, in truth I would not want their attention. The gods will do as the gods wish. Only priests and fools believe otherwise, and I do not always distinguish between those two." He smiled thinly at his own jest.

"Who, then, is this Crom? Often do you name this god."

"He is the god of my people. Crom lives in a great, icy mountain of gray stone, Ben Morgh. When a Cimmerian is born, Crom breathes into him the strength to strive and to slay. We ask naught else from him or any other god, and Crom would not hear our prayers anyway."

Sajara shivered. "He sounds like a god whose heart is ice and stone, like his mountain. Asusa is a kind god who has done much for our people."

"He seems content enough to watch you die." Conan observed rather brusquely.

"We do not blame him for what has come to pass. Asusa cannot help us if we do not heed his wisdom. And the spirits of Ganaks who die—save our warriors—are taken up into an island beyond the skies to be united with the spirits of our ancestors. It is a place of joy, the elders say. Of course," she added hastily, "I have no wish to go there yet."

"What becomes of your warriors, then?"

"Muhingo welcomes their spirits into his lands of gray, where they can keep our spirits safe from those of our enemies."

"The lands of gray," he repeated. "Your Muhingo is perhaps not so different from our Crom. When death claims a Cimmerian, his soul roams a realm of gray mist, where icy winds blow and clouds forever darken the sky. There we wander for all eternity. It is a wonder that with a cheerless afterlife awaiting them, more of my people do not take to adventuring. I would see what life has to offer before my soul is condemned to such a bleak fate."

"You are a man with courage, Conan of Cimmeria. To know that such a fate awaits you is a burden to your spirit. Its weight would crush a man without bravery. You make light of it, I think."

Their conversation lulled as they neared the tower. All the while, the vines became increasingly evident. At first, Conan had merely seen the occasional stalk growing along the ground near the domed buildings or perhaps working its way up their cylindrical sides. But gradually the dark green growths seemed to be everywhere, nearly covering some of the smaller structures.

By Conan's way of thinking, they had an unwholesome look. He imagined them as thin, leafy serpents who slept amid the ruins.

"These stems have a scent of evil," Makiela said, looking at them suspiciously. "I do not think that we should touch them."

"Aye." Conan's gaze flickered ahead. The vines thickened, infringing on the stone pathway. "It were prudent to stay in the middle of this path." He could not shake the sense of dread that had suddenly come over him. He slowed, eyes searching the jumble of vegetation for any signs of movement. Shrugging his brawny shoulders, he continued.

Barefoot, they moved as silently as a wisp of smoke. Had their steps not been so stealthy, Conan would not have heard the faint rustling behind them. Glancing over his shoulder, he halted in midstep, breath whistling between clenched teeth. In a smooth, sweeping motion he drew his sword, eyes widening in dread at what he saw.

Sajara spun about, as did Makiela, both drawing their shell-spikes and gasping in shock. "Avrana, Kanitra—no!" Sajara whispered.

Swiftly as striking cobras, the vines nearest the path lunged at the two, coiling wormlike tendrils around the unsuspecting Ganak women. Leafy bonds encircled their faces, closing over their mouths and nostrils, twining about their necks to choke off their screams. So tightly did the vines grip them that blood welled up everywhere from furrows in their skin. Their spears had been snatched from them; Conan saw those shell-tipped sticks being dragged away by a few of the waving weeds. They struggled violently, tearing some of the things, but others quickly shot out to replace them. Before they could move, Kanitra and Avrana were ensnared in a wriggling web.

Two leafless stalks the thickness of a man's thumb pushed out from among the small leafy branches. These squirming, serpentlike horrors were a sickly pale green. Clusters of lidless yellow eyes sprouted like leaves from the stalks, bobbing or dangling on slender connective fibers. But that was not what made Conan, Sajara, and Makiela cry out in revulsion.

At the tip of each stalk, puckering pink mouths opened, each extending a milky green tongue covered with noxious red lesions. These arm-length appendages lapped greedily at the blood that oozed from the Ganak women's vine-gashes. In a smooth, slow motion, the speckled tongues slid under the flesh *into* the wounds, eliciting muffled screams of agony from Avrana and Kanitra.

Faster than a pouncing lion, Conan sprang toward the

sickening stalks, raising his sword in midjump. Makiela seized one stalk, wrenching it away while Sajara reached for the other. The stalks writhed defiantly, tongues flailing; mewling hisses issued from their blood-smeared mouths. At the sound, vines that had lain quietly near the path leaped into motion, encroaching upon their victims.

In the blink of an eye, more vines were looping themselves around ankles, calves, legs and arms. Conan was instantly enmeshed in a mass of constricting coils. His sword-stroke, aimed at one of the leech-stalks, instead sheared through a dozen of the grabbing, groping vines that surrounded him.

Sajara and Makiela were faring no better than he, though Sajara had managed to keep her arms free. Makiela, thrown off-balance by a bundle of the things that wrenched at her ankle, went tumbling into a writhing mass of virescent doom. Her defiant screams were cut short as a score of rustling vines smothered her upper body.

Tearing himself free, Conan laid about with his blade, hewing like a demented harvester in a field of hell-spawned wheat. Five more of the thick, putrescent stalks were crawling toward him and the others, pink lips parted, slimy tongues sliding out hungrily. Strands swarmed from between buildings and lashed at the struggling defenders from all directions, binding whatever limbs they reached.

Swathed in vines, Conan hacked furiously to keep his legs and arms free. When severed, the tendrils relaxed their grip and ceased their tugging. Panting, he stood unmolested for an instant, realizing that he and the others would be overwhelmed unless they fled. But where to go? Between them and the outer wall, the stone pathway was blocked by a waist-high hedge of wriggling death, and before them lay a crawling carpet of leafy doom. The Cimmerian wondered how far these things could reach; he had yet to see their roots. From what garden of Hell had they sprouted?

Slashing through a half-dozen shoots that had wrapped themselves around Sajara's arms, he stepped closer to the others and aimed a murderous blow at the stalk that was feasting on Makiela's wounds. His blade parted it with a rubbery snap, its detached length convulsing. Conan's flesh crawled when he saw that a crimson flush now tainted its length. Droplets of blood flew from its severed ends. Like a leafy leech, the thing was sucking blood into its unseen roots.

Simultaneously sickened and enraged, Conan chopped and hacked until shredded leaves flew from his steel. This was hack-and-slash fighting, not swordplay; his sweat-drenched chest heaved as his blade rose and fell in count-less sweeping motions.

Sajara, recovering from the shock of the ambush, had drawn her shell-knife and was slicing through stems that neared her while frantically tearing with her free hand at other tendrils that clung to Makiela. Avrana and Kanitra lay on the stones nearby, their struggles growing weaker either from lack of air, lack of blood, or both.

Conan heard their gasps for breath over the ceaseless rustling of fronds. The stems encircling their faces and in-explicably loosened. Then a sickening revelation dawned on Conan. Their attackers were deliberately letting the women breathe . . . *they wanted to keep them alive*. But try as he might, Conan seemed unable to reach them. Every time he cleared his legs and arms of the things, a fresh wave seemed to wriggle out from nowhere. Together, he and Sajara kept one another free of the constricting plants, but they were tiring. Their opponents seemed to feel nei-ther fatigue nor pain; mindlessly, they continued their as-sault, though their severed shoots were piled thigh-deep on the stones.

Vines tore and flew from Makiela's body as she finally broke free. All along, her height—longer legs and arms, bigger targets for the striking stalks—had been a hin-drance. Sweeping her knife from her girdle, she spun in a frantic half-circle, slicing at anything in range of her sharp-edged shell-blade. "Run!" she screamed hoarsely at Conan. "If you fall here, our people are doomed!"

"Never!" Conan shouted as he and Sajara battled their way toward her. But even if he had wished to flee, there was no avenue of escape. They were surrounded. Wearily swinging his steel, Conan fought on. He would cut through them and free those women or die trying!

Makiela's knife wreaked havoc among the vines as inch by inch, she battled her way to the prone Ganaks. "No! It . . . cannot . . . be!" she shrieked between slashes.

"What?" Conan bellowed the question, severing one of the bloodsucking stalks with a vicious downward stroke. But her outburst had drawn his eyes from the vines around him to what she had seen. He watched with dismay as Avrana and Kanitra were dragged slowly onto opposite sides of the stone pathway. Just as their spears had been hauled away, the vines were now pulling their prey toward some unknown destination.

Forced to turn his attention back to the weeds that writhed at his ankles and knees, Conan momentarily lost sight of the women. He looked up again, catching a glimpse of a weakly twitching foot vanishing *into* the wall of a one of the pillar-buildings. "Crom curse me for a fool," he groaned. Obviously, not all those cylindrical walls were solid—the doorways of some they had passed had simply been concealed by dense growths of vines! A shiver ran down Conan's spine as he wondered what manner of menace he might meet inside.

"Avrana!" Makiela screamed, rushing toward one of the buildings. In her haste she became entangled, her hand caught in a lashing limb. She quickly succumbed to the swarming green horde, shell-blade dropping from her hand. Makiela howled in helpless fury as the vines dragged her through a leaf-choked doorway.

"We—cannot—save them—all," Sajara panted in frustration, breathing shallowly from exertion, nearly slipping on what had become treacherous footing.

Conan could not disagree. Inevitably, he and Sajara would be dragged to a nameless grave if they stood their ground. Nonetheless, he stubbornly refused to retreat.

"Follow me," he rasped, clearing his legs of vines with a series of well-placed cuts. With all the speed he could muster, he sprinted toward the wall into which Avrana had been pulled.

Sajara sped after him, vines flailing at her legs and grasping at her ankles. Stumbling, she fell and rolled forward, narrowly escaping their clutches. Smoothly regaining her balance, she caught up to Conan with a few leaping strides. The Cimmerian's blade swept before him as he ran, clearing a path of sorts through the writing vegetation.

Without slowing, Conan jumped toward the now-visible gap in the cylindrical wall, twisting sideways to fit through it. Small holes in its dome dimly lit the interior: a smooth stone floor littered with rocks that had apparently crumbled down from the ceiling. A pit gaped open in the center. Conan grunted as he fell painfully onto a large chunk of stone, the impact nearly jarring his hilt from his grasp. Sajara landed behind him.

Shaking his head to clear it, the Cimmerian faced the crevice through which they had entered. The vines could approach from only two directions: the pit and the crack in the wall. Grabbing the largest hunk of stone in reach, Conan crammed it into the gap, squashing a half-dozen tendrils in the process. With furious strokes of her shell-knife, Sajara drove back what few weeds rushed at them from the pit.

Slamming a few more lumps of rock into the opening, Conan hammered them with blows of his pommel to jam them together. He stepped back for a moment to see if his hastily built barrier could withstand the weeds' assault. No more vines were issuing from the pit; Sajara stared at its black mouth expectantly, knife upraised.

Conan's patch held; they heard no scraping of rocks or rustle of leaves outside.

For the moment, it seemed they were safe.

"Avrana must be down there," Sajara whispered, walking slowly toward the rim.

Still catching his breath, Conan shuffled across the floor and peered into the dark hole. He picked up a pebble and dropped it in, almost immediately hearing it clatter to a surface below—stone, from the sound. "It is shallow," he told Sajara, swinging his legs into the darkness and lowering himself slowly. His feet touched naught but air.

Pulling himself up, Conan selected a few lengths of severed vines, tying them together in a makeshift cord. He fashioned one end of it into a loop. "Hold onto this," he said, handing it to Sajara. Hand over hand he descended, keeping his feet in contact with the wall of the pit until its sides suddenly curved away. He kept going until the soles of his feet eventually touched stone. He tested the footing, which seemed solid.

Conan's eyes had gradually adjusted to the gloomy blackness, and he could see vague outlines of a corridor around him. He guessed that he was facing in the general direction of the tower at the center of the ruins above. The corridor stretched before him as far as he could see, which was no great distance, to be sure. He had no shortage of standing room; the Rahaman builders must have been a tall folk indeed. Behind him, some light radiated from regularly spaced openings in the ceiling. He judged that these were pits in other pillar-buildings; the visibility was better, but he did not think that Avrana had been taken there. She had been bleeding, and no stains glistened on the corridor floor behind him.

The trail lay ahead in the darkness.

"Stay here," he said to Sajara, his voice echoing eerily.

"What do you see?" she asked.

"The hallway to Hell," he answered grimly. Much was clear to him now, especially the reason why they had encountered no insect or animal in the ruins above. He knew not what waited at the end of the corridor, but if it could not be slain with steel, this tunnel would become his tomb.

Listening for any sounds and watching for any movement ahead, Conan crept toward the dark heart of the ruins.

Sixteen
Hell's Hallway

Conan moved forward on his hands and knees, cursing his slow progress. He had to creep along like a dog on a hunt, sniffing the floor. It was his only means of following Avrana, for the sole sign of her passing was the scent of her blood. He knew now the frustration that a sightless man must feel. For some time the tunnel had been utterly devoid of light; he had relied on touch to guide him.

The Cimmerian wondered why had had not encountered more of the vine-beasts. He had passed the last ceiling-pit a while ago, tensing in expectation of an attack from above. Never had his tracking ability been challenged thusly.

The tunnel had not been straight as he originally surmised. He had passed nine intersections so far, each connecting with corridors that apparently led to buildings above. It was little wonder that they had found no doors in those cylindrical structures—the Rahamans had entered from below.

The droplets of blood were fewer and farther between.

His knees were rubbed raw and it was cursed uncomfortable to carry his sword in this position. Further, his ridiculous posture put him at a disadvantage if he should be ambushed.

A pebble lodged itself into his kneecap, and he paused to pick it out. Presently he encountered larger rocks. He stopped, his nostrils twitching. Did he smell Avrana's blood or only imagine it? His hands felt along each wall to the side, finding openings left and right. He decided to follow his instincts and rose to a crouch, flexing his knees to rid them of stiffness. He forged directly ahead, this time certain of his course.

At first it was only a faint odor of decay, but with his every step the smell worsened. Standing upright and stretching, he realized with a start that there were still openings above him. No light streamed through, rendering them nearly invisible. Perhaps he had not traveled so far yet. This irksome darkness disturbed his ability to sense the passage of time.

Thump.

The sound echoed, nearly stopping his heart.

Hastening forward as quickly as caution permitted, he felt his stomach churning from the increasing vile stench. He could not name the reek that filled his nostrils. He knew from experience that after prolonged exposure, he could become accustomed to almost any stink, however foul it might be. But this odor worsened until his eyes began to water.

Then he heard the whispering rustle above.

He reached upward, his hand flinching as it touched a vine. But the vine was taut, unmoving. He ran his fingers across a score of others that clung to the ceiling. He lifted his blade to sever them but stopped, his brow furrowing. They did not seem aware of his presence. Would not his sword-stroke alert them somehow? Hurrying forward, eyes streaming in irritation, he came to another bend in the tunnel.

Light! Around the corner, he could see it, far away but

encouraging nonetheless. Its distant glow was enough to illuminate the corridor. Wiping at his face, he blinked and stared upward, grimacing. A wide ribbon of leafy tendrils covered the ceiling, again stretching tightly against the stone. As he stared toward the light, he was overwhelmed by the sheer number of the stalks; they thickened and spread down the walls, nearly reaching the floor.

Concentrating with difficulty, Conan tried to envision where he stood in relation to the ruins above. If the tower itself was the source of this light, then these tunnels would be ... strands, radiating from a giant, circular web.

And he was nearing the center of that web.

The thick clusters of vines set his teeth on edge. Apparently, they had no senses at all except at their tips, or they would have reacted to his presence by now. To his gratification, he had seen none of the repulsive bloodsucking stems with their myriad eyes. But he had formed a unwholesome impression of what he might discover upon reaching the light ahead.

His eyes adjusted to the dim glow, narrowing fiercely when he studied his surroundings.

Earlier the rustling of tiny leaves had been almost unnoticeable, the movements imperceptible. Now, the sheer number of vines created a reverberation in the tunnel, and their slight shifting gave them a rippling quality like waves of water.

When he arrived at the source of the light, his breath was taken away by the bizarre scene before him.

In the center of the high ceiling, a circle of crystal glittered overhead, catching the rays of sunlight from above. Bright beams shifted in dazzling, shimmering rainbows of color, shining upon the floor of the chamber. Other corridors, similar to the one in which Conan stood, radiated from this vast, round room. *Not strands of a web*, he realized, *spokes of a chariot's wheel*. For the crystalline circle was also the floor of the chamber above. He was looking *up*—through a transparent ceiling—at the fountain of the gods.

It was diffusing the light, imbuing it with scintillating hues while filtering it to the room below. Numerous tiny holes perforated the crystal basin, passing completely through from its floor to the ceiling of the chamber in which Conan stood. Pierced thusly, how could the fountain have held its contents? Then he understood—this circular chamber and its connecting network of corridors must have once been filled with water, enough to rise up through the holes. The pits in the cylindrical buildings had been wells, doubtless fashioned by Rahaman stoneworkers.

Everywhere else, obscuring the walls and floor, were rippling masses of vines numbering in the thousands at the very least. Among the leafy variety were nestled crimson stalks with proliferate orbs, wriggling on fibrous stems . . . hundreds of fishlike eyes stared at the awestruck Cimmerian.

Looming before Conan was the source of all those vines . . . and the most loathsome abomination of nature to ever offend his eyes.

It squatted on the chamber floor like a pulsating pineapple, fat and green, thrice Conan's height. Thousands of vines, like those he and the others had fought, jutted from dark green slits in its mottled skin. Scarlet lumps rose from it like bloody warts, pulsating in the light. The thing had no eyes save those on its attached stalks. Before it, wrapped in those reddish shoots, lay the prone forms of Avrana, Kanitra, and Makiela.

They were barely recognizable but for their unnaturally pale, exposed faces. The thick, eye-covered stems had burrowed their tongues deeply into their victims' torn flesh— four each in Avrana and Kanitra, five in Makiela—and their color made the ghastly nature of their feast all too apparent.

With a start, Conan realized that all of the vines in the ruins sprouted from this single abomination. The pale stalks were akin to roots, but instead of drawing sustenance from the soil, they drew it from above . . . from the bodies of hapless prey. For how many centuries had this abhorrent behemoth skulked beneath the ruins, spreading outward, feasting on anything that came within its reach?

So unholy was the nature of this creature that the fact of its existence sent a violent shiver of disgust through his body. The thing belonged in the nightmares of deranged demons, not in the world of the living. Conan's mind reeled and his arms and legs refused to move; the blasphemous plant-beast gripped him in invisible bonds.

Makiela's eyes snapped open, meeting Conan's slack-jawed stare with an expression of mingled terror and agony. She opened her mouth, but a stalk shifted its coils from her neck to cover the lower half of her face, smothering her cry.

She's alive ... as the others may be! Appalled but galvanized by new hope, Conan clenched his Akbitanan sword tightly and sprang toward that hunkering monstrosity.

A mouthlike gap opened in the thing's bloated base. A noxious cloud of pulpy spores belched from the maw, splattering the Cimmerian. The cold, slippery globs burned like fire, immediately turning his flesh a hue of virulent red. Had his eyes not closed instinctively, the caustic stuff would doubtless have blinded him. Its pungence alone would have knocked down most doughty warriors, but such was Conan's rage that he ignored both the stench and the pain that stabbed at every pore of his flesh.

He was halfway to the thing, dashing madly across the vine-bedecked floor.

The mouth-slit parted again, but Conan jumped to one side, dodging its greasy discharge.

Swinging with fury that lent him the strength of ten men, he struck a mighty blow at the thing's distended belly. The blade sliced through thick, fibrous membranes and sheathed itself in the soft vitals beneath. Another spray of spores fountained from the slimy maw, narrowly missing him. A thousand leafy tentacles writhed and thrashed, and the wounded thing squirmed. It lifted itself from the floor with a prolonged ripping sound that was followed by a loud pop.

Vines flailed at Conan, but he heeded them not, thrusting his steel into the lacerated belly with such force that blade, hilt, and arm sank into the monstrous innards. A nameless organ burst with wet flatulence, spewing clammy green sludge from the puncture. But the thing's appendages were unrelenting. They hung from him like a living robe, constricting his limbs and spoiling his balance. Flexing mightily, Conan extended his arms and kicked outward with his feet, snapping dozens of vines and loosening others. Before they could regroup, he hacked at the bulbous creature with powerful blows that would have felled a stout tree.

Oozing from a half-score of slashes, it slumped to one side, its tendrils slackening, the crimson stalks hanging limply from its body. Like a punctured wineskin it sagged and flopped over, unmoving. The chamber was silent but for Conan's ragged breathing and the burble of muck that still trickled from the obscene husk.

Conan took an awkward step backward, chest heaving. The vines had scrubbed the acidic spores from his skin, leaving marks that resembled rope burns but naught else. He had feared the deadly effects of poison, but the spores had apparently lacked any such danger. His whitened knuckles loosened around the hilt of his sword as he regained some of his composure. Prodding the fibrous, glistening remains, he allayed his concerns that any life remained in the green devil. He bent down and began yanking at the vines that still encircled the stricken Ganaks.

Makiela coughed and stirred, her movements feeble. Avrana and Kanitra still breathed, but the pale hue of their skin made apparent their severe loss of blood. Incredibly, Makiela struggled to her feet, hand gingerly rubbing her throat. The paint that had once covered her body was largely rubbed away, her skin indented everywhere with vine marks but deeply cut in only five or six places . . . where the plant's tongues had fed.

Makiela shook off a pale, limp stalk that still clung to her leg. The eyes on it stared lifelessly at her, and she kicked it away in disgust. "Thank you, warrior of Cimmeria," she rasped weakly.

Nodding, Conan tore the last of the stalks from the unconscious women. His brow furrowed as a new problem presented itself. He stood ankle-deep in a puddle of slick green slush. A moment ago, the same clammy muck had not even covered his toes. He labored to breathe as if inhaling and exhaling something thicker than air. The overpowering reek was the essence of putrefaction, as if the sewage of an entire city had been pumped into the spreading puddle that lapped at the tops of his ankles.

Apparently, the malignant growth had blocked the flow of water to the fountain above it and the wells in the buildings above. Conan remembered the ripping sound and the subsequent loud pop. Without the beast stoppering the subterranean well, this room and its connecting corridors would soon fill up with the stagnant seepings from below. If it were merely water, Conan would be less concerned with the slow influx. But however clear and pure it might have been, centuries of contact with the hideous plant-monster had fouled it. The Y'Taba had spoken of a terrible curse laid upon the fountain by Jhaora's gods . . .

"Can you walk?" Conan asked Makiela.

"I—I think so," she answered groggily, steadying herself against a wall.

Conan reckoned that she would manage under her own power. The other Ganaks were another matter. Carrying two women of normal size would present only minimal difficulty for Conan, but exhausted as he was, he did not think he could bear these two giants all the way back through the tunnels. He had no choice but to try. Crouching, he lifted Avrana over one shoulder and Kanitra over the other. Straightening his bent knees, he took ponderous steps across the vine-choked floor.

The stems were no longer taut. Some of them had slid down from the walls, others were strewn in disarray at his feet. Near the edge of the room where the puddle had not yet risen, there were now gaps in the thick, leafy mass. Through them, Conan could see the ancient remnants of countless feasts. The floor was covered with myriad remains—bones from birds of small and large species mingled with those of tall humanoids, either Rahaman, Ganak, or both. There were husks and carapaces of huge insects—even the fibrous skeletons of stalkers. How many victims had been dragged into this den and sucked dry . . . and had Kulunga been among them?

If the *atnalga* lay in this corpse-pit, it would stay there. There was no time to rummage through the pile of bones, even if Conan had been so inclined. He would have to hope that Kulunga had avoided the clutches of the vines. When he and the others reached the surface, he would first see what was in the tower directly above.

Makiela followed him out of the room, glancing once over her shoulder.

Behind them, the pool spread like green blood from a slashed throat, ebbing inexorably toward the corridors that it would soon pervade. The light from the crystal basin receded as they wended their way through the tunnels. Progress was agonizingly slow. Laden with weight nearly twice his own, Conan had no choice but to pace himself. He stooped and shuffled all the way, retracing his footsteps by relying on a combination of memory and instinct. When darkness utterly engulfed them, he found it necessary to stop at intersections. They could not afford to become lost in these corridors, and finding one's way was damnably difficult in this stone maze.

It was at an intersection that Conan stepped into a shallow puddle. Cursing, he kicked at the wall, nearly overbalancing and dropping one of the women. "We should be well ahead of this by now," he muttered.

"In this place, even I cannot tell how far we have walked or what direction we have taken." Makiela's voice wavered, lacking its usual assurance despite her words. Though she carried nothing, she could scarcely maintain Conan's pace. Loss of blood had all but robbed her of strength.

But more trying than this, or so Conan judged, was her dread of the dark corridors themselves. He could sympathize, for she had spent her whole life outside under an open sky. There were people who could simply not abide enclosed spaces, and if she was of this sort, he was sure that only sheer willpower kept her going. He, too, was weary of the tunnels and longed to feel the sun's rays.

He had unburdened himself and tried to climb some of the vines that disappeared into ceiling-holes, but the unattached tendrils were too slack to support him.

Perturbed by the unexpected wetness, he shifted the weight he carried and plodded on. They returned to the last intersection. Makiela stumbled and fell; Conan had to help her up, his hands encountering her blood-slicked arm as he did so. "Crom, girl!" His exasperation made his voice more gruff than he had intended. "Why did you not say you were still bleeding?"

"It is not so bad," she mumbled. "It stopped for a while, but when I fell . . ." she trailed off, slumping back to the wall.

"Makiela? Up, girl!" he urged, gently shaking her. She responded with a long sigh.

"Ishtar! We are so close . . ." He shook her again, but could not disturb her deep breathing. He knew that he could not carry all three of them. His back had begun to cramp and even his legs ached. He propped Kanitra and Avrana gently against the wall and stretched his weary muscles, wondering if he should scout ahead for their destination while Makiela rested. No, he could not leave them all here.

Moments later, he slid down the wall and dozed off, his course of action still undecided.

* * *

Soaked in cold sweat, Conan awakened. His eyes snapped open, but it made no difference; all around him was the impenetrable gloom of the tunnel. His nightmare had been bad, but he remembered no details, just waking up before he drowned . . .

"Crom!" the curse tore from his lips as he jumped to his feet. It was not sweat that drenched him—it was oily slime that had risen to the level of his chin. Shivering, he grabbed Makiela's arm and hauled her up but could not revive her. Her breath was faint, too shallow for his liking.

He hated to do it, but he had no choice. Gathering what vines he could, he wrapped them loosely around her and the others to secure them in a standing position. The vines were loose, and he prayed that they would hold until he could find Sajara. He should have thought of it before— *she* could carry Makiela.

He sloshed doggedly through the swampy muck. The vines overhead began to thin as he had hoped, and a dim residue of light became visible.

"At last, by Crom," he breathed in relief, his spirits lifting as he hastened toward the dim glow emanating from far ahead. "Sajara!" he shouted. When the echoes faded, he called out again, hoping that she would respond.

"Conan?" the whisper reached him, rebounding from the walls ahead. Sajara stepped into view.

"Quickly!" he shouted, gesturing for her to follow.

"Where are the others?" she asked breathlessly.

"Safe, I think. Come on!" They splashed along at a half-run. In between breaths, he gave her an abbreviated account of the harrowing battle.

"I would have sought you sooner, but the face of Asusa had sunk behind the wall. I could see nothing down there. The sky became dark, then light again. Finally I climbed down to look for you."

Conan and the others had spent the whole night in that wretched tunnel, oblivious to the threat rising around them. Snorting in annoyance, the Cimmerian forged on. He would never forgive himself if the Ganak women died.

He had been more weary than he realized, but that was a poor excuse. And to lose even one of them after all they had been through . . . he clenched his fists as they hurried into the gloomy tunnel where he had left them.

But his makeshift knot of vines had held them up, and they all still breathed, albeit shallowly. He hoisted Avrana and Kanitra onto his shoulders; Sajara strained with the taller, bulkier form of Makiela and succeeded in lifting her. They proceeded back to the bunch of vines hanging from the wide opening in the ceiling. Conan gave the leafy rope a tentative tug.

"I wrapped it around a large stone and piled others on top," Sajara said. "It should bear your weight."

Conan carefully hauled himself up, relieved to be out of the stinking swill at last. He reminded himself to clean his sword thoroughly.

One by one they raised the unconscious women, Sajara tying them to the vines and Conan lifting. It seemed to take forever, but at last they were out of the corridors. He kicked down the barrier of stones that blocked their exit and stepped out, drinking in the sunlight like a parched man gulping water.

The lifeless vines, looking somewhat thinned but no less menacing, lay all about them. They made straight for the pool of water near the entrance, washing the greenish scum from their bodies and cleansing their wounds. Sajara had nothing that would serve to bind their cuts, but the skin had puckered around the ragged edges and closed them off anyway. She dabbed gently at the welts with some of the *yagneb* leaves they had left by the pool.

"We cannot leave them alone," Conan said. "You must stay here while I explore the tower."

Sajara shook her head. "We should not separate. Wait here with me until Makiela awakens. She is strong. Her body will heal quickly. By morning, she will be fit to watch over the others. Then you and I can face the tower together."

"Better to face it now, even alone. We have lost too

many days already, and these ruins are empty now. Can you not feel it?" He gestured toward the tower. "The guardian is slain, and nothing else dwells in these desolate walls. What if the Kezati strike your village in the morning? We an afford no further delay!"

"And if you never return from the tower, what then? I go where you go, Conan of Cimmeria. A *Ranioba* may not always choose her destination, but she may choose any path that leads to it—or make her own. Stay here, or venture into the tower, whatever you will."

Conan had little doubt that this stubborn wench would leave the others behind if she had to. He fumed for a moment before throwing himself heavily onto the ground beside the pool. He could not abandon the Ganak women, and he would not waste further effort bickering with Sajara. He sat brooding, staring at the distant tower.

The stone path, no longer so choked with vegetation, led directly to an arched portal in the base of the tall tower. Inside he would find the fountain of the gods and other remnants of the Rahaman civilization. Was the *atnalga* there, simply lying on the floor amid the bones of Kulunga? Conan prayed that the legendary Ganak warrior had not met his doom in the plant-beast's lair—a lair now submerged in bilious muck. Conan would be a graybeard by the time he sifted through *that* pile of skeletal scraps. The Cimmerian turned his attention to his sword. He had just found a suitable stone to hone the sword's edge when Makiela finally opened her eyes.

"Asusa," she mumbled, stretching.

"Makiela!" Sajara jumped to her feet, her eyes lighting. "How do you feel?"

The tall Ganak groaned, managing a terse smile. "Alive," she replied.

Conan and Sajara explained the situation to her, and she assured them that she could stand watch over Kanitra and Avrana, who were still unconscious. "I have slept enough," she added, "and we must return to the village before the Kezati. Go!"

Sajara left her shell-spike with Makiela, who had lost hers earlier while battling the plant-beast. Conan examined his blade critically as he and Sajara headed toward the tower. Akbitanan steel was well worth the price it commanded in what few markets he had seen it. How Khertet had come by it, Conan could only guess. The nearly unbreakable blade could fetch its weight in gold for one who was fool enough to sell it.

"Did the gods give that weapon—*sword*," Sajara corrected, stumbling over the word, "to you?"

"In a way," he said with a dark chuckle. "It is a long tale."

"Tell me."

Conan briefly recounted his capture and the dire events that followed it, leading up to the melee with the Kezati. He omitted the details of his ape transformation; even the memory of that slaughter still made him uncomfortable. Sajara shook her head in bewilderment throughout most of his account, interrupting frequently with questions. The Cimmerian did his best to explain, but he was no teacher. The ship seemed most difficult for her to grasp, despite his efforts to illustrate it.

"Only our warriors use the log-boats," she commented when he was comparing those crude Ganak craft to the ill-fated *Mistress*.

For Conan, the conversation was an awkward reminder of the gulf of differences that separated his world from hers. The Ganaks were in ways more primitive than the tribes in the deepest recesses of the Black Kingdoms, but their society at times seemed as complex as any he had encountered. They seemed to lack any real ability to read or write; Jukona's crude but nonetheless accurate map in the sand had been the only indication of any literate capacity. Yet they were rich in history and legends, passed down from elders to the young.

Moreover, they had lived without the benefits of fire or metalworking, which were basic but essential tools of survival for most cultures.

It seemed incredible that Jhaora and her people had not brought knowledge of these things to the Rahamans. Perhaps they had; the engravings on the pathstones demonstrated the Rahaman's ability to write, a skill lost to the Ganaks. Whatever lore the Rahamans acquired had become a casualty of the war between Jhaora's gods and those of the Rahamans. The Ganaks had been fortunate to survive that conflict, even if only to become a stagnant race imprisoned on this primal island.

Shaking these musings from his mind, Conan scanned the short stretch of pathway separating them from their goal. Aside from the jumble of slack-stemmed vines and a few large cylindrical buildings, he saw nothing remarkable about the region in the center of the ruins. The only feature of note was the tower itself, a wide spike of stone that narrowed smoothly to the worn spire and rose above the impressive outer walls. It was a dazzling piece of work. One might expect to pass by it while strolling through the aristocratic districts of civilization's more splendid cities. On this isle, however, it could not have been more out of place.

When they drew closer to it, Conan could see that spiral strings of symbols like those on the undersides of the pathstones adorned its weather-worn surface. Near the base, he saw evidence of attempts to deface those symbols. As Y'Taba had said, Jhaora's people had scoured many of the Rahaman writings from the stones. But farther up, the interlocking spirals had been subjected only to the gradual weathering of wind and rain.

A narrow ramp wound partway up the tower, ending at a tall, arched door. Conan judged its height to be half again his own. The Rahamans might well have been taller than their Ganak descendents.

At last they stood before the door. It was a pristine slab of stone without any feature resembling hasp, hinge, or handle. Conan found it curiously unmarred.

"How are we to enter here?" Sajara asked, befuddled.

"Unless your Rahamans magicked it with nameless arts, we shall pick its locks, whatever form they may take."

After studying it carefully, Conan found no opening mechanisms. Setting his shoulder against its edge, he threw his whole weight into a shove that would have burst the hinges of an oaken door.

He might as well have tried to topple a Stygian pyramid.

"Bel curse it," he said, running his hands all around it for a hidden means of entry but finding nothing. "We can try again to force it open," he told Sajara.

She nodded.

"On three," he said, beginning the count. When he reached three, they shoved in unison.

Veins knotted in Conan's temples, his face reddening from effort. Sajara's sleek muscles tensed, and she dug in her feet to bring the full strength of her legs to bear on the door. She shut her eyes as she and Conan strained against the unyielding stone.

"What in the fiery fifth hell of Zandru—" the Cimmerian exclaimed, backing away, eyes wide with astonishment. The surface of the door had rippled like water, swallowing up Sajara. Or so it seemed, until he heard the loud smack that was unmistakably made by her body slamming against the stone floor.

"Conan!" she cried out. "Where are you?"

"Out here, Crom curse it! Why did this blasted thing let—ha!" he suddenly shouted triumphantly. He understood now why the door had been unmarred by weather or vandals. It was illusory . . . a phantom existing solely in the eyes of those who beheld it. Pressing against the portal with his palm, he closed his eyes and cleared his mind of the portal's image. He pushed again, not because he hoped to open it himself but rather in the hopes that his efforts would blind his mind's eye.

Stone became air beneath his sweating palms; overbalancing, he sprawled unceremoniously to the floor. Avoiding the impulse to break his fall with his hands, he forced his body to roll with the impact. Sajara nimbly leapt aside.

From inside the tower, the door was invisible. They looked out at the ruins. The effect reminded Conan of mirrors he had seen once in a decadent inn of Shadizar, where all manner of fleshy delights were available for a price. The depraved proprietor had fitted many rooms with these mirrors, transparent from one side, and charged patrons for the privelege of watching the room's occupants while remaining unseen. Of course, this Rahaman door went one step further. He speculated that many, if not all, of the cylindrical buildings surrounding the tower might boast of similar portals. It would explain why his earlier searches had revealed nothing.

"Look," Sajara pointed downward.

Conan immediately recognized the fountain, though he had seen it only from below. They stood in a high-ceilinged chamber positioned directly above the vine-beast's den. Before them sparkled the fountain of the gods. Its countless facets reflected the sunlight onto the tower's walls, which glittered as if set with living jewels of ever-shifting hues: glowing greens, luminous blues, fiery reds, iridescent yellows . . . a dazzling rainbow of shards. Never had Conan seen its like; even the most opulent Ophirean palace had no fountain as stunning as this one.

The effect, however, was spoiled by the shallow puddle of green mire that just covered the bottom of the basin. The chamber below had apparently filled completely with that contaminated swell from the plant-creature's lair.

A cleverly built stone ramp spiraled upward along the tower's inner wall, forming a tapering path to the lofty spire far above. Conan moved warily along it, looking in all directions for any sort of traps. More of the cryptic spiral script adorned the walls, but Conan scarcely gave it a glance. Sajara stayed at his side, gripping her knife in one hand and Conan's free arm in the other.

As they neared the top of the winding walkway, it narrowed, forcing them to turn sideways and edge along it with their backs to the wall. Its irregular, broken state suggested that it had once been considerably wider. An awkward climb took them so high that the fountain below looked no larger than a crystal goblet. Conan, who was at home in such lofty environs, showed no discomfort, but Sajara trembled at every step, as she clutched at his hand, looking everywhere but down.

The slender pathway ended at a chamber once covered by the worn spire. Now Conan could see that its condition was worse than he originally thought. The remnant of a crack-ridden ceiling seemed ready to cave in at any moment. All that remained of the roof was an overhanging fragment of rock which cast a thin shadow across the sparsely furnished room. It seemed austere in comparison with the antechamber below.

But to Conan, its contents were no less fascinating.

Rubble covered half of the floor, partially burying three large chests that stood against a curving wall. In front of these trunks sat a fourth, similar in construction but much smaller. All featured metal corners and bands that secured pitch-smeared wood planks. Rounded lids topped the chests' square sides. On the wall opposite these, seeming entirely out of place in the wrecked tower, was an ornate chair fashioned from what looked like solid opal. No rubble had accumulated around the incredible object. It was elaborately carved in seamless designs, suggesting that it had been sculpted from an enormous block of that iridescent white stone. If it were truly opal, Conan could not hazard the vaguest guess of its worth. The thing was on par with the extravagant furnishings one might find in the lavish palaces of Khorshemish, Belverus, Luxur, or even Aghrapur and Tarantia.

Upon it sprawled a skeleton.

The skull had tumbled from the bony neck, landing, by a droll quirk of fate, in the skeletal lap. The throne clearly had been built for someone much smaller than its present occupant. The pelvis scarcely fit between the throne's arms, and the thigh bones jutted far beyond the edge of the seat. Blades of broad shoulders rose well above the ornate chair's slender back.

Resting on the ivory knees was an exotic scimitar. Its shape mimicked that of a serpent's fang, but its composition was wholly different. It was as if a blacksmith—no, a *stonesmith*—had molded a piece of basalt into a sword. Puzzled, Conan suppressed the urge to snatch the thing by its gleaming black hilt. A basalt blade would be a poor weapon indeed, bound to shatter against even the basest of bronze weapons or armor. And he doubted if even the most skilled artisan could have fashioned such an incredible work from basalt, smoothing every chip and chisel mark from the surface to bring out the luster like that of polished steel.

What stayed Conan's hand was a superstitious dread of the scimitar's dead owner. Bony fingers rested on the blade, and empty sockets glared from the huge skull as if promising a dire fate for any would-be thieves. As a youth, Conan had once faced such a menace, a corpse that rose up when the Cimmerian had taken away its sword.

But of course this was different.

"Kulunga?" Sajara's voice was an awed murmur. She knelt in the doorway, lowering her eyes from the skeleton to the floor.

"Aye, or so it seems," said Conan. He crossed the rubble and examined the scimitar closely. It *looked* like basalt. He reached toward it, hesitating for a moment. By Crom, if he was the chosen one, he was entitled to it.

Grasping the smooth, cool hilt, he slid the scimitar out. It rasped against the aged bones. When no immediate doom came upon him, he breathed a sigh of relief. "The *atnalga* is ours at last!" he grinned, brandishing the peculiar weapon. It felt nothing like it looked—indeed, the *atnalga* was lighter and more flexible than his sword. If anything, it seemed to lack sufficient weight to be suitable for its purpose. Slender, lightweight blades were useful only for thrusting. They were typically chosen by foppish aristocrats who pranced and played at swordfighting but dared not venture within a league of a real battle. Only a fool would pit such a weapon against a western broadsword of the sort favored by Conan.

He tested the *atnalga's* edge against his thumb and grunted in surprise. It slipped through his thick, calloused skin before he even felt the fiery tang of its bite. A normal sword cut would not have stung as this nick did. The blade's lethal sharpness and pristine condition impressed him. It had been lying here for Crom knew how long, exposed to rain, moist air, and other elements that would have rusted even oiled, finely tempered steel into a worthless hunk of metal.

Its hilt tingled in his palm. The hairs on his hand and arm stood up as if a chill were creeping up his arm, but the blade felt warm to his touch. The tingle traveled, too, into his side and neck until it reached his head. A sudden shock of pain jolted him, crashing like a wave from his palm to his arm and searing his brain. He fell to one knee and tried to release his grip, but his muscles met with unseen resistance, as if an invisible giant had clamped a hand around his own.

"Conan! What is the matter?" Sajara was at his side, an alarmed expression on her face.

"Must ... let ... go ..." he began, his tongue swelling inside his mouth and robbing him of his speech. Intense heat flared up in his head, searing his brain until he could barely stand to be conscious. Conan struggled to drop the hilt, his sweat-beaded face reddening. Twitching, he writhed on the floor, bearing down on his fingers with every shred of willpower he could summon.

Sibilant whispers slithered in his ears. *False one,* an accusing voice shrilled. *Infidel!* another shrieked. *Die!*

The unseen choir hissed in a chanting crescendo, their voices piercing his eardrums like needles. Blood seeped from his nose, so hot that he smelled the scorching of his nostrils and upper lip. Tendons thick as cords rippled along his arm as he labored to relax his grip.

Sajara was shouting at him, but her words were

drowned in a sea of wailing voices. She grasped his face in her hands, snatching them away, grimacing and shaking her fingers.

Conan mustered his last surge of strength, expelling hot breath from his lungs. At the same instant, Sajara grabbed a head-sized chunk of rock and brought it down on Conan's vibrating hand.

The *atnalga* flew from his nerveless fingers, rattling against the wall before it lay still. The hideous howling ceased at once. Conan felt the heat subsiding quickly, though twinges of pain tingled from his hand to his sweat-drenched head. He rose, limbs still shaking, breathing labored. "Crom," he said thickly, licking the dried smear of blood from his lips. "Y'Taba was wrong."

"Oh, Conan! If you are not the chosen one, what are we to do? The gods have turned away from us. We have failed!" Tears ran from her eyes.

"Not while we still live," he said fiercely, a measure of his strength returning. "By Crom, a Cimmerian never gives up." He rubbed at the lump of flesh swelling on the back of his hand, flexing the fingers slowly, his teeth clenched.

"But without the *atnalga* we are doomed." Sajara suddenly turned her tear-stricken face toward Conan, as if the meaning of his words had only just struck her. "You . . . you would still help us, Conan?" she fixed her pleading gaze on him.

He nodded. "We shall yet deliver this blasted *atnalga* to Y'Taba, though I see no use for a demon-haunted relic that bites the hand of its wielder! Y'Taba made a bargain with me and I shall keep it, by Crom—as will he. But with or without that thrice-accursed black blade, your people will *not* fall to the damned Kezati, not even if I must hew a hundred vulture-necks myself."

"What befell Kulunga, I wonder?" Sajara mused, wiping at her eyes.

She was regarding the skeleton in either morbid fascination or reverent awe, Conan could not say which. "Mayhap he escaped the monstrous beast below and holed up in this tower, only to starve. There are a thousand nameless graves such as this, in all corners of the world, marked by the bones of heroes who sought to restore past glories of their peoples." The Cimmerian spoke absently as he stood beside Sajara, running a hand along the opaline throne and studying it with a practiced eye. "Opal, or I'm a Pict," he murmured. The sight of it tickled at his memory.

With a rasp, the bony occupant slumped forward, tumbling out of the throne with a crash. Sajara sprang backward, gripping a wall in wide-eyed terror. Conan, in spite of his numbness, leapt a foot into the air and landed in a crouch beside the rubble. He snatched up his fallen sword and held it at ready.

The skull, which was half again as large as a normal man's, thumped onto the stone and came to rest near Sajara's feet. But otherwise the bones lay in an unmoving jumble at the foot of the throne.

Conan gawked at the likenesses engraved in the smooth, iridescent stone. Sculpted in painstaking detail were the twin faces of a two-headed elephant, adorned with resplendent collars and fringed caps. Huge eyes stared outward at Conan; tusks curved upward, framing a coiled, upraised trunk. The sight lit a lantern in a dim corner of the Cimmerian's memory. "Vendhyan!" he exclaimed. He had seen it before while adventuring in that land of glittering jewels and ancient gods. He knew the thing represented an obscure god, though he could not recall its name. But in that instant he mentally assembled all the clues about the island which had thus far stumped him. Like torn pieces of a treasure map, they fit together. He even recalled the name of the goddess whose macabre image loomed above the doorway in the outer wall.

"Kahli," he said grimly. "Jhaora was the high priestess of Kahli whom King Orissa banished from Vendhya."

Sajara looked at Conan in utter befuddlement. "I do not understand, Conan. Vendhyan . . . Kahli . . . King Orissa?"

Her tongue stumbled over the unfamiliar words. "What—
or who—are they?"

"You remember the glimpse you had of the devilish
goddess whose graven effigy broods on the outer wall?"

Sajara nodded, shuddering at the memory of that glance.

"Well, years ago I was traipsing through the two-
millenia-old ruins of Maharastra, a once-glorious city of
Vendhya."

"Vendhya?"

"A kingdom far east and south of Cimmeria—at least a
year's journey on foot, were one hardy enough to attempt
it. Anyway, the face of that ten-armed she-devil was chiseled on a gigantic stone that lay among those ruins of
Maharastra. At the time I was forced to travel in the company of a treacherous Vendhyan wizard, and I half-listened
to his account of the legend behind that cruel goddess's
face.

"Maharastra had once been the capital of Vendhya. The
city's founder was King Orissa, first true king of Vendhya.
He had vanquished many foes in his day. Only one rival
was known to have survived: the high priestess of Kahli.
She claimed kinship with a race called *pan-kur*, the spawn
of a human woman raped by a demon. The priestess was
powerful, holding sway over thousands of worshipers who
reveled in degenerate rites. She had built a small empire
that spread like blood from a slit throat, staining the southern coast of Vendhya. All feared to oppose the priestess,
for Kahli was the most bloodthirsty goddess in the
Vendhyan pantheon. Her long-forbidden rites had been a
red blasphemy. The abominations that took place in
Kahli's temples were recorded once in crumbling scrolls
which that Vendhyan wizard had read. He related a few of
them to me, but thankfully I remember them not. According to the wizard, the most ghastly rites were unreadable;
some scrolls had been soiled by the vomit of their
scribes." He paused, rubbing his chin and dragging his rec-
ollection of the tale from the dark recesses in his mind.

"The priestess's army of zealots once sacked a city

ruled by Orissa's brother, whom they sacrificed to Kahli. This"—he tapped the opal chair with his sword-point—"is surely the famous opaline throne of Orissa. Treasure-seekers and plunderers all over the world still swap tales of its whereabouts or sell false maps which supposedly reveal its location." He made a wry face, remembering that as a once-naive youth, he had wasted a dinar or two on those shams.

Conan ran a hand over one of the elephant's ears. "She must have taken this with her ... Orissa eventually drove her out of Vendhya. Angered by the grotesque butchery of his brother, he appealed to the priests of mighty Ihndra, the god whose icon you see graven hereupon.

"By inciting a holy war, Orissa closed his powerful fist around the priestess's realm and crushed it, though she somehow slipped through his fingers with a few devout followers. No one knew what became of her—until now. Doubtless she hired mercenaries and ships, fleeing to the safety of the seas ... perhaps hoping to build a new base of power."

Sajara gazed thoughtfully at the throne. "When Y'Taba spoke of Jhaora, did her name not bring this tale to your mind?"

He shook his head. "Her name was stricken from all writings and banned by Orissa. It was death to utter it. For years he searched for her, seeking vindication for his brother's murder. He died a bitter graybeard on that vain quest."

"What now, Conan?" Sajara asked, gesturing at the ebony blade lying upon the floor. "How shall we bring the *atnalga* to the village?"

"In one of these chests," he replied, clearing away the rubble that buried one of the smaller trunks. He was curious to learn of their contents anyway ... without arousing too much suspicion. On the island, Jhaora would have had no way of spending the loot from her empire that she had surely taken with her. Conan was of a mind to haul it away with him when he left this island. And now he was reasonably certain where the mainland lay.

Jhaora could not have strayed too far from the coast of Vendhya. Vessels of those times were ill-suited for long voyages. Further, the Vendhyans had never been a people noted for their seamanship.

And he would not return empty-handed. Not if these chests contained even a tithe of the wealth rumored to have been in the priestess's possession. Licking his lips, Conan slid the point of his sword under the bronze hasp and gently worked it loose. The lid was wedged in tightly, probably warped by prolonged contact with rain and sun. He pried it off with his blade, standing aside and as far back from the thing as he could. The absence of locks often indicated the presence of insidious traps.

In this case, however, it simply indicated the lack of valuable contents. Conan frowned as he leaned over the mildewy mass of tomes stacked in the trunk. The humidity had all but destroyed them. He peered at the cover of one and withdrew it carefully, as it seemed ready to crumble between his fingers. He squinted at the ghosts of characters with which it was haunted. Conan had gathered the general sort of knowledge that accumulates in the memories of those who travel the length and breadth of many lands. He had acquired skill at the speaking and reading of so many tongues that many a chairbound scholar would have been amazed by Conan's abilities. To thief, warrior, mercenary, or adventurer, the difference between life and death can lie in the meaning of a single syllable or a simple rune.

These writings were incomprehensible, though the characters that formed the words were unmistakably Vendhyan. He was loathe to abandon them, yet he deemed this neither the time nor the place to peruse the moldy old manuscripts.

He picked up an arm bone and wedged the *atnalga* into it. Holding it as if it were an irate asp, he set the bizarre weapon atop the pile of books. The lid closed neatly over it, and he hefted the low-sided chest onto one of his brawny shoulders. It was heavy but manageable, though he doubted he could run far or fast while burdened with it.

Setting it down, he kicked aside some of the jagged chunks of rock that half-buried the other three trunks. Cracks in the floor spread from under these to the opposite wall, suggesting weighty contents that fired the Cimmerian's imagination. He bent apart the latch securing the center chest and lifted its lid, grinning at the golden coinage within. It was a haul that a year of piracy could not have matched. He groaned inwardly, frustrated by the presence of such a hoard when he had no means to haul it away. The winding ramp to this room had crumbled away, and he had no rope to fashion any sort of conveyance.

"Conan!" Sajara screamed, shrinking against the wall as she stared past his shoulder.

A shadow suddenly enveloped her; Conan instantly dropped to the floor as the rush of air came from behind him.

The chest saved his life.

Spiny forelegs seized the bronze bands and hardened wood, crushing the trunk like a bug. Green jaws snapped in the air a finger's breadth from Conan's neck, sunlight glinting wickedly on razorlike edges.

"Crom curse it!" he growled, crawling forward to clutch his dropped sword.

The gigantic stalker filled the room, easily thrice the size of the deadly predator they had faced before. Its antennae, tall as two men, swept backward from the top of the bulbous-eyed head, twitching. The spines on the monstrous forelegs jutted like rapiers, and three men of Conan's size would scarcely have filled the thing's segmented abdomen. Its carapace gleamed like emerald armor.

Bending down, the stalker shot out pincerlike legs toward the prone barbarian, who rolled for cover under the throne. The spines clacked against the opal, gouging chips from its edges and lifting it into the air, exposing Conan.

A loud crack sounded from between the stalker's forelegs, and a shower of opal shards rained down from the throne's ruined arms.

Dumbfounded by this display of strength, Conan looked at the puny blade in his hand and sprang from his crouch toward the doorway, grabbing the petrified Sajara. "Come on!" he shouted, pulling her with him.

The stalker tossed the wrecked throne. It struck the wall above the ramp, bouncing off and nearly squashing Conan, who avoided it by twisting in midleap. Lunging again with the speed of a lighting strike, the creature's deadly legs struck, their spines raking the wall where Sajara had stood moments before.

They were cut off from the ramp. There was no other exit from the chamber.

Galvanized into action, Sajara followed Conan's evasive moves. They began a shuffling, diving dance, avoiding attack after attack with desperate dodging and rolling. With uncanny precision, the stalker began to anticipate their maneuvers, forcing them to change tactics. Time and again they leaped toward the exit, only to be driven back by the powerful swipe of those lethal spines.

Conan knew that they could not keep up the pace; the footing was poor and their foe seemed tireless. The slightest slip would result in a bloody death between the stalker's snapping forelegs. To worsen matters, the cracks underfoot were spreading as the aged floor vibrated from the strain. A distant rattling filtered up to them, as if pieces were falling from the ceiling and crashing onto the fountain below. The clattering echoes brought cold sweat to Conan's brow. If the floor gave way . . .

Better to fight than plunge to a horrible death. Conan knew that his own sword had been of little use against these things. The Cimmerian seized a desperate chance. Rolling forward, he groped for the hilt of the *atnalga*, snatching it from the wreckage of the smashed trunk. The warm tingle returned at once, but he risked the pain for a brief span, coming out of the forward roll on his feet and springing straight for the stalker.

As he had hoped, the beast's tactics did not change. When it lowered its head to snap at him, his jump brought him up to the pair of shiny, sinister eyes. His powerful downward stroke drove the *atnalga* right between those orbs, razorlike edges parting fibrous green tissues as the blade sank to its hilt. As before, he felt his muscles clenching; in a moment they would refuse to let go of the thing in spite of the searing pain he felt.

With a surge of strength he wrenched his hand from the weapon's grip, letting himself fall to the floor. A massive foreleg batted him across the room; he skidded, scattering chunks of rock and crashing into a wall.

The stalker's unearthly wail filled the air with deafening tones. The enraged monster flailed about with its forelegs, whipping its head from side to side, trying to dislodge the deadly spike. Its eyes glowed like a pair of huge, hot coals, wisps of smoke rising from their red-orange surfaces. The stalker's head glowed, swelling, changing from green to a scarlet blister as its frenzied spasms weakened and its shrieking subsided. Its head burst in a messy spray of steaming pink muck, splashing the walls with scorched matter so foul it made Conan's eyes burn. The gigantic body collapsed, twitching feebly; its head naught but a ragged, smoking stump.

The floor collapsed beneath it, giving way with booming crack.

Trapped in the center of the room, Conan had no place to go but down. He slid forward, feeling the sickening rush of weightlessness as the supporting stones dropped away from him.

Sajara's fingers hooked onto the ledge they had used to enter the ruined chamber.

Conan threw out his hand, nearly dislocating his shoulder. His fingers brushed Sajara's calf before grasping her ankle.

She winced as the Cimmerian's mass nearly tore her

hand from its grip on the ledge. They swayed together like a pendulum, their combined weight gradually forcing her fingers to straighten.

Sajara held on with waning strength, slipping downward slowly, inexorably. She craned her neck and shouted at Conan, her pained expression telling of the strain she was under. Her words were lost in the booming crash of chests bursting against the crystalline fountain, and the din of rocky debris pelting floors and walls. The opal throne struck a ledge on its way down; spinning, it shattered against the floor in a shower of iridescent shards.

Staring down along the wall, Conan saw the ledge beneath them. It looked wider than the one above . . . a silent, stony dare. His sweaty hand relaxed its hold on Sajara's ankle; he braced himself to grab that beckoning edge, hands sliding along the wall as he plummeted. His clutching fingers at last encountered it, breaking his fall. He clung to it for a moment, savoring the reassuring feel of unyielding stone.

Without Conan weighing her down, Sajara maneuvered along the thin ribbon of rock, improving her hold. Moving hand over hand, she descended the ledge, pulling herself up when it widened sufficiently.

The clattering and crashing subsided, leaving only a dull ringing in Conan's ears. He hauled himself up onto the stone ledge and sat there, tilting his head backward against the wall and panting from exhaustion. After catching his breath, he stared down at the jumble of stones atop the stalker's crushed carcass. Coins gleamed everywhere, sprinkled across the chamber like golden drops of dew. The contents of the other chests were buried beneath the wreckage.

Conan joined Sajara, his eyes flashing a silent thanks to her for hanging on. She wiped her brow and smiled at him.

"Gods, but that was close. We'd be filling that beast's belly were it not for the *atnalga*. But now we must prolong our stay in this damned tower and pick through yon pile there to retrieve that strange sword. Surely it survived the fall."

"Twice we have escaped death in the jaws of a stalker," Sajara mumbled. She seemed dazed by their harrowing escape. "Although you are not the chosen one, the gods must hold you high in favor. Either that, or your Crom bestowed upon you a measure of fortune far beyond that granted to most men."

"Ha! Spend an eve at my side in a gambling den whilst I roll the dice and you'll say otherwise. Ill fortune follows at my heels like a stray hound seeking food. This time, though, the bones rolled and came up winners. But what we need now is haste, girl! The sunlight fades, and our task awaits us. With luck"—he almost bit his tongue as he said it—"we can rejoin the others before sunset." *Before a stalker finds them* was the unspoken fear that stewed in the back of Conan's mind.

Seventeen
The *Ranioba*

Y'Taba, another night comes. Why have they not returned?" Jukona fretted, pacing in the dirt outside the door
to Y'Taba's hut.

"Be at peace, Jukona. A sky of clouds clears not while
one stares up at it. Worry will not serve you as well as rest—
you have not slept since the morning of their departure."

"The Deadlands will devour my daughter, and Conan,
and the others. I should have accompanied them," he
groaned, ignoring the spirit-leader's admonishment.

"To what end? Those whom you have sworn to defend
are here—our women, our children, the elders, and your
handful of warriors, wounded or dying but yours to protect. If the Kezati come—"

"Then they will face not one warrior but two," a somber
voice sounded from the doorway to the hut, causing the
two old men to turn and stare. Ngomba strode up to them,
muscles rippling under the afternoon sun. He looked like
anyone but a man who a few days ago had lain upon a
deathbed. Aside from some scabs and bruises, his body

showed no evidence of the beating it had taken. His bright, fierce eyes radiated exuberance.

"Ngomba! By Asusa, you look fit as ever," Jukona marveled.

Y'Taba regarded the young warrior with a stern gaze. "You must be careful, Ngomba. Your vigor may wane when you most need it. To you I say what I said to Jukona: rest."

"Not while the Kezati hover nearby, waiting to prey upon us. Dreams of them darken my sleep, Y'Taba Spirit-Leader. When I close my eyes I see them hover like winged clouds, waiting to rain down upon us in a storm of beaks and claws. And who shall stand before that rain of doom?" he snapped, jabbing a finger at Jukona. "You?" Snorting, he shook his head disdainfully.

Jukona stiffened, eyes flashing. "Hold your tongue, Ngomba. I have suffered it to wag with your words of scorn, but no more!"

"I see. You will punish me if I do not show proper respect for a warrior-leader who is no longer even fit to follow?" His laugh rang harshly, bitterly.

Jukona's open palm struck the young warrior's face with a resounding slap, so forceful that it knocked his head backward.

Snarling, Ngomba balled his huge hands into clublike fists, cocking his arm backward.

Y'Taba caught Ngomba's fist with a meaty smack, wrapping his hand around it. The imposing spirit-leader bored his eyes into Ngomba's. "Be silent, insolent one!" Y'Taba boomed, his eyes narrowing in anger. "Once I banished you; I shall do so again if you disobey me. Your heart is true to our people, I think, but your mind is a pit into which I cannot see. You are strong, Ngomba. The gods have granted you a boon that you must not abuse. Apologize to Jukona."

Ngomba glowered in silence, tugging at his fist to loosen it from the spirit-leader's powerful grip.

Jukona stood expectantly, his arms folded across his chest.

Y'Taba's muscles quivered as he forced Ngomba's arm

down. "Apologize," he insisted. Cords rippled along his forearm, and his biceps bulged as he pushed back the younger warrior's upraised fist. But if he felt any strain, his voice did not show it.

Ngomba's lips drew back across his bared teeth. Then his shoulder slumped as he seemed to give up the struggle. "Forgive me, Jukona Warrior-Leader," he mumbled, bowing his head.

Y'Taba let go, planting his hands on his hips.

"You need me. Our people need me," Ngomba said to the ground. "You dare not banish me, and if you did I would not go. As for the stranger, Conan, we need him not. If he returns, send him away. If she who will one day be joined with me has perished, I shall not forgive you, Spirit-Leader. You should have not let her go."

"She is *Ranioba*, and by our custom the right is hers." Y'Taba slowly flexed his fingers, setting his jaw as if to conceal a grimace of pain.

Ngomba watched him. "How shall you wash your hands of her blood, Spirit-Leader? How? My heart tells me that like Jukona, you have faded. It is dusk for you, Y'Taba; the sun that was your wisdom is sinking from the sky. But you are still Y'Taba, and you have strength I did not guess at." He unclenched his hand, rubbing the palm, then shaking his fingers. "So we wait. Who will return first? Our enemies, or the stranger who—you say—will save us?" Tight-lipped, he clasped his hands before him, tapping the forefingers together.

Jukona stood impassively, his face a block of chiseled stone.

Y'Taba's eyes flickered between the trees that bordered his village and the darkening sky that loomed above it. He did not answer the question.

"Where in the blazes of Zandru's seventh hell are they?" Conan asked, surveying the area by the pool of water as they neared it. The midmorning sun provided excellent visibility, but he did not see anyone in the expected place.

Sajara quickened her pace. "Maybe they sought shelter—from a stalker, perhaps."

Conan hurried along the stone pathway, glad to put the tower behind him. The search through the rubble had taken longer than he had hoped, forcing them to stop when the light failed. At first the prospect of spending a night in the tower soured Conan's mood further. His flaring temper had been more than assuaged when Sajara had, in gratitude, kissed him. Their lips lingered in an embrace that preceded an evening of passion. The beautiful Ganak huntress had herself seemed surprised by desires that Conan awakened in her.

The Cimmerian felt somewhat bruised and battered this morning, but he doubted he would have slept anyway. In spite of the rough comforts of the tower, the amorous encounter had been just what he needed.

Sajara, for her part, also seemed to be in much better spirits. When the dawn's bright light filled the tower's interior, they had resumed their search and located the *atnalga* beneath a heap of splintered wood. Conan had found some interesting object among the debris, which he tucked into the pouches he had originally fashioned for the rubies. After divining that those crimson gemstones represented eyes in a carven image of Kahli, he had given up his plan to pry them loose. Such treasures bore the stench of black magic upon them, and his experiences with such loot had brought nothing but trouble in the past. He might return for them one day, but for now he was content with some of the baubles retrieved from Jhaora's hoard.

He had also picked up the small chest. One side of it had been smashed, but not too badly, and he stuffed it with a few books that remained more or less intact. A casual flipping of pages revealed some interesting contents, further brightening the Cimmerian's mood.

Carefully they placed the *atnalga* into the chest and wrapped the burst corners with vines to secure it.

Laughing and joking, they left the tower with renewed hope. Only now a new concern had arisen.

"If anything happened to them, we shall see the signs," Conan said.

When they reached the area by the spring of water, they drank their fill quickly before searching the place for signs of the Ganak women. While Sajara splashed water on her face, Conan studied the dirt and rubbed his jaw in bewilderment.

"No signs of a struggle, but I count *four* sets of footprints leading toward the doorway."

"Four?" Sajara was at his side in a few supple strides.

"Come on. We'll follow them."

They hurried toward the tall, arched exit, slowing when they heard the wall.

"Did they—" Sajara began.

Conan raised a finger to his lips, then pointed at the doorway.

Outside, a shadow lay across it . . . a colossal shadow with an all-too-familiar shape.

Conan whispered. "That portal is too narrow for the thing to come through. We're safe enough, but . . . "

"Makiela . . . Kanitra . . . Avrana," she moaned. "No. It cannot be."

"Aye, I hope not," Conan said fervently. "What of this fourth set of footprints?"

"Sajara?"

They both nearly fell over backward in surprise when a head appeared in the doorway.

"Makiela!" shouted Sajara.

"By Crom, what—"

Makiela walked into view, followed by Avrana and Kanitra. "Sajara!" they called out. "Do not worry. We are safe."

The shadow shifted its position, unmistakably belonging to a stalker.

Sajara rushed through the archway, Conan following her and cursing. *Ranioba* and her hunters hugged briefly while the Cimmerian gaped at the green-bodied monstrosity. He stayed back a few paces, respectful of the creature's astonishing speed. His sword was in his hand by instinct.

Astride the stalker's neck sat an old Ganak woman with

a sun-wrinkled face. Her skin was not painted in typical Ganak fashion, though she wore a necklace similar to Sajara's. A braid of gray hair swept down past her waist; tied to the end of it was a white, cylindrical seashell the size of a man's forefinger. Smiling down at them, she turned, revealing that her left arm was entirely gone.

The old woman's smile turned into a stare as Conan walked into view. She seemed as startled by his appearance as he was by hers.

Sajara blinked, her eyes registering both recognition and disbelief. "Nyona *Ranioba*?"

"Yes, child. Your eyes were ever keen, as befits a *Ranioba*. Though when I last beheld you, you were a girl with only a stub of hair. Has it been so long? It has, I suppose. The passing of sun to moon means little to us here. There is much to tell, but first"—she waggled a finger at Conan—"I must know by what name this one is called, and from where he has come. My tale is for the ears of Ganaks, not *njeni*!"

"He is called Conan, from the land of Cimmeria that lies faraway. He is not *njeni*! He fought the Kezati with our warrior-leader, drank *kuomo* with our spirit-leader, and he has saved me and these others from death—more than once." She glared at Makiela. "As Makiela should have told you," she added in an icy tone.

"There was not a chance—" Makiela began to protest.

"Nyona *Ranioba* came to us just after sunrise, Sajara." Kanitra offered.

Nodding, Avrana joined in. "We were about to explain why we had come to the Deadlands when—"

"Silence, children!" the old woman commanded. "Sajara, speak. The rest of you, hold your tongues."

Conan was burning to know why the stalker did not simply devour them all, but he suspected that this strange Ganak rider would brook no further interruptions. He stood uneasily, fidgeting with his sword while Sajara related an abbreviated account of recent events, beginning with Conan's arrival at Ganaku. Nyona seldom interrupted for more details, seeming curiously well-informed of much that had transpired—particularly in the Deadlands.

While they spoke, the Cimmerian studied the stalker. He had seen them often enough before but never had the opportunity to examine one at leisure. The thing had made no hostile move, but its bluish-green eyes—their hue different from that of the other stalkers—glittered with unnatural intelligence that still made his flesh crawl. He saw that this stalker had narrow, leathery forewings and large, fan-shaped hindwings. The latter were folded neatly beneath the forewings. Spots of red and white adorned its thick forelegs. Conan was certain that the others had lacked these colorations. A sheaf of bark had been fitted around the treelike neck, upon which Nyona was seated.

While listening, Conan deduced that Nyona had vanished into the Deadlands while Sajara was a young girl. Another *Ranioba* had taken her place and was later succeeded by Sajara. Conan was still uncertain of the exact privileges of a *Ranioba*, though the title seemed to convey authority over a select group of women—"huntresses and seekers," he had heard them called. He guessed that a *Ranioba* was at least the equal of a warrior-leader.

Finally Sajara satisfied the last of the old woman's curiosity.

Nyona nodded approvingly to Conan. "Your eyes and skin are of a man from Cimmeria, I do not doubt. But the gods gave to you the heart and spirit unseen since the Ganak warrior-leaders of old walked upon the soil of Ganaku."

Conan made no thanks for the compliment, instead seizing the opportunity to speak. "Whence come you, then? Surely not from this accursed place of old stones!"

"Old? Yes, the stones are old," she agreed. "More than you know. Accursed? Perhaps once, though no longer. You slew the last—and worst—of the denizens born in the war of gods. Life may again rise from these stones." A tone of regret softened her voice. "I have been hiding in the Deadlands, not here, mind you, for you have seen only the part of the Deadlands that is outermost. Where I come from is deeper, beyond reach of Ganak—or Cimmerian. Even the *anansi* do not dwell there.

"When I was of the same age as Sajara, I sought knowledge in the Deadlands as had many before me. Fools all, we were, those of us who followed the path of Kulunga—yet so proud, so brave. Like so many, I ran afoul of the *anansi*. They chased me through the sward, to a place of trees not far from here. I was trapped; it was impassable. No," she grinned at Conan, who was nodding. "The place is not this circle that surrounds Rahamji. Where I ran the trees are thicker and grow against each other. Only from above can one enter. And then only on the back of a *mzuri vugunda* like this one," she tapped the tree bark. "Rasangwa rode upon a *mzuri* when she saved me from the *anansi*. Rasangwa was a Rahaman . . . the last of her race."

"A *Rahaman* saved you?" Sajara's awed whisper echoed Conan's thoughts.

"The fountain of the gods flowed with water that gave her this gift of life—or curse, Rasangwa called it. She was one of few who escaped from Rahamji when the gods of Jhaora fought those of the Rahamans. They knew many secrets of this land." She lifted the shell tied to the end of her long braid and raised it to her mouth as if blowing into it. The shell made no sound, but the stalker stirred and changed its position, like a monstrous steed guided by invisible reins. "The *mzuri vugunda*—those who bear marks of red and white—obey the wind-spirits who haunt these shells, if one knows how to command them. Rasangwa taught this art to me.

"You see, she spared me from death in the jaws of those *anansi*, though my arm was torn away as I escaped. She took me to the place of which I spoke and treated my arm. It was there that I later gave bir—gave her my vow to not reveal her to the Ganaks, but to remain with her, for she was alone.

Never shall I return to her.

"Twenty times has the face of Asusa risen since Rasangwa fled to the lands of gray. Yet her face was smooth, her hair as black as the night. She had been lonely for so long, her life empty but for the memories of those she loved . . . they all passed into the lands of gray before her, broken and lonely." Nyona swallowed, wiping briefly at her eyes. "I do not wish to die as she did, from a heart broken in sorrow. It was time for me to return to my people, and my vow to Rasangwa no longer kept me away.

"In the night I have flown over Ganaku to see the village. I watched when you entered Rahamji. But I arrived too late to warn you, and I could not save you from the terror of old that Conan defeated. It slew even the *vugunda* who strayed too near. And Dawakuba, whom you see before you, is almost as old as I. *Mzuri* are rare; they do not prey upon each other as the other *vugunda* do. That is a sight to sicken you, should you ever witness it. The female slays the male even as they mate, biting his neck in twain and devouring his head."

Conan flinched at the vivid image. "Can you not teach us to command these wind-spirits? Mounted on an army of stalkers, those Kezati hellspawn would stand no chance against us."

Nyona shook her head. "The boys in the village would reach manhood before you learned the art. But I will do what I can in the battle that we must fight." She looked over the Ganak women and Conan as if sizing them up. "Though Dawakubwa does not fight well, she flies like no other of her kind." She blew into the shell, and the stalker lowered its huge body to the ground. Makiela, Avrana, and Kanitra squeezed themselves onto the bark-covered neck, but there was no room for Conan or his vine-wrapped trunk.

The Cimmerian eyed the stalker dubiously. "I can walk," he said, content to forego his ride. He still harbored some mistrust toward the stalkers, however obedient this one might be. The harrowing encounter in the tower was too recent a memory.

Sajara nodded agreement, evidencing similar feelings.

She, like Conan, had carefully distanced herself from the winged mount.

Nyona smiled knowingly. "I felt the same once. Do not worry. Dawakubwa and I shall come back for you. Stay inside, near the spring of water where you will be safe from any *vugunda*. Only those who are vicious fly within the walls at all, and even those do not get close to the ground. They do not know that the vines can snare them no more. The face of Asusa will yet be above us when we return."

Much of the day had passed during their encounter; morning had become afternoon. But Conan did not doubt Nyona's claim. He had seen how swiftly those beasts could move. He and Sajara watched as the old *Ranioba* blew soundlessly into the shell, the *mzuri* ascending with powerful beats of its wings that raised a small cloud of dust beneath them. Conan averted his eyes from the image of Kahli that filled the wall above him, reentering the ruins that Nyona—or rather the Rahamans—had called Rahamji.

Sajara headed straight for the spring, taking a drink and splashing herself liberally with its refreshing water. Conan knelt near her, cupping his hands to get his fill. He was completely off-balance when she shoved him in from behind. He plunged in headfirst but grabbed her slender, muscular forearm as he fell, dragging her in with a splash.

"We should not be covered with dust when we return," she said when she recovered from the unexpected soaking. "And the way you smell, even that stalker may refuse to bear you upon its back." She laughed, slapping the water with her palm and dousing Conan.

He dunked his head and yanked it out quickly, shaking his hair and spraying water at Sajara as he flipped it back. Dewy beads caressed the smooth, olive skin of her face, dripping onto full breasts that were partially submerged in the sparkling waters of the spring. Sajara smiled coyly at Conan, still laughing, and they embraced.

The wait for Nyona's return passed quickly.

Eighteen
Duel in the Dark

Night had fallen long ago, and Conan had consumed considerable quantities of *kuomo* before retiring, as had Jukona and the elders, even Y'Taba. Ngomba had surprised everyone by publicly apologizing to the Cimmerian for both the theft of his sword and the subsequent misdeeds he had committed. Sajara and the women, who by custom did not drink *kuomo*, had nevertheless been in as jovial a mood as the others. The successful return of Sajara, Conan, and the others had polished the tarnished hopes of the Ganaks, it seemed.

Y'Taba had seemed distracted all night, more reticent than usual. He had avoided Nyona, averting his eyes from her for reasons beyond Conan's grasp. The spirit-leader had reacted with some consternation when learning that Conan was not the chosen one; the *atnalga's* usefulness in the upcoming conflict was now in doubt. But a handful of wounded warriors had begun to recuperate from dire injuries sustained in battle, and Ngomba seemed completely recovered. Nyona and her stalker would surely be unstoppable, they agreed.

Further, Conan had pledged to lead the Ganaks in their decisive battle. Y'Taba and many others seemed satisfied that the stranger from Cimmeria, who they deemed beloved of the gods, would turn the tide and ensure their victory. Confidence flowed like *kuomo*, and for the first time in many days, the fog of despair lifted from the villagers.

But now Conan stirred restlessly, staring at the ceiling of Jukona's hut. The warrior-leader had consumed an incredible volume of *kuomo*; he snored like a bellowing Corinthian buffalo.

The Cimmerian knew the reason for his sleeplessness. He was anxious for morning to come; Y'Taba would summon the shell-spirits and rid him of the shaman's curse that lingered in his mind like an everpresent thundercloud. Through one of the many holes in the hut's roof, he could see the moon staring down at him. How long had it been since his bestial night of butchery aboard the *Mistress*? The moon looked nearly full again. He turned away from it onto his belly, burying his face in his crossed arms. The pile of leaves under him was far from comfortable, but he had slept upon beds much worse in his travels.

Closing his eyes, he imagined the heady smell of Sajara's hair and skin, which had lingered delightfully long after his tryst with her in the pool. Eventually he slipped into a light doze, then a heavy slumber . . .

He was racing through the underbrush, the fetid smell of his breath rising hotly in his nostrils. From the sward ahead rose other smells; leaves, rain, bugs, snakes, a medley of odors that he keenly and instinctively distinguished from that of his prey. He loped relentlessly onward, faster and faster, until he heard the animal ahead. Its fear rolled from it in waves, whetting his appetite. Saliva dripped from his mouth onto his chest as he closed in, charging madly after his victim. He paid no attention to the whipping of leaves against his face, the venomous serpents under his feet. They were nothing to him.

He hungered for the hot blood that would gush from a slashed throat, a torn belly, a still-beating heart ripped from the splintered ribs of a heaving breast.

Seizing a thrashing hind leg of the galloping beast, he pounced onto its back, crushing it to the ground, enjoying its squeals and struggles. His claws shredded its flesh, digging into its vitals and he snarled and roared, reveling in the kill.

Its anguished face looked up at him, crying out in terror . . .

Conan bolted up, choking back a scream. Sweat covered him like a soaked blanket, and his heart hammered in his chest.

The face in his crimson nightmare had been Sajara's.

"Crom," he groaned, brushing off leaves that stuck to his drenched body. He would not even attempt sleep after that grisly dream. The morning could not come soon enough for him. For the twentieth time since their arrival at Ganaku on Nyona's stalker, he wished that the shell-spirits would do their work at night. But Y'Taba had insisted upon waiting for his sun god to awaken before attempting his cure.

A fresh snore from Jukona blasted across the hut, the reek of sour *kuomo* assailing Conan's nostrils. He stepped soundlessly outside for fresh air, inhaling deeply and trying not to look up at the moon. He rubbed his face tiredly, strolling toward the place of gathering. The bench would be as good a place as any to pass the night.

To his surprise, Sajara was there. She held a flower in her hand, spinning its stem between her fingers and staring at petals whose cheerful hues seemed dimmed by the moon's dull glow. After his dream, he was reluctant to sit by her, but she saw him and smiled, beckoning him to her side.

He planted himself glumly upon the bench, summoning a forced smile.

"Conan, are you not happy that Y'Taba will cure you tomorrow?" she asked, looking into his eyes.

"By Crom, of course I am," he said gruffly.

"And after we defeat the Kezati, you will leave . . . to return to Cimmeria."

"More likely to Vendhya, if those books we found—" He stopped, biting his tongue. He should have recognized the nature of her question, having heard it before. Had he not been so muddled from the *kuomo* and the disturbing dream, he would have noticed the signs and been better prepared.

Sajara continued, staring at the flower in her hand. "You may stay as long as you wish. Back at Rahamji, when you told me that you must go back, I did not realize how much I would miss you."

Conan gave the matter some thought. Sajara was a treasure, of that there was no doubt. She was as comely a wench as any Conan had known, and a spirited fighter besides. With her as his mate, he could set himself up as a prince of sorts among these people. When they rid the place of the damnable Kezati, Ganaku would be an island paradise. Many a rogue would cheerfully sacrifice any of his limbs to live there.

But not Conan. He was as different from most rogues as a lion was from jackals. And he was far from ready to consider settling down. He would have none of the domestic life, surrounded by squalling brats, bound to one place and one woman—even a woman as voluptuous as Sajara. Further, most of the excitement would vanish from this place without the Kezati to stir things up.

"You do not have to fight for us again," she said.

"Only a knave would depart tomorrow, when your need is great." Conan had vowed to see this through to the end, when the blood of the last giant vulture flowed down his blade. "I think I shall stay here, at least for a while," he told her. When the curse was banished, a few days would

make little difference. Preparing for his northward voyage
would take time anyway, and he would peruse Jhaora's
books in hope of finding his exact whereabouts. He even
had half a mind to go back for the rubies at Rahamji and
take his chances that Kahli's vile clerics had not bedeviled
them. He had risked his neck for smaller rewards, by
Crom.

Sajara's eyes shone in the moonlight as she smiled,
throwing her arms around Conan's brawny torso, leaning
her head upon his chest. The Cimmerian held her in silence, his thoughts about the events of the morrow distracted by the feel of Sajara's supple body. She kissed him
fiercely, but he pulled away at the sound of a rustle behind
them.

Ngomba stood there watching, his face a twisted mask
of menace. He gripped his sharpened oar so tightly that
tremors ran from his clenched hands to his massively muscled shoulders. "She is mine," he hissed, savagely baring
teeth that gleamed in the moonlight.

"Ngomba, no!" Sajara protested, leaping to her feet.
"Do not challenge him—once I loved you but no more.
You fight for nothing! Conan saved me and——"

"No!" the immense Ganak bellowed, head snapping
sideways as if her words had slapped him in the face. Eyes
blazing, he turned his face from Sajara back to the Cimmerian. "You are to blame for this, *njeni*! Meet your
gods!" Spear outthrust, Ngomba approached, his dark eyes
glittering like icy orbs of polished steel.

Conan immediately adopted a pit-fighter's stance, rue-
fully wishing for the sword that rested against the wall in
Jukona's hut. Interposing himself between Ngomba and
Sajara, he stood with flexed knees, arms out, ready for the
spear. "Get back, girl," he said. Earlier, he had been willing to forgive the warrior for his offenses. But new ire
burned hotly in Conan's breast, flames that could be
quenched only in blood. "Ngomba will have neither you
nor any other, unless he courts a she-devil in Hell!"

Swifter than a leaping panther, the Cimmerian sprang straight for the spear.

Ngomba's vicious jab met only air. Conan seized the sharpened oar and jerked it backward, hoping to pull his foe with it. Incredibly, the Ganak warrior kept his balance, wrenching away the spear by brute force and whirling it around in the same motion, slamming it against Conan's outthrust head with a loud thwack. Knocked to his knees by a blow that would have split a lesser man's skull, Conan grunted but grabbed again for the spear, grasping it in both hands and tugging. Straining, legs braced, the warrior played a deadly tug-of-war, the moonlight etching the bulging muscles of their sweaty frames. Ngomba suddenly stopped pulling, instead shoving the spear forward while angling its point toward Conan's neck.

Craning his head to one side, Conan felt the shaft scrape his neck, its point sliding past him. He flexed his legs and jumped backward, finally upsetting Ngomba's balance. The Ganak toppled forward, huffing as his fall knocked the breath from his lungs. Conan whipped the blade of the oar against Ngomba's back, then reversed it in his hands and stepped backward, gripping the spear like a strange quarterstaff. Gasping, Ngomba rolled and sprang to his feet, jumping nimbly to avoid the oar as Conan swept it under him.

Sajara stood rooted in place, unable to tear her eyes from the combatants, her mouth frozen open.

The Cimmerian rained a series of rapid blows on Ngomba's arms and legs, none of which slowed the Ganak in the least. Like a rabid beast he advanced, seemingly unstoppable. Conan backpedaled to keep the spear out of reach. The oar pummeled Ngomba again and again. Blood streamed from a cut above his eye, but the brutish warrior kept coming, forcing Conan to retreat toward the village. His heel banged into the vine-wrapped trunk from the tower, which lay where Y'Taba had left it earlier.

Sajara found her voice and began calling for help, rushing toward the two men.

"Stay back!" Conan shouted, eyes flickering toward her. Cocking his arms backward, he switched tactics, lunging at Ngomba to stab him with the spear's point.

The battered warrior snatched the spear in a deft, powerful motion, ripping it from Conan's hands. Ngomba brought it down against his knee, snapping it in twain, pouncing onto the Cimmerian while tossing aside the pieces. The Cimmerian twisted, catching Ngomba's neck in the crook of his arm.

Grunting, Conan tightened his hold, his biceps flexing like iron against the Ganak's windpipe. Ngomba's elbow rammed into the Cimmerian's belly, loosening his armlock. Conan coughed, staggering backward. He kicked out, his foot connecting solidly with Ngomba's groin. The Ganak doubled over, groaning in agony. Reeling, fighting for breath, Conan swept his foot into Ngomba's jawbone, where it struck with a crunch.

Spitting blood and teeth, the Ganak warrior reached out toward the vine-wrapped trunk, stretching for something that lay just within his reach.

It was the hilt of the *atnalga*, jutting from the side of the wrecked chest.

The Cimmerian aimed another desperate kick at Ngomba, hoping to stop him before he grabbed the length of black death. But Conan's hasty move shifted his weight awkwardly, twisting his ankle painfully beneath him. He thumped to the hard ground as Ngomba shouted triumphantly, thick, powerful fingers closing around the *atnalga*'s grip. Whipping it from the trunk, Ngomba rose to his feet and whirled, planting his foot hard on the prone Cimmerian's ribs.

"No!" Sajara screamed as she raced toward them, arms pumping. Confused murmuring and cries of surprise issued from the huts nearest the roof of celebration, their occupants stirring from deep *kuomo*-induced slumbering.

Sweat and blood dripped from Ngomba's fierce face onto Conan, who struggled vainly to dislodge the huge foot holding him down. The Ganak sneered, raising the blade and slashing downward with a murderous blow.

In the corner of his eye, Conan saw Sajara sailing through the air, propelled by a powerful running leap. She was heading straight for them, and in the instant that he realized her intent Conan smashed his malletlike fists against Ngomba's ankle. At the same moment Sajara collided with the tall Ganak's calf. Ngomba's foot slid across Conan's sweat-slicked flesh and his stroke went wide, flashing downward toward Sajara's neck.

The Cimmerian shoved her away as the blade bit deeply into the soil. Ngomba roared, raising the weapon again. Its edge flashed down at Conan, whose legs were pinned under Sajara. He flung up an arm in a futile gesture as the *atnalga* swept toward him.

Then Ngomba froze, checking the motion in midswing, his snarling countenance suddenly tranquil. He stared in wonder at the *atnalga* and took a step backward, squeezing his eyes shut and pitching forward to his knees. His eyelids lifted slowly a moment later, tears welling in pupils that had changed from a dark brown hue to silver-speckled black. Laying his blade gently upon the ground before him, he covered his face with his hands.

Conan wasted no time getting to his feet. He kicked the blade out beyond Ngomba's reach and shoved the warrior to the ground, pinning him and seizing his throat, thumbs pressing in. Ngomba offered no resistance, but the Cimmerian's blood was up; he could show no mercy to one who had tried to kill him, one who had nearly murdered Jokuna and Sajara.

"Yes . . . slay me," Ngomba wheezed, his body slackening. "The spirits . . . in the *atnalga* . . ." He paused, gasping for breath. ". . . spoke to me. *I* am . . . chosen one."

Conan lessened the pressure on his thumbs, though he did not relax his grip on Ngomba's throat. He remembered in the tower when the strange voices within the blade had screamed at him, how the touch of that weapon had seared him, nearly sending him to Hell. The Ganak warrior had apparently not felt the fire of the blade. What if he were Kulunga's chosen one—should he spare the treacherous warrior?

Ngomba coughed. "Spirits commanded me . . . to yield. *atnalga* will not serve one . . . whose heart is . . . impure."

A small group of Ganaks, led by Jukona, came running toward them. They stopped in their tracks, staring at the scene.

"By Asusa, what has—" Jukona began.

"Shh!" Sajara rose, raising her hand and pointing toward the two fighters.

"Slay me . . . man of Cimmeria," Ngomba pleaded, sensing that Conan's resolve was ebbing. "Sajara is yours. I am . . . not worthy of her. I could have saved my people, but my folly has doomed us all."

Staring into those silver-flecked eyes, Conan took his hands away, letting Ngomba's head slump to the ground. A seasoned veteran of countless face-to-face battles, Conan had come to recognize a look of hopelessness that creeps into the eyes of an utterly defeated man. He had seen that in the Ganak's gaze. Though not one to show a foe any mercy, Ngomba had seemed a changed man, not the man with whom Conan had fought. He wondered fleetingly if he would regret his impulse to release the Ganak. He lifted his knee from the prone warrior's gut and stood, stepping back a few paces.

Sajara looked at him in amazement. "You would spare him?"

Conan nodded. "I am not his executioner. Let him burn in Hell when his gods see fit to end his miserable life." Stretching and bending down, he worked the stiffness from his twisted ankle. "Though I trust him not, I deem that he hates the Kezati more than me and will fight them to the last."

"Will one of you tell me what has happened here?" Jukona demanded, his fists planted on his hips. He was bleary-eyed from his *kuomo* excesses but did not slur his words. "And what has become of Y'Taba and Nyona?"

Conan and Sajara exchanged blank looks as Ngomba finally picked himself up.

"The *vugunda* no longer waits near the hut of Y'Taba." A prune-faced, yellow-painted elder commented. "They may have gone together, perhaps to speak where their words cannot be heard by others."

"It was strange that they spoke but little to each other this night," Jukona said absently, ruminating. "Well, I would hear your account now, though Y'Taba should know of this at once." He watched Ngomba with a stony-faced look as the downcast warrior stood in place, shoulders slumping, arms dangling at his sides.

Wordlessly, Ngomba shuffled over to the dropped *atnalga* and picked it up, still hanging his head in shame. He shuffled over to the bench at the edge of the place of gathering and sat down.

Incredulous stares followed him as the Ganaks watched the once-proud youth.

Sajara and Conan began their recounting of the fight, eliciting a raised eyebrow from Jukona when he learned of Sajara's affection for Conan.

Y'Taba, Nyona, and her stalker did not return to the village.

Nineteen
Four Against Hundreds

A sliver of indigo appeared on the horizon, brightening to a band of azure as the rising sun overpowered the sinking moon.

Conan munched absently on a large chunk of raw fish, spitting its bones onto the ground near the roof of celebration. Weary from his pitched clash with Ngomba, he had managed to fall asleep last night—without dreaming—and felt rested, though a few bruises and aches lingered from his scuffling. In hand-to-hand combat, these Ganak warriors were fearsome foes.

Jukona seemed surprisingly energetic in spite of the staggering amout of *kuomo* he had quaffed. He sat nearby, glancing up at the morning sky. Though he spoke no more of it, Conan could see that Y'Taba's absence worried the old warrior-leader.

"You have my blessing to become joined with Sajara, if you wish it," he said unexpectedly.

Conan choked on his food. "We have not decided," he

said, clearing his throat. "But she is *Ranioba*. Would she not forgo this role if she were to take a husband?"

He nodded. "This is our way. Y'Taba could forbid the joining since you are not Ganak, but I do not think he would object, after all that you have done."

Conan looked away, watching the Ganaks go about their morning routine. Women and children worked diligently, cleaning the catch brought in by the hunters that morning, cracking open clams and oysters to dig out the meat inside, and smashing coconuts with stones to drain their milk into large, bowl-shaped clamshells. The *kuomo* stock had nearly run dry after last night's swilling. Boys and girls worked together to fashion nets used in the snaring of fish. Elders milled around the place of gathering, sometimes huddling into groups to discuss matters of importance.

One of the wounded Ganak warriors was able to walk, though not without some assistance from his woman. Another still tossed in the throes of fever, his condition worsening, while the others lacked the strength to do aught but nibble their food and sip water.

Ngomba sat by herself upon a large stone, fashioning a new oar to replace the broken one. The young Ganak had regained some of his composure, though he maintained an embarrassed silence, avoiding Conan and Sajara altogether. He seemed absorbed in his work on the oar, a process that Conan realized took a very long time indeed when all one had was tools of stone and shell. The *atnalga* rested nearby; either Ngomba deemed its blade unsuitable for the working of wood, or its usefulness in that process had not dawned on him.

Remembering that his own blade needed some tending, he laid it across his knees and began scraping at it with a shell of shape and size appropriate for smoothing out minute nicks and honing its edge. If the Akbitanan blade had one drawback, it was the difficulty of sharpening and conditioning. It needed oiling, too ... he supposed that the fish carcasses would provide a functional amount. Conan was mainly just passing time while he waited for Y'Taba to return.

Sajara, Makiela, Avrana, and Kanitra emerged from a tall patch of reeds near the place of gathering, returning from their scouting foray. The wounded women had healed quickly, courtesy of the *yagneb* leaves and Y'Taba's considerable skill.

Jukona looked at his daughter, his face inquisitive, but Sajara simply shook her head. They had sought for any signs of Y'Taba or Nyona, first studying the tracks leading away from Y'Taba's hut, then scaling trees near the village's edge. Makiela had been convinced from the onset that Y'Taba had ridden with Nyona on the stalker, but none could say to where they had gone.

Conan turned his attention back to his sword, tossing aside the shell when he realized that the tempered steel was grinding it away. He wondered if a whetstone would have fared any better. Glancing toward the chest of tomes salvaged from the tower, he supposed he should start browsing through them.

Jukona watched with interest. "What do you call those?" he asked, pointing at the bent sheaf of weathered pages in Conan's hand.

"Books," Conan replied in a surly tone. His mood was worsening as the morning wore on.

Wrinkling his brow, Jukona gawked at the faint scribblings. Conan's curt manner, however, put off any further questions he might have phrased.

Indeed, throughout the village, the only conversations that seemed to continue were those of the elders. A web of tension seemed to have entrapped the Ganaks in its invisible bonds. On everyone's mind was Y'Taba's mysterious absence, the imminent Kezati threat, the strangeness of Ngomba, or any combination of all three.

Conan dropped the fourth book in annoyance, its contents as undecipherable as the previous one. Age, heat, and humidity had combined to render these tomes into pulpy masses of stained, crumbling parchment. Some of them practically disintegrated at his touch, though the first and second volumes had contained informative if unexciting scrawlings.

A shout of excitement from Makiela turned heads throughout the throng. At first, Conan could not see it, but moments later the speck on the horizon became distinguishable as a swiftly flying stalker. It sped through the sky above the jungle, bearing its riders to the place of gathering. Ganaks everywhere dropped what they were doing and flocked toward the mound upon which Dawakubwa set down. Even Ngomba trailed behind the others. Conan noted that he brought the *atnalga* with him.

Y'Taba climbed off, somewhat shakily, his usual confident demeanor returning when his feet touched the soil. Nyona remained upon her immense winged mount, peering back toward the sky above the jungle. The stalker's eyes swiveled in that direction as well, antennae twitching like windblown reeds.

Darkness ringed the spirit-leader's drooping eyes, marking a sleepless night. But if he were weary, his manner did not show it. He raised a hand to still the murmuring. "Forgive me for departing in the night," he began. "Nyona *Ranioba* and I had much to discuss; we tarried longer than planned." He surveyed the villagers with a reassuring smile before adopting his usual somber expression. "Of what we spoke, there is no time to relate. Our enemies of old approach even now. Our day of victory is at hand!"

Gasps rippled through the gathering, though some of the villagers accepted the news with stoic silence.

"Nyona *Ranioba* saw the Kezati coming from afar as we flew over the Deadlands. Even in the distance, the sky was thick with them, but do not despair. Though we do not have the *atnalga*, the mighty Asusa and Muhingo War God have bestowed upon us the means to defeat the children of Ezat. Conan, Ngomba, Nyona, and Dawakubwa——"

"Y'Taba," Jukona interjected, "perhaps we *do* have the *atnalga*."

The spirit-leader paused, face clouding. "How, Jukona? Hasten your tongue!"

Jukona pointed to Ngomba, shrugging. "He fought Conan and nearly slew him with the *atnalga*, but the spirits within it stayed his hand, and then Conan spared his life. Ngomba said the spirits will not serve him, for his heart is impure, but they suffer him to bear the blade. He is the chosen one after all!"

Y'Taba's eyes narrowed, his gaze burning into Ngomba's strangely transformed eyes. "What say you, Ngomba?"

"I have failed, spirit-leader. I shall wield the *atnalga* against the Kezati, but the spirits who empower it have become silent. They spoke to me once, commanding me to yield and calling me unworthy. Perhaps they have fled."

Conan noticed that Nyona looked upon Ngomba with affection that seemed unwonted between two strangers. But words she had uttered before, words he thought had been a slip of her tongue, tickled in his ears. He rubbed his chin contemplatively, recent events taking on new meanings. An intriguing notion had arisen, but it was too outrageous for him to vouch. Besides, he had other matters to concern him. With an inward groan, he realized that Y'Taba's fulfilment of their bargain would be postponed until the battle was done.

"We shall soon see, Ngomba." Y'Taba's tone seemed to soften for a moment, his expression unreadable as he regarded the young warrior. "The women and children must seek safety with the elders. Sajara, prepare your huntresses. Hasten! The Kezati will strike as before, I do not doubt. We must ready our spirits also. Nyona, who accompanies you astride the back of the *mzuri vugunda*?"

"Alone we shall fly," she smiled, "as one we fight, and swifter with no burden of two."

Y'Taba nodded. "Conan, I am sorry. If you wish, we shall go now to my hut, where I can command the spirits. You have kept your vow to me and I am bound by words of promise. What say you?"

"I fight first," Conan set his jaw grimly, gripping the hilt of his sword.

"Side by side, once again," Jukona nodded, lifting a sharpened oar from the pile near the benches.

"We are ready, Y'Taba," Sajara added. She and the others, each toting several extra spears, dashed into the tall reeds near the place of gathering. Conan divined their tactics at once and approved. He had seen the accuracy and force with which they hurled those spears. They would throw their weapons from the cover of the marsh, accounting for perhaps a few score Kezati before resorting to knife-work.

"I do not deserve the honor, Conan of Cimmeria," Ngomba implored, "but I would beg of you and Jukona that we fight as three, back to back. The children of Ezat will drop like a rain of blood before us, while we three falter not." A wisp of the old Ngomba reappeared, and Conan mulled it over for a moment. "Fight where you will. I care not, so long as you hew only Kezati necks with that blade." Conan briefly regretted that he and Ngomba were by necessity at odds. There had been no time to teach the lad proper swordsmanship.

"Four will stand upon the mount," Y'Taba intoned, hefting a spear. *Four against hundreds,* he thought resignedly.

Nyona smiled momentarily at Y'Taba, glancing at him over her shoulder as she blew into the shell and Dawakubwa took to the air. She, like the others, would hide away and emerge when the Kezati approached. Conan grinned at this, knowing from experience that the stalkers were masters of the ambush. He wondered how many Kezati heads would roll before the vultures could muster a counterattack against Dawakubwa. An Aquilonian general would trade a legion of footmen—even a score of mounted knights—for such a formidable ally.

Makiela alone did not seek cover with the rest; she had climbed partway up a tree near the clearing, scanning the horizon whence the last attack had come. Conan, knowing her keen eyes would see the Kezati long before even his, waited upon the mound with the others. Back to back, the four silent warriors held their ground, forming a square as they listened for the signal that would warn them of the winged army's approach.

Y'Taba stood at Conan's right, Jukona at his left. Ngomba waited directly behind, his back to the Cimmerian's. An absolute silence settled over the village. In the mild, still air of late morning, not even a breeze stirred the leaves, no bird chirped, no insects buzzed. Conan watched a bead of sweat trickle from Jukona's nearly bare scalp to join others that glistened on the huge warrior's burly shoulders.

After an unbearable eternity, Makiela whistled, jabbing her spear into the sky. She darted into the reeds to join Sajara and the others, vanishing in the thicket as the Kezati horde appeared.

"Crom," Conan muttered under his breath. He would have thought it a storm cloud descending, so dark and expansive was the approaching menace. The Kezati easily numbered twice that which they had fought on the shore of skulls . . . if not thrice. And many more Ganaks had stood against the Kezati then. But Conan felt no fear at their approach. No man could live forever, by Crom, and it were better to die on the field of battle than on a sickbed of straw!

His heart pounded, blood singing in his veins. The thrill of battle was upon him; his aches, his grudge with Ngomba, his dread of the curse, fell from him like melting icicles, evaporated by the fire that burned in his breast. Legs braced in a wide stance, gleaming blade upraised, Conan uttered the fierce, eerie cry that was a Cimmerian's call to battle.

Swooping toward the mound, the Kezati fanned out, moving in unison like a well-drilled legion. A crescent formation encircled the four men, its curving points soaring ahead of the others as if to close like mandibles about their prey.

At the rear of the airborne mass, Conan glimpsed a

spreading shape that looked like three or four Kezati interlocked, wings beating in unison. But that brief sight was instantly obscured by the diving assault of the foremost vultures. Talons extended, beaks snapping menacingly, they hurled themselves like bolts of feathered lightning. A deafening din of shrill, predatory cries shattered the silence as man met beast in a frenzied melee.

A hail of spears showered the Kezati as they dived, impaling a dozen or more. Several others plunged to the ground, flapping weakly; some died in midair. Squawks burst out from the center of the crescent as Dawakubwa flew into the thick of the horde, wreaking havoc. Savage green jaws beheaded one Kezati in an effortless snap as spiny forelegs grasped another and crumpled it. A flurry of blood-slicked feathers dropped in the stalker's wake.

Undaunted, the airborne beasts plunged downward, some twenty stabbing beaks converging on the defending foursome. Kezati bodies met spears and swords raised against their charge.

Conan's blade flickered twice, lopping a leathery head from its plummeting body and gutting another Kezati who flopped to the ground, twitching. Jukona's spear-point skewered a ferocious face even as he whipped the oar blade around, smashing it into another beast. Y'Taba impaled one through the belly, but the screeching beast slid down the shaft, its talons and beak furrowing the Ganak's chest before it succumbed to its wound.

As five of the winged devils neared Ngomba, he lifted the *atnalga* and prepared to strike. As he did so, a madness overcame the five attackers, their piercing stridulations rising to an unbearable pitch. They wheeled desperately as if to avoid the weapon, whose blade suddenly flickered a silvery blue. Crackling strands—like miniature bolts of lightning—shot from the tip of the blade, forking as they arced through the air toward the twisting Kezati. Five feathered corpses thumped to the ground as wisps of smoke rising from their unmoving bodies filled the air with the stench of scorched flesh.

Ngomba's knees buckled; he slumped forward, gasping. The bolts had traveled from blade to hilt, stabbing at his flesh like lances of cold fire. Groaning in pain, he lurched to his feet, his arm shaking as he once again lifted his blade.

Unimpeded, four vultures plowed into Y'Taba, knocking him to the ground. Conan spun, his blade striking like a steel cobra. Blood jetted from the stump of a Kezati neck. Then three of the beasts overwhelmed the Cimmerian, one fleshing its talons into his unprotected back while the others flayed his exposed head and side, their beaks burrowing into muscle. Bellowing in rage, Conan laid about him with his blade. His vehement sword-stroke sheared through a midsection, momentum carrying the blade into the body of another attacker. Wrenching loose the dripping steel with a howl of fury, Conan reached behind his head, seized a scrawny neck in a massive fist and snapped it with a single powerful twist of his arm.

He turned again to the band that tore at Y'Taba, clubbing one Kezati with a vulture's body while sweeping his sword back to strike another lethal blow. Jukona, unfazed by the beasts surrounding him, dropped his spear and pummeled his enemies with powerful blows, cracking ribs and crushing a skull. Beaks and talons ripped at his flesh, but he seemed oblivious to the blood that dripped from his wounds as he battered feathery bodies with sledgelike fists.

Y'Taba strangled the last Kezati. He pushed its hooked beak away from his throat and standing, kicked away the corpse. Flaps of torn flesh hung from his head and chest, blood seeping from punctures where beaks had gored him. He grabbed his spear and set it just in time to meet the rush of a fresh swarm of vultures.

The new wave of Kezati struck like a storm of demons. They screeched in fury at the deaths of their kin as they pressed upon the badly outnumbered defenders. Again Ngomba lifted the *atnalga*, whose uncanny power felled three vultures before he reeled back on his haunches, stunned by the very force that slew his enemies.

Conan met head on the diving attack of six feathered devils, his blade weaving a wall of razor-sharp steel before him. His eyes blazing with blue fire, his thin lips asnarl, the Cimmerian fought like a cornered wildcat. Kezati fell like ripe grain in a ghastly harvest of blood, none passing through Conan's whirling gauntlet of death. Chest heaving, he stepped back from the knee-high mound of bodies, wiped blood from his eyes and glanced upward with a dark smile.

At last, the winged host had begun to thin.

Nearby, Dawakubwa dispatched several more Kezati. Nyona clung to his neck with her legs, fending off the vultures who made repeated dives for the stalker's eyes. She bled from a score of wounds but bravely fought on without faltering. Directly below her, the frenzied knife-strokes of Sajara and her hunters dispatched several Kezati. The vultures had taken their toll, however; Avrana lay motionless amid a heap of slain Kezati.

Determined to end the battle, Conan halved one foe at the waist, grunting as others ripped at his flesh. Crimson flecks flew from his steel as he hacked his way free of them, a giant beak nearly ripping out his throat.

"Crom!" he roared, as the thing's head fell upon the carrion-mound at his feet with a wet plop. He had not expected this sort of close in-fighting from the Kezati, who on the shore of bone had dived upon them and retreated upward before striking again. What had driven them to sacrifice themselves so recklessly? Now was not the time to ponder! Lashing out with his sword, Conan clove the breastbone of the diving, wailing vulture. Pivoting to face the expected attack from behind, he blinked in surprise.

A single speck hovered high in the air above them, but the sky was otherwise clear. The Kezati were beaten.

Sajara limped toward the mound, supporting Makiela and Kanitra, who looked half-dead. A handful of other hunters, injured too severely to walk, waited beside the reeds. Several Ganak bodies lay motionless around them.

Jukona extricated himself from a mound of crumpled bodies and rose unsteadily to his feet with a deep grunt of pain. Ngomba lay beside the deepest pile of the dead, breath wheezing from his bloody lips in ragged gasps. His hand still clasped the *atnalga*'s hilt.

Y'Taba propped up the young warrior's head, whispering into his ear. Ngomba's eyes widened in surprise. He sat up, coughing fitfully before lapsing back to the ground. The spirit-leader stood, facing Conan and the others. Though he smiled, the Cimmerian could see the pain in his eyes. Behind him, with a rustle of wings, Dawakubwa set down gently.

"One Kezati yet lives," Nyona cautioned, pointing upward. "It soars well beyond the reach of Dawakubwa, whose wings took hurt in the battle. But something about it is different; it keeps at a distance, as if to avoid being seen."

Y'Taba shrugged. "One enemy against many Ganaks is but a single cloud in a sky of victory. There can be no more of them, at least for another generation. By then, our young will be grown. Then we shall seek them out as they sought us and make certain they never trouble the sons of our sons. Never again!" The old Ganak, in spite of his numerous wounds, stood proudly atop the mound, his presence as commanding as ever. "And now, Conan of Cimmeria, shall I honor my promise to you." He brushed the crusted blood from his necklace of shells, lifting it in his hand.

A flickering shadow passed over the mound, moving so swiftly that had Conan blinked, he would have missed it. A rush of air swept past him, stirring his hair. Sajara shouted a cry of warning, and Jukona raised his fists defiantly. Nyona gasped, lifting the shell pipe to her lips.

It plunged from nowhere, or so it seemed. The Kezati that had been a speck rushed past them with blinding speed. Conan's flesh crawled at the sight of the winged

monstrosity thrice the size of its kin. It occurred to him
that he had doubtless seen it briefly at the onset of battle,
mistaking it for a cluster of Kezati. Its talons and beak
were terrifying at those gigantic proportions. Its belly
bulged with a strange roundness, and Conan was sickened
by a sudden revelation—this Kezati was a pregnant female
. . . perhaps their queen.

Soundlessly she attacked Y'Taba from behind, before he
was even aware of the approaching menace.

Galvanized, Conan sprang toward her, sword in hand.
But he might as well have tried to catch an archer's bolt
in flight. Seizing Y'Taba's arms with enormous talons, the
she-devil soared upward. The Ganak's yell of mingled
pain and astonishment faded as the Kezati's wings carried
Y'Taba away. But burdened by Y'Taba, the monster flew
less swiftly.

"Conan, Sajara—quickly!" Nyona called frantically.
"We must try to catch them!"

"What about me?" Jukona shouted.

"These two will slow us down enough, but they are the
lightest burden and the only ones fit for more fighting,"
Nyona snapped, blowing into the shell almost before
Conan and Sajara had secured themselves on the strip of
bark.

"Is Dawakubwa not injured, then?" Sajara asked.

"She fed," Nyona answered. "She may tire ere we catch
Y'Taba, but we must try."

Wings flexing powerfully, the stalker took off in pursuit
of the fleeing Kezati while Jukona stared upward, jaw
hanging open in shocked silence.

Twenty
The Kezati Queen

Ishtar and Pteor!" Conan swore, watching helplessly as the Kezati slowly increased its lead. "Can this infernal beast go no faster?" Y'Taba was vanishing from sight, and with him was vanishing the Cimmerian's hope for eradicating the shaman's curse.

"Perhaps, if you jumped off," Nyona shot back.

"Look," Sajara interrupted, pointing down. "Conan, is that the shore of skulls?"

He recognized the crescent-shaped isle at once, the ivory piles of bones prominent on one end. "Aye," he said, nodding. Dawakubwa was moving more swiftly than he had thought; they had not been at the chase for very long.

Fascinated, Sajara watched the island shrink behind them. "No huntress ever left Ganaku—until today, that is."

"Why?" Conan asked, his eyes still locked onto the distant form of Y'Taba, which now looked ant-sized.

"There is no time for it," Sajara answered regretfully. "The hunting of food, the making of spears and shell-spikes, the constant laying of nets to snare fish, the seeking of *vanukla* fruit and plants for Y'Taba, and the training and practicing of our skills, these occupy our days." She sighed. "But the ways of the past may change, for now we must be warriors, too."

Conan shrugged. "For the women of Cimmeria—aye, for the men also—it is much the same. Seldom do my people travel beyond the borders of their tribe's land, unless a blood feud is afoot or the bloody spear calls forth our tribes to battle a common enemy."

"Someday, when the village is restored to order, I would like to see the lands of which you speak," Sajara said.

Conan nodded sympathetically. Any place he stayed in for too long took on the feel of a dungeon, prompting him to move on. Admittedly, he often exited with the local soldiery at his heels, but when one intended to leave anyway, why not add some profit—or at the very least some excitement—to that departure?

The stalker began to lose speed, earning a frown from Nyona. The elderly *Ranioba* blew into her small shell, fingers gliding along its notched holes. Her silent ministrations went unrewarded; the stalker was now losing not just velocity but altitude as well.

"Dawakubwa is exhausted," Nyona said, her shoulders sagging. "We have lost Y'Taba."

"Not yet," said Conan. "There the Kezati descends, upon yon rock. By Crom, if I have to swim there, so be it."

Sajara and Nyona saw it, too. From afar it looked no larger than a fist-sized stone, but as they approached, its true size became evident. Perhaps only a quarter of the Ganak island's size, their lair of the Kezati was naught but a sheer-walled islet, rising from the sea like a craggy fortress.

Behind them, faltering wings ceased beating without warning. Conan had time to draw in a lungful of air before the stalker and its wide-eyed riders splashed into the shimmering water. Before he plunged below the surface, Conan caught a glimpse of the hulking Kezati setting down atop the isle, Y'Taba still clutched in her talons. The Cimmerian prayed fervently that the spirit-leader still lived.

Swimming as if pursued by every shark in the sea, Conan propelled himself toward the islet. Sajara followed closely, though she could not match the Cimmerian's frenzied pace. Nyona remained with Dawakubwa. The stalker was clearly out of its element, floundering to keep itself above water. Nyona treaded water beside the terrified creature, blowing into the shell in an effort to keep the stalker afloat.

The Cimmerian emerged dripping from the ocean at the edge of the rocky islet, sword clenched in his scarred fist. The sting of salt water in his wounds had subsided, and though he had endured a battle and a swim that would have exhausted the sturdiest of men, weariness clung to him no longer than did the seawater. Nimble as a mountain goat, Conan clambered up the rough face of the cliff that rose above him. He was halfway up before Sajara reached the shore below.

She eyed the daunting slant of stone before her and began working her way up. Her ascent was not nearly so rapid or smooth as Conan's, but few people in the world possessed his honed talents or experience. Furthermore, his reckless pace was driven by urgency. A moment's dalliance, and he might confront the Kezati only to find her feasting upon Y'Taba's innards.

A final stretch brought him to the top of the cliff. With a grunt he hauled himself up to peer over the top. The sheer walls of the islet tapered near the top, and weathering had smoothed it like a plate. So small was its diameter that Conan could easily hurl a stone clear across it. A pit gaped near the edge to which Conan clung.

A few spatters of blood stained the rock near the mouth of that pit. Y'Taba's necklace of black shells rested on the rock, just beyond his reach. Swinging a leg over the cliff, he grabbed the necklace and tied it about his neck. Then he crawled toward the hole for a closer look. A shriek from below turned his head. He reversed his direction and looked down to see if Sajara had fallen.

Staring over the side, he witnessed a strange sight: Sajara was disappearing into the face of the cliff! Her cry of surprise and horror was cut short as she vanished. Damn his haste! He should have stayed at her side! Sajara had taken a different path up the cliffside and must have found a cave undoubtedly occupied by a Kezati.

Cursing, Conan descended the wall, going straight to the place where Sajara had been lost to sight. Sure enough, he found a narrow opening there, a third of the way up. Her knife lay upon the stony floor of the tunnel beyond, which was barely wide enough to accommodate a man. Beyond the entrance, its ceiling rose rapidly to thrice Conan's height. A scraping echo sounded faintly from within, then the cave fell silent.

Conan stepped in without a moment's hesitation. His eyes adjusted to the deepening darkness, nostrils twitching at the pungent air wafting past him. A shuffle and a thump echoed from somewhere far ahead. Fortunately, the sun offered dim, indirect light, even as Conan crept deep into the upwardly sloping tunnel.

Irregular niches pocked the cavern walls. With a start Conan realized that he had blundered into the Kezati aerie. He peered into a jagged recess, his hand feeling along the wall and encountering the rough edges of a large nest. He snatched away his fingers as he realized that its sides were not made of sticks and mud, as he had thought, but of bones—large, human bones, mixed with the stranger bones of the Kezati. No wonder the Ganaks carried away their dead from the shore of skulls.

At the very back of the niche, wedged in place above the nest, a single Kezati skull leered at him. He moved on, glancing into the other macabre beds of bone to be certain that no vultures lurked in the shadows. Rounding another bend, he saw that the tunnel spiraled upward, probably all the way to the top where he had seen the pit and was sure that he would find the winged she-devil.

He continued upward past scores of empty nests. It seemed Y'Taba was right; the place was deserted. Perhaps the Ganaks had slain all but the last of this abominable race.

Ahead the winding corridor widened and reflected sunlight from above. He slowed, sword raised in readiness, his footsteps as stealthy as the padding of a stalking panther.

Where the corridor ended, the tunnel opened into a vast chamber. Bright rays of sunlight filtered from a hole in the roof—the pit that Conan had seen atop the islet. The scene inside filled him with nausea.

Hundreds, nay, thousands of lumpy eggs the size of ale barrels lay upon the floor. Among them, a few speckled red shells were quivering slightly. One shivered violently before splitting. The puckered, slimy head of a Kezati infant emerged, its tiny but sharp beak cawing.

A few paces away lay the prone forms of Y'Taba and Sajara. Y'Taba's chest rose and fell with ragged breathing, reviving Conan's hopes. Sajara stirred weakly; Conan could see her nasty head wound from across the chamber.

The giant Kezati squatted near them, her back turned away from Conan. As she straightened, a wet plop sounded above the faint screeching of the newborn Kezati. A muck-encrusted egg wobbled on the floor beneath her.

The young Kezati emerged, tearing away the rest of its shell with its hooked beak. It was the size of a fully grown eagle, though its wings showed only minimal development. Waddling on its revolting legs, it wobbled toward the fresh meat brought home by its mother.

Conan had seen enough. Blade whirling like a steel cyclone, he bounded into the chamber, smashing eggs beneath his feet, hacking apart the repulsive Kezati weanling as the vulture-queen turned to face him.

So baleful were the crimson pupils of her weirdly human eyes that their very malevolence stopped him for a moment. In their red depths lurked ageless evil, an undying and cosmic hatred so intense that it pierced Conan's soul. In that awful instant, he knew he faced no mere over-sized Kezati, but a diabolic fiend spawned in Hell's most blasphemous breeding pit.

The reason for the desperate sacrifices of the vultures at once became clear. This she-devil had fresh hatchlings to feed, and she cared only for the future of this new brood. In those eyes he had seen lust for pain and blood, for the suffering of anything that lived. She had deliberately not slain Sajara and Y'Taba, out of vengeance—to watch them suffer, to hear their tortured screams as her brood devoured them . . . alive.

The moment ended abruptly as the Kezati queen struck, her talons lashing out in a disemboweling sweep beneath Conan's upraised sword. He sprang backward, narrowly avoiding them, his defiant shout ringing in the chamber. He threw Sajara's knife in a smooth motion, burying it in the queen's side. She plucked it out with her beak and tossed it aside, screaming in rage as she lunged at Conan.

So tall was she that her neck rose beyond the tip of his blade. The reach of her talons exceeded that of his sword, forcing him to weave his way through her slashing assault. When she lowered her beak to strike, he rolled onto the floor, eggs crunching under his back, thrusting the sword toward her underbelly. Sajara stirred nearby, rising to her elbows.

A quick beat of the Kezati's wings carried the she-devil above Conan's attack, then she dropped back onto him, talons ripping into his shoulders. A desperate blow lopped off her leg, her enraged screeches of pain nearly bursting his eardrums. He struck again, shearing a chunk of feathered flesh from her side, exposing her quivering vitals before a gout of black, oily blood gushed over them.

The sweep of her talons knocked Conan through the air and slammed him into the opposite wall, spinning his sword away. Clutching his gouged side in an effort to stem the flow of blood, he scrambled for the blade.

Although his stroke had wounded the queen severely, it was not enough. She glared at him maliciously, then took to the air, flapping slowly toward the opening in the ceiling.

From where she lay, Sajara reached out, her fingers grasping the remaining leg of the retreating queen. Ignoring the Ganak, the Kezati continued her flight, pulling Sajara with her.

Bellowing curses, Conan lumbered toward them, blood streaming from his side. He jumped and caught Sajara's foot in a one-handed grab. Such was the queen's strength, even wounded, that she continued to fly, clearing the edge of the hole. Once outside, the shrieking Kezati began shaking her leg, trying to kick loose the Ganak who clung so tenaciously.

Conan maintained his tenuous hold on Sajara's foot by sheer strength and willpower, hooking his own feet under the edge of the opening to prevent the queen from rising further. His other hand was still wrapped around his hilt.

Unable to either ascend or to shake loose the clinging woman, the enraged Kezati bent forward, her beak stabbing downward toward Sajara's exposed head.

Conan howled savagely. Releasing his toe-hold on the aperture below, he swung himself up to meet the queen's attack. His flashing blade struck the queen's lunging neck, slicing through leathery flesh and cleaving bone.

The beak stopped a handspan from Sajara's face, as the queen's severed head bounced off the rock to splash into the sea far below.

Conan's hand slipped from Sajara's ankle. He landed on his feet, swaying at the edge of the cliff before recovering his balance. The Kezati's final shuddering convulsion dislodged Sajara. Talons slashed across Conan's chest, ripping loose the necklace he had tied there ... sending Y'Taba's string of shells flying outward in a wide arc toward the sea.

The moment froze before Conan's eyes.

Sajara's arms flailed, missing the cliff's edge as she fell in the direction of the Kezati queen's headless body— away from that of the plummeting necklace.

Without hesitation, Conan threw himself after Sajara, his powerful hands closing around her slender wrist and pulling her to safety. He heard a faint splash below, but put all thought of it from his mind. Leaning down into the pit, he called to Y'Taba, hoping that the spirit-leader was still breathing.

He climbed down carefully, dropping to the floor. Sajara followed, still numb with shock. Conan stomped every egg in the chamber. Sajara managed to revive Y'Taba, although the old Ganak's shoulders were a shredded ruin. He was weakened from the loss of the blood and barely able to stand, so Sajara and the Cimmerian supported him on their shoulders, winding through the tunnel to the opening in the rocky wall.

Nyona and Dawakubwa waited below on the jagged rocks at the base of the cliff. The stalker clutched a huge, half-eaten carcass in its forelegs—one that Conan recognized at once. He deemed it appropriate that the last Kezati would itself wind up in the belly of another beast.

"Dawakubwa will yet bear us home," Nyona said, breaking the silence. "She needed food."

Y'Taba coughed, clutching at his neck. "Conan of Cimmeria, I shall fail to keep my vow. All that I have is yours, but I cannot cure you of the curse. The spirit-shells must have fallen from me as I was borne by that—"

"Do you mean these, Y'Taba?" Nyona lifted the string of black shells from her lap.

Conan's heart leapt into his throat. "Ha! So the gods do have a sense of humor!"

"I saw them fall as we watched from below." Nyona smiled.

"And this time, warrior of Cimmeria, you shall not wait," Y'Taba vowed. His typically somber lips were curled in an ear-to-ear grin as he took the shells from Nyona.

Twenty-one
Unfettered

Conan wiped his brow and peered ahead, shifting uncomfortably on the bark between him and Dawakubwa's back. At first he thought it to be a trick of his mind, but he blinked and looked again.

Land! He grinned as Nyona blew into her shell, the stalker angling downward. Sajara's arms were flung around his muscled waist, her eyes alight with anticipation. They had recovered completely from the day a fortnight earlier, when the last Kezati was slain.

After a brief rest, Dawakubwa had borne Conan, Nyona, Y'Taba, and Sajara back to Ganaku. The elders, the *Raniobas*, and Jukona, had witnessed the ceremony that night in which Y'Taba had summoned the spirits in his necklace of shells. The ritual had taken little time—the spirit-leader had mumbled no arcane nonsense, nor had he gesticulated wildly, like a Pictish or Kushite shaman. Eyes closed, brow furrowed, he had clasped the shells of his necklace and concentrated until sweat dripped from his face. A loud hum droned from his fist—then a booming crack followed by utter silence.

Conan shivered at the memory of the spirits summoned forth—watery specters that had swirled around him. Before he could move, those dewy ghosts had flown *through* him, driving out a red mist that had quickly dissipated into the air. Then the spirits had vanished. Awestruck, the Ganaks and Conan turned to face Y'Taba, who stood wearily as crushed pieces of shells fell from his palm. Conan had felt a brief flash of pain, then a tingling in his head that quickly abated. That night, though the moon had shone brightly, he had been visited by no malefic dreams.

A few weeks of resting at Ganaku under the tender care of Sajara had healed his body and given him time to study the aged books from the tower. Among them he had found log books and with some difficulty had divined Ganaku's position: due south of the Islands of Pearl, which in turn lay to the west of Vendhya.

Ngomba had recovered from the battle a changed man. Either his brush with death or the voices of the spirits in the *atnalga* had transformed him. Gone had been his impetuousness and pride. In their place emerged a personality that had reminded Conan of the spirit-leader, which indeed made sense, if the Cimmerian's feeling about Y'Taba and Nyona was founded in truth. At any rate those two had taken the young Ganak under their wing.

Sajara, overcoming only mild objections from Y'Taba, had decided to accompany Conan on his journey. By mutual agreement, Nyona would come back for her at the next full moon.

Conan had managed a grin when hearing of the appointed time. He was relieved to be free of the curse and felt a new man: unfettered by enchantments, snakeskin sack bulging with loot from the tower at Rahamji, sword hanging ready at his hip, and a beautiful, spirited girl at his side. What more could a man ask for?

No sooner had Dawakubwa set them down on the beach than the locals approached. Their garments bore a look familiar to Conan, and he laughed boomingly. As he had hoped, they had landed upon the isle occupied by the Gwadiri, a friendly tribe of pearl fishers. He had chosen this destination for its proximity to Ganaku, doubting that Dawakubwa had the endurance to fly them all the way to Vendhya.

Conan had other reasons, too. Not long ago, back in Iranistan, he had saved the Gwadiri chief's daughter from a horrible fate.

The heavyset, deeply tanned chief approached, spear in hand but its point raised skyward. "Conan of Cimmeria?" his deep voice asked incredulously.

"Aurauk!" the Cimmerian replied heartily. "How is Nanaia?"

"Fine, fine, already she has married a chieftain of the Bajris. We can speak of that later, eh?" The big man's eyes lit up excitedly. "First you must tell me who these lovely women are, and what manner of beast is that?"

"It is a long tale," Conan said. "Better told over a gourd of wine."

"Wine we shall have, and a feast fit for kings! How glad I am to see you. I owe you more than that for the rescue of my daughter. And you could not have come at a better time."

"Only a rogue would have—" Conan began.

Aurauk waved aside Conan's protest. "Anyway, I was going to tell you that the Bajris are now our friends. But the three tribes of Udwunga threaten to attack—a territorial dispute in which I must offer my aid. What say you, Conan? Lead us to victory, and I'll give you all the pearls that your winged monster can carry!"

"What more could a man ask for?" mused Conan. "Why, with such a haul of loot, I could buy myself a kingdom. And after battling beasts that fly and crawl, I relish the prospect of pitting myself against men of flesh and blood. Aye, by Crom," he rumbled. "Ready your men, chieftain, and hasten—we have Udwunga blood to spill ere the sun sets!"